DYING TO MEET YOU

RICH AMOOI

To Robert, my brother from another mother.

CHAPTER ONE

LIZ

Google told me I was forty-five times more likely to die from flesh-eating bacteria than win the lottery, so it seemed only natural for me to ignore the winning numbers on the television screen and inspect my body for abnormalities. My search ended when my pinky toe cramped up, causing me to lose my balance and fall off the couch.

I stared at the TV screen from the floor, feeling a little nauseated. The pukey sensation wasn't a symptom of any rare skin disease, but something brought on by the lottery ticket clutched in my sweaty hand.

I decided to confirm the winning numbers again. This time, I would start with the Mega number and then work my way backwards through the rest.

I glanced up at the TV and back down at my ticket.

Back and forth.

Six times.

A minute later, I took a deep breath, confident I had the information necessary to conclude I wasn't delirious or delusional. I had overcome the doubts and disbelief that had been cutting off the oxygen to my brain.

I, Elizabeth Parker, had won the lottery.

$575,000,000.00.

Grabbing the remote, I turned up the volume on the TV, eager to get as much information as possible from the local news before I passed out.

"The winning ticket was purchased at this Stater Brothers location on Carmel Mountain Road in San Diego," the reporter said, gesturing to the supermarket behind him. "Since there was only one winner, the lucky ticket holder will receive a cool two hundred million dollars after state and federal taxes, if they choose the lump-sum cash amount."

Two hundred million dollars.

It was mine.

All mine.

A few minutes ago, I had barely twenty thousand to my name—not including the six dollars in quarters I kept in the center console of my car for parking meters.

Now I had two hundred million dollars.

I had visualized this day in my head countless times, the way I would feel, the celebration, the people I would call, and in what order.

Honestly, I was disappointed with my reaction so far.

I should have been jumping up and down.

I should have been screaming my head off.

I should have been peeing my pants.

Nope.

Nothing.

Not a peep out of me.

Nor a pee.

"Lottery officials urge the winner to sign the back of the ticket in ink and claim the prize at the nearest California Lottery district office as soon as possible," the reporter continued. "Otherwise, anyone who has the ticket in their hands can claim the jackpot as their own."

"What?" I said to myself, not even realizing someone could take my ticket and cash it in for themselves. Who would do such a thing? It was hard to know who to trust these days.

A noise in the front yard got my attention.

Cranking my neck hard to the right, I listened for anything that seemed out of the ordinary.

Nothing.

Had I imagined that? I had never had a problem with my hearing.

A little investigation wouldn't hurt.

I turned off the TV, threw the remote on the couch, and ran to the window. I peeked through the living room blinds, making sure no one was outside staking out the house, on the verge of chopping me into pieces and stuffing my diced bits into their trunk.

The ice cream man was sitting in his converted van right in front of my driveway.

It was almost dark. There were no kids around.

It was suspicious.

Wait a minute . . .

The bush in front of my living room window moved, and it wasn't windy.

I jumped back and screamed when a blue-haired woman appeared on the other side of the glass.

Dolly Pearson, a professional busybody and all-around snoopster.

Everyone within a two-mile radius of our street called her Snoop Dolly Dog.

She was always in other people's business, asking questions, sharing information, stirring up things. She insisted she wasn't doing anything wrong since she had always come with the truth and nothing but the truth, so help her God.

I placed my hand over my heart to calm it down and swung the front door open. "Can I help you, Dolly?"

She huffed and pulled a leaf off her flower-patterned, full-skirted swing dress that buttoned up the full length of the front. "You have spiders in that bush. Did you know that? I'm allergic to spider bites, for goodness sake. If I die, it'll be on your conscience."

"Then stay out of my bushes."

"I was trying to check up on you!"

I pointed to the doorbell. "Try pressing that little gizmo right there. It's amazing how the ding dong is so clear throughout the house." I crossed my arms, wanting to tell my neighbor she was the one who was a ding dong, but resisted, opting to get to the point. "How can I help you?"

She got on her tiptoes and peeked over my shoulder. "Uh . . . you okay in there?"

I closed the gap of the open door, paranoid she would knock me over, run inside, and grab my winning ticket. "Everything is fine. Why wouldn't it be fine?"

"Well, it's Wednesday."

"And?"

4

"And after your salad you go for your evening walk before watching reruns of *Frasier*."

It was true.

Was I that predictable?

Okay, maybe I was.

I liked my routine. I liked my ordinary life.

Change was something I had never learned to appreciate.

"I was worried since you hadn't left on your walk yet and you're almost always back by now," Dolly continued.

I sighed. "Well, I'm fine. You have a nice evening, Dolly."

Too bad she stopped the door with her foot before it shut all the way. "Did you hear someone bought the winning lottery ticket at the Stater Brothers? It could be someone we know!"

"I doubt it," I lied. "Take care. Gotta go."

Closing the door, I rushed to the kitchen, grabbed a pen from the junk drawer, and signed the back of the lottery ticket. I snapped a picture of both sides and a selfie with the ticket next to my face, before emailing the images to myself.

Okay, I'm being a little paranoid, but you can never be too sure.

Relax.

I opened a bottle of my favorite wine and poured a tall glass, wondering if I would continue to buy the same seven dollar bottle I have enjoyed for a decade or if my tastes or habits would change because I had enough money to buy the entire winery.

It would be a good idea to come up with a plan.

No impulse purchases.

Practical was the way to go.

Sure, maybe a new car, but who needed a Ferrari or a

Lamborghini? Not me. I didn't need a mansion, either, although it would have been nice to have a house where it didn't take the hot water ten minutes to heat before getting in the shower.

Simple things.

I grabbed a pad and pen and slid onto the barstool.

I wrote the first two things that popped into my head:

1) Wine.

2) Cheese.

I nodded, appreciating my simple list.

That should do it.

I'll spend two hundred million dollars on wine and cheese. I'll be set for life.

Geez, I'm already nuts, and I haven't even received the money yet.

The best thing to do would be to see what other lottery winners have done with their money.

I took another sip of my wine and asked Google for help again, but this time my interest was in the history of lottery winners in the US.

"Oh, boy," I muttered aloud.

The results of the search weren't very encouraging.

There were stories of past winners blowing all their money and ending up worse off than before buying the ticket. Stories of close friends and loving family members who turned into vampires, trying to suck the life and money out of the lottery winner. Winners who bought enormous properties, then didn't have enough money to pay the property taxes and were forced to sell for a huge loss. Lottery winners who'd been robbed, taken hostage, or even killed.

Slamming my laptop shut, I took a giant gulp of my wine,

and twisted my body around on the barstool toward the sliding glass door leading to the backyard.

Was it locked? Was there movement in the backyard?

The sound of my ringing cellphone startled me and sent me skittering backward on the barstool. Luckily, I didn't fall off, but wine splattered on the counter and floor.

I glanced at the caller ID on my phone. My brother, Joshua, was calling.

I tapped the answer button and the speakerphone. "Hi, Josh." After sliding off the barstool, I yanked a long string of paper towels from the roll and started wiping up the wine.

"Hey," Josh said. "You sound far away."

"I'm cleaning up a mess."

"Sorry, but I must have the wrong number because my sister never makes a mess."

As nervous as I was, Josh still made me smile, but he was right.

When was last time I had spilled something?

And my house was always spotless.

Josh had always joked it was as clean as a hospital and that you could eat food off just about any surface, including the floor.

I was a little OCD, but you'd never hear me admitting that in public.

"I spilled wine—no big deal," I said. "What's going on?

"Did you see on the news that someone bought the winning lottery ticket at the Stater Brothers by your house?"

"Yeah," I said.

"I wonder if it's somebody we know."

I can guarantee you it is.

1

"For a moment there, I was hoping it was you, but you would've called me right away if you had won."

I sat there, silent for a moment.

I wanted to tell Josh, but now I was paranoid my phone was being tapped and someone would break down the door any moment, hit me over the head with a coconut, and take my ticket. Okay, the coconut thing may not have been realistic, and I only brought it up because I had also read that I was more likely to be killed by a coconut than win the lottery.

Wait a minute.

I decided I should give the ticket to Josh and he could guard it. It was the perfect plan since he was a cop—one of San Diego's finest for over twenty years.

That would take the pressure off, so I could sleep.

"Meet me for dinner," I blurted out.

There was silence on the other end of the phone.

"Josh? Are you there?"

"I'm here," Josh said. "And now I'm worried."

"Why?"

"You're never spontaneous. What's going on? You're scaring me."

"Nothing is going on!" My lying voice must have gone up a thousand octaves, so I did the first thing I could think of to distract my brother and throw him off the scent. I banged a wooden spoon on one of the frying pans hanging over the kitchen island and sang "Beat It" by Michael Jackson.

"Sis? Are you taking any new medication I should be aware of?"

He suspected something.

It was not a surprise Josh was being promoted from police officer to detective.

He had always been good at smelling rats.

Today, I'm the rat.

Like Remy in the movie Ratatouille, except I was fifty years old, couldn't cook to save my life, and was now a paranoid millionaire who would never leave the house again.

"Liz. Talk to me. Today is green salad day. Don't tell me it's not sitting on the counter in front of you at this moment."

I glanced at my mixed green salad with cherry tomatoes, avocado, hard-boiled egg, garlic butter croutons, and my favorite balsamic vinaigrette. I had been eating the same salad every Wednesday for the last eight years.

I turned my back on the salad, wondering if everyone in the world knew my business.

"So, why do you want to go out to eat?" Josh continued his interrogation.

My brother would make a damn fine detective. Of course he would know I was a non-spontaneous rat who had meals planned years in advance.

I felt paranoid telling him over the phone, so the only thing I could do was lie again. "I got a bag of bad lettuce from the store. I'm just not in the mood to die from salmonella, you know? Anyway, are you going to meet me for dinner or not? My treat."

"Why didn't you say so?" He chuckled. "Where do you want to meet?"

"Meet me at Vintana in a half hour."

"Vintana? Wow. What's the special occasion?"

"I'll tell you when I see you. Oh—and make sure you bring your gun."

"My gun? What the—"

I hung up on my brother, so I wouldn't have to explain.

He called back, but I let it go to voicemail.

Josh would understand my sudden case of psychosis and paranoia when I told him his sister was now a millionaire.

My life would change, and I needed to figure out some things, for sure. But for now, I needed to get to the restaurant without crashing my car.

CHAPTER TWO

LIZ

Vintana was located on the second floor of a Lexus dealership in Escondido, a city just north of San Diego. I glanced over at the shiny cars in the showroom as I headed upstairs. Maybe I would buy one soon.

I waited for Josh inside the restaurant and waved to him as he entered.

"You sure know how to freak a brother out, hanging up on me like that." He hugged me.

"What did I do?" I asked, even though I knew the answer. "Everything is fine."

Josh pulled away from the hug, but kept his hands on my shoulders, inspecting my eyes. "You asked me to bring my gun. Everything is not fine. You're not yourself. I could hear it on the phone, and I can see that right now. Is another student stalking you?"

"No."

"Are you in trouble?"

"No!"

"Do you need money?"

I snorted. "Definitely not, but I need food, so let's eat."

After we sat and ordered, I lifted the cloth on top of the breadbasket in the middle of the table, pulled out a slice of the sourdough, and buttered it. I took the first heavenly bite, feeling Josh's eyes still on me.

"This is so good." I ignored his suspicious stares and waved my piece of bread in the air. "You have to try some."

"Sis."

"Don't tell me you're watching your carbs."

"Sis."

"Hang on."

The waiter brought us each a glass of wine.

Wasting no time, I lifted mine in the air for a toast. "To life."

"To life?" Josh hesitated and clinked my glass.

"Yup. Life. Actually—I have a better one. To a life full of surprises."

"You hate surprises." He glanced at me. "Spill the beans or I'll take you downtown and hook you up to a lie detector machine."

"You don't even have one."

"I'll find one on eBay. I'll get the truth out of you."

"Always being silly . . ." I took a sip of my wine, preferring not to say another word or make eye contact.

He placed his wine glass on the table and crossed his arms, waiting.

Okay—it looked like I had stalled long enough.

"Fine." I sighed.

I opened my purse and pulled out the winning lottery ticket, looking around the restaurant for undesirables or suspicious-looking mafia types who would tie cement blocks to my ankles and drop me in the ocean.

It looked like I was safe, for the moment.

I set the lottery ticket on the table, kept it covered with my hand, and slid it in his direction.

"Please guard this for me," I whispered and looked around again. "Just for tonight."

Josh's gaze dropped to the ticket.

He arched an eyebrow when he realized what it was. He reached for it, and inspected both sides of the ticket, pausing on the back side that had my signature.

"Okay . . . no problem." Josh slid the ticket into his wallet and leaned forward on the table with his elbows, a smile growing on his face. "This is why you're acting like a nutjob?"

I nodded.

"Now it's making sense. How many numbers did you match?"

A smile grew on my face. "All of them."

Josh jerked his head back. "Holy crap!"

Every head in the restaurant turned in our direction.

"Shhh!" I leaned across the table. "Keep it down."

He chuckled. "How can I keep it down when you won one of the biggest lotteries in the history of the US? Damn." He stared at me for a moment and looked back toward the kitchen. "I should have ordered the lobster."

I laughed. "You should have."

"And an appetizer." He pointed to me. "You're a freaking millionaire and can have anything you want on the menu. You ordered a salad?"

"First, it's Wednesday, salad day, you know that. Plus, I don't have the money yet. And what? Millionaires aren't allowed to eat salads?"

It was weird calling myself a millionaire.

"Salads with caviar on top, sure. Or something else us peasants and commoners can't afford. And the food should be served on a twenty-four-carat gold plate by someone who bows to you and calls you Queen Elizabeth."

That made me smile.

I stopped going by Elizabeth years ago since it was much faster to write Liz.

Efficiency. That's what my life was all about.

I took another sip of my wine, feeling such a strange combination of emotions running through my body at that moment.

Shock.

Anxiety.

Fear.

Happiness.

Guilt.

Yes, guilt.

Did I deserve all this money?

I mean, I bought the ticket, so I won fair and square. And people buy the tickets to win the money, so I shouldn't feel guilty at all. But what about the fear? What was that all about?

Fear of being judged?

Fear of making a big mistake like the other lottery winners?

Fear of turning into someone I don't like and becoming an uncontrollable shopping monster where I run through department stores grabbing everything in my path like it was Black Friday?

I didn't want to be one of those rich people who thought they could do whatever they wanted because they had money. I would still obey the speed limit, hold the door open for people, and say thank you when somebody did something for me.

"I'm not going to change because of a little more money." I hoped it would become an affirmation.

"A little more money? I can't believe you said that."

"Me, either." I laughed and cupped my hand over my mouth.

The laughter became louder, almost hysterical as I tapped my foot on the floor like I was trying to kill a cockroach.

People in the restaurant were looking in my direction again.

I was losing it.

I wanted to win the lottery, but now that I'd won, I didn't know how to handle it.

Luckily, the perfect solution came. "I need to be sedated."

"What?" Josh said.

"Or maybe you need to use your stun gun on me."

Josh chuckled and pointed to my glass. "That'll work right there. Drink. I'll make sure you get home okay."

I took another sip of the wine.

Josh shook his head and sat back in his seat. "I can't believe my sister is a—"

I held up my hand. "Don't say it."

"Fine, but you need to think about some things. You'll need a financial adviser, for starters. And don't look to me for advice. You need a real one. And you need to quit your job."

I can't believe I hadn't even thought of that.

Of course, I would quit my job.

That's what everybody did, right?

Not that I hated being a high school history teacher, but it was hard work. On one hand, it was rewarding because I was shaping kids' lives for the future. On the other hand, it had never been my real passion. I was good at it, and I had been teaching for almost twenty-five years. But becoming a history teacher was more because I was fascinated with history than it was for the actual part of wanting to teach it. I figured it was a good fit and something I could easily do.

Well, my career counselors in high school had decided it would be a good fit, and I had agreed because no other career seemed appealing at the time. Except for zookeeper, but then there was the poop to deal with, and I wasn't going to have any of that.

The waiter brought the food. "Enjoy."

I took my first bite of the salad and set down my fork. "What about you?"

Josh looked at me, confused. "What about me?"

I shrugged. "Well, you know . . . you don't have to work anymore, or worry about money either. Whatever you want, it's yours. I can take care of my baby brother from now on."

I smiled because I still called him my baby brother, even though he was forty-five years old.

"No way," Josh said. "I'm excited about becoming a detective. Now, if you want to spoil me while I become the best detective this city has ever seen, I won't have a problem with that at all. Detectives look good in shiny black BMWs with plush leather seats, from what I hear." He chuckled and took a bite of his swordfish.

I nodded. "You can choose any color and model BMW on the lot. Anyway, I had a feeling you would want to keep working, but I had to offer. And the offer will always be there if you ever change your mind."

"Thanks, sis." Josh chewed and wiped his mouth. "Have you thought about what you want to do with the next chapter in your life?"

"No."

He held up his glass. "Well, I guess you have some serious contemplating to do."

"No doubt about that."

We finished dinner and dessert and headed back downstairs to the parking lot. I ended up not drinking too much, so I could drive myself home. Josh had agreed to pick me up at nine in the morning and escort me over to the lottery district office in his squad car.

I hugged him and thanked him for guarding the ticket for the night.

He turned to walk to his car.

"Josh." I took a few steps back in his direction.

"Yeah?" He swung back around.

"Don't forget to bring your gun in the morning."

He laughed and shook his head. "You're crazy, you know that?"

Maybe I was, but there were some big changes coming my way and I didn't want any surprises.

CHAPTER THREE

LIZ

The next morning, I waited in my driveway for Josh to pick me up, eager to go to the Lottery District Office and claim the prize. Fortunately, I could sleep knowing Josh had the ticket. The second glass of wine at home had helped with the sedation I had been longing for in the restaurant since he'd refused to use his stun gun on me.

I had called the school to let them know I couldn't come in today, so at least I wouldn't have to worry about work. The plan was to claim the prize and figure out what I wanted to do with the rest of my life. It was odd thinking in those terms considering I was already fifty years old and I had another fifty years left to live.

Snoop Dolly Dog strolled out of her house in her gold gangster robe and white bunny slippers, grabbing her newspaper from the driveway.

Please go back inside. Nothing to see here.

Dolly picked up the paper, pulled it out of the plastic bag, and glanced at the front page.

A few seconds later, she looked up and spotted me.

Just wonderful.

She arched an eyebrow and crossed the street in my direction. "Looks like you're playing hooky today." She eyed my jeans and my San Diego State T-shirt. "You haven't missed a day of work since your second divorce trial."

Of course she would know.

"I have errands to run," I said, which wasn't exactly a lie.

"Really?" She stared at me, most likely trying to get me to blink. "Taking a day off to run errands?" She turned and watched as Josh pulled up in front of my house. "Sounds fishy. Who runs errands in a cop car?"

Josh lowered his window. "Good morning, Dolly."

"Good morning." Dolly's gaze popped back and forth between me and Josh. "Where are you off to so bright and early?"

I shook my head at Josh, hoping he would get the hint not to say anything.

He glanced at me and back to Dolly, smiling. "We just have to take care of some things."

Two hundred million things.

"You in trouble, Liz?" Dolly asked, placing her hand on the window of the back door, and inspecting the back seat.

"I'm not in trouble," I said.

Josh glanced at me. "We should get going."

"Ready." I cut in front of Dolly to get in Josh's car.

"Josh, did you hear Lawrence DeCarr got into trouble with the law?" She pointed to Lawrence's house across the street. "He wasn't picking up his dog's poop, and the bastard was finally caught in the act on video. He got a big fat fine. That'll teach him."

"Who took the video?" I asked, getting in the car.

"I did," Dolly said, proudly. "Hey—you never told me where you're going."

I smiled. "To buy a video camera. There have been people trespassing on my property recently and I'm going to catch them in the act. Thanks for the idea!"

Dolly opened and closed her mouth.

I glanced in the side mirror on the passenger side as we headed down the street.

Dolly was standing in the same spot with her hands on her hips, watching us drive away.

"She's a piece of work." Josh laughed. "You can always move if you're tired of her. You can live anywhere you want now. Maybe a beachfront property?"

"Who knows?"

When we arrived at the lottery office, Josh swung the front office door open and waved me in. "After you, Queen Elizabeth."

Something told me it wouldn't be the last time he called me that.

I smiled and stepped inside, looking around. The lottery office had an armed police officer, and video cameras on the walls. Three employees worked on the other side of what appeared to be bullet-proof glass. The lottery was serious business.

"Hey, Dave." Josh approached the cop and shook his hand. "How are things?"

It was amazing how many other cops he knew.

Officer Dave nodded. "I'm good, I'm good. Did you win something big?"

Josh pointed to me. "My sis did."

Officer Dave nodded again. "Good for you. Congrats."

"Thanks," I said.

"We just had someone come in with a hundred-thousand-dollar ticket. Imagine that?"

I preferred to imagine what I had won.

Fortunately, Josh pointed to the counter in front of the glass, so I wouldn't have to say anymore. "We're going to check in."

"Of course," Officer Dave said.

I approached the glass and held up the ticket for the woman to see. "Hi, I would like to claim this."

She inspected the ticket through the glass and looked up at the latest winning numbers illuminated on the wall, her eyes opening wide. "Congratulations!"

"Thank you."

She swung around toward the other two employees, gesturing back to me. "This is the big winner."

The three of them smiled and clapped for me, which felt odd since I hadn't done anything that required skills to get this win. I had just spent a couple of bucks, that's all.

I filled in my information on the winner claim form and slid it through the opening under the glass, along with the winning ticket.

The woman confirmed the information on the form. "Just so you're aware, California law states we need to release your name immediately to the public. TV, radio, newspapers, just about everyone will know you won the jackpot."

"Oh." I thought about it. "There's no way to remain anonymous?"

"I'm afraid not." She shook her head. "Not in California. The public needs to know the winners are real people. Otherwise, we could say we have a winner and just keep all the money for ourselves with no one the wiser. I wouldn't have a problem with that, but theft and fraud are frowned upon around here for some reason." She laughed. "I'm sure you understand."

It made sense, but that didn't mean I had to like it. Everyone in the world would know I had two hundred million dollars.

"Change your phone number," the lottery woman said, reading my mind. "Take a seat. Someone will be with you shortly to interview you."

"Interview me? Why?"

She nodded. "It's part of the security measures in place to prevent fraud."

"Oh . . ."

A few minutes later, the inside door buzzed, and an armed man came out holding a clipboard. "Liz Parker?"

I stood and took a few steps toward him. "That's me."

He smiled. "I'm Matt, lead investigator. Please follow me."

Lead investigator? Did they think I stole the ticket? Was he going to grill me in a dark room under a bright light until I cried and admitted to something I hadn't even done?

My paranoia was taking over again.

Relax.

Breathe.

He's on my side.

"I'll wait for you here." Josh pointed to a chair in the waiting area and grabbed a magazine from the table.

"Sounds good." I smiled at Officer Dave as I passed him and followed Matt through two doors to a back office.

Office was probably the wrong word.

More like a junkyard, if you'd asked me.

Documents, folders, and mail were piled high all over his desk, mixed with pens, pencils, and loose paper clips all over the place. In the middle of the disorganized madness was a balled-up cheeseburger wrapper from McDonald's and an empty bag of Flamin' Hot Cheetos. The untidiness made my eyes twitch and almost seized up my brain.

I could never go out with a man like that.

He gestured to the chair with his red fingers. "Please take a seat."

"Thank you."

He studied the information on the clipboard and nodded a few times.

"Is there a problem?" I asked.

He shook his head. "Shouldn't be. It's standard procedure that we interview the big lottery winners to make sure everything is on the up-and-up. There's a lot of greed and fraud, people trying to cheat the system, you know? So, where did you buy the ticket?"

"Stater Brothers on Black Mountain Road."

"Did you get a Quick Pick or did you choose your own numbers?"

"I chose my own." I pointed to the ticket attached to his clipboard in front of him. "Doesn't it show on the ticket that I chose the numbers myself?"

"Yeah, but I still need to ask. Procedure and all that. How did you come up with the six numbers you chose?"

"Seriously?"

He nodded. "Yeah. Let's go through them one-by-one."

"Okay." I thought about the numbers.

"Start in order with the first number," Matt said.

"Two is how many times I have been divorced," I answered confidently.

Matt scribbled on his clipboard. "Seven?"

"My shoe size."

Matt peeked under his desk at my feet but didn't comment.

"Do I need to take off one of my shoes and show you?"

He shook his head. "No, no." He hesitated. "It's just . . . I've never heard someone pick their shoe size as one of the numbers." He wrote on his form again. "Okay . . . thirteen."

"Thirteen is the number of hot dogs I ate in a hot dog eating competition," I said.

Matt looked up again. "You ate thirteen hot dogs?"

"Back in college."

"Impressive." He sat up in his chair. "Did you win?"

"Not even close. The winner ate fifty-three."

Matt thought about it. "Just forty-one more hot dogs and you would have won."

I laughed. "So close."

He glanced at the clipboard. "The next number is twenty-five."

"That's how old I was when I got my master's degree at San Diego State."

"Good school," he said. "Thirty-four."

"That's my—"

Oh no.

I just realized how I had come up with the next number, and never thought in a million years I would have to share that with someone.

Maybe I could make something up.

No.

He would know I was lying.

I glanced up at the camera on the wall in the corner of the room behind his desk.

Somebody was watching me, too. I was sure of it.

What to do, what to do, what to do?

"Thirty-four, Liz?" Matt said.

"Look . . . you probably already figured out by now I'm the person who bought the ticket. Do we need to continue?"

He nodded. "Actually, we do. Like I said before, this is procedure. You need to answer all the questions, or you don't get the prize."

"Well, when you put it that way." I would never see him again, anyway. "I chose thirty-four because . . . it's . . . my . . . bra size."

Matt glanced down at my chest, then his eyes shot back up to mine. "Right. Okay. And the last number?"

"Fifty is my age."

"Of course." Matt smiled. "Okay, that should do it. I'm also required to tell you that your full name and city and the amount of your winnings, including your gross and net installment payments, will be matters of public record."

I shook my head in disbelief. "I heard. Are you sure there's no way around that?"

"Sorry," Matt said. "Oh—and you may be asked to participate in a press conference, but that's totally up to you.

Everything looks good from my end. Typically, the check takes a few weeks, but you may get lucky and get it sooner depending on the load of the controller's office in Sacramento. A press release mentioning you as the winner, your city, and occupation goes out within the hour and it's picked up by every major news agency in the world. We recommend you hire a financial planner and also change your phone number immediately."

"The woman at the reception area mentioned that too, but my number is unlisted. Not too many people have it."

"Trust me. They will find it. They always do. And this is not official advice, but you may want to consider moving or at least going on an extended vacation."

"Why is that?"

"Because people will show up at your front door, asking for money. They're not shy about it. Some are even aggressive. Call nine-one-one if it gets out of hand and you fear for your safety."

I stared at Matt. "Seriously?"

"Seriously."

Matt escorted me back to the lobby, said goodbye, and wished me good luck.

Josh stood and dropped the magazine he was reading on the table. "Ready?"

"Ready," I said.

Back in the car, Josh convinced me that the best thing to do was to go directly to the Poway school district office to quit my job. It would be too much of a distraction for my students with reporters and TV crews showing up, looking for an interview during finals. It felt a little weird quitting with just three days left until summer vacation, but it wouldn't be an inconvenience for the school because a substitute would be basically babysitting during the finals and could easily handle that.

I called the principal on the phone first to let her know the plan. She totally understood and was happy for me. I would miss my students dearly, but the good news was that the school had a wonderful part-time history teacher who had been eager to teach full-time.

Twenty-five minutes later, Josh pulled into the Poway Unified School District parking lot and turned off the engine. I reached for the door to open it when my phone rang.

I eyed the caller ID but didn't recognize the phone number.

"Hello?" I said.

"Liz! It's me, Lars! How are you?"

I shrugged at Josh when he glanced over at me. I did my best to remember who this person was, but I was drawing a blank. The only Lars I recalled had been the principal of the first school I had taught over twenty-five years ago. It couldn't have been him, since we hadn't spoken since, which was a good thing.

"Liz?"

"Yeah. I'm sorry—who is this again?"

"Lars. Lars Duggins? From Canyonville Middle School in LA? It's been such a long time!"

Not long enough.

It was him.

My stomach turned, thinking about him.

Why was he calling? And how had he gotten my number? I didn't have this phone number back when I had been working there. In fact, I was pretty sure I didn't even have a cell phone back then.

"How can I help you, Lars?"

"Straight to business . . . no problem."

Business? What was he talking about?

"I'm living in San Diego now, taking care of my mother," Lars said. "She's dying."

"I'm so sorry to hear that."

I may not have liked the man, but I didn't like to hear about anyone's parents dying.

Especially since Josh and I had lost both of our parents.

"Thank you," Lars said. "It hasn't been easy. Especially since her insurance is no longer covering her illness, those bastards. Sorry for my language, it's just, I'm forced to pay everything myself out of pocket. And frankly, I'm going broke."

I was certain I heard sniffling.

Was he crying?

How was I supposed to respond to that?

"It's a horrible situation to be in," Lars continued. "What's worse is I found out that I will need at least three hundred thousand dollars to keep her comfortable during her last days on this blessed earth of ours. Are you healthy, Liz?"

"Uh . . . yeah."

"Good. Good for you. Not so good for my mom, as you could imagine. But luckily, I have friends with big hearts available to help. Can you help a friend out, Liz?"

Friend? Help?

What was this guy smoking?

"It's been a while since we last chatted, but I was hoping

you would find it in your heart to help me out in my time in need, I mean, in my mother's time in need."

I stared at the phone.

Did he really think I was going to cut him a check for three hundred grand?

Like it was no big deal?

"What?" Josh whispered, looking over at me again with his eyebrows squished together.

I waved him off with my free hand, trying to figure out how to tell Lars to take a hike.

"Liz? Are you there? Look—I'm desperate."

I let out a deep breath. "I can't believe you're calling and asking me for money. How did you get my phone number, anyway? It's private."

"I work at the California Department of Education. I have access to over a quarter million teachers' records with the click of a mouse. Anyway, what's the big deal? Three hundred thousand is a drop in the bucket when you have over five hundred million big ones. Besides, you owe me."

"What?" My pulse was now pounding in my temples. "How do I owe you? You fired me when you had no good reason. Oh wait, you had a good reason. Your girlfriend at the time wanted to teach history, and I was in my probation period since it was my first year. You didn't think twice about firing me, even though I had done nothing wrong."

"I know—I'm sorry about that, but you need to understand it had to be that way to preserve my relationship. Anyway, it all worked out for the better, since I'm the one responsible for your becoming a millionaire. By the way, are you single?"

I blinked twice.

This is why they warned me to change my phone number. News traveled fast.

As much as I wanted to hang up on Lars or hurl every curse word in the book at him, my curiosity got the best of me. I had to know how he thought I couldn't have been a millionaire without him.

"Please do tell, Lars. How did you help me become a millionaire?"

Josh looked like he wanted to reach through the phone and rip Lars' head off.

I tapped the speakerphone button, so Josh could hear.

"It's simple, really. I fired you, and because of that you moved back home to San Diego to live with your parents again. Then you got the job at Westview High School, where you've been ever since. And because of that job you bought your house down the street from the Stater Brothers, and *that* is where you bought the winning ticket."

"How do you know I live near Stater Brothers?"

"Like I said—I have access to the info through my job. I looked you up on Google Maps. Anyway, none of that would've happened if I hadn't fired you. You get it now? You would still most likely be teaching in Los Angeles and definitely not even close to a millionaire. And you know what? I knew you would be okay when I fired you. I did! I knew you would bounce back because there has always been something special about you, Liz Parker. Very special. So, how about we meet up for a cup of coffee? Or maybe dinner? You can afford that."

I hung up without responding.

Josh turned to me. "Block his number."

"Good idea," I said, going to the call history on my phone

and tapping two buttons to block Lars' phone number. "Man, they weren't kidding about changing my phone number."

We went inside the district office to turn in my resignation, which took about thirty minutes.

I turned to Josh after we got back in the car and put on our seat belts. "I'm unemployed now."

He chuckled. "You poor thing."

My phone rang again.

"Don't answer that," Josh said.

I glanced at the caller ID. "This one's fine. It's the substitute teacher who's covering for me today." I answered the call. "Hi, Josie. Is everything okay?"

"Hi, Liz. Well, yes and no. The students are great. I don't have to do much when they're taking finals. I only have a minute before the next period comes in, but I need your help with my daughter. I'm so worried."

"If you need to talk to someone about leaving the school, I can't help you with that."

"No, no, no. It's nothing like that. My daughter got a perfect score on the SAT. Sixteen hundred."

"That's amazing. So, what's the problem?"

"Well, the college she had her heart set on doesn't give merit scholarships for high SAT scores and you know it's impossible to pay for a college education on a substitute's wages."

Oh no. Please don't tell me she's going to ask for money.

"I was hoping you could help me out," Josie continued, confirming my suspicions. "You know, since you won the lottery and have *all* that money now. Everybody is talking about you here at the school. You know I've always been available for you, and I'm sure that has made your life so much easier. I'm hoping you can return the favor. The tuition is seventy-five thousand dollars per year for four years. It isn't that much, considering how much you won. You won't even notice the money is gone."

You have got to be kidding me.

The woman wanted three hundred thousand dollars.

Just like Lars.

Was three hundred thousand the sweet spot for begging? Was there some handbook on begging that suggested this amount, so they didn't sound like greedy fools?

"Sorry, Josie. I can't talk right now."

"But—"

I hung up on her, blocked her phone number, and turned off my phone.

I hadn't hung up on a single person in my entire life, but I had hung up on Josh last night and two more people today.

Was the money already changing me?

There was a painful tightness in my throat. "Unbelievable . . ."

"Something tells me it will only get worse," Josh said.

"Looks like I need to change my phone number right now. Do you have time?"

"No problem." Josh pointed to my arm. "What happened there?"

I twisted my arm around to see what he was talking about. I had a huge bruise that traveled the length of my tricep.

"I have no idea."

It was the oddest thing because the only thing I remember bumping into recently was the coffee table in the living room when I had fallen off the couch, but that was my shin.

Curious, I slid my pant leg up to take a look at the spot

where I had bumped it. There was another bruise there, and it was a giant.

I stared at it for a moment. "Okay, this is weird."

"Whoa . . ." Josh leaned closer and inspected my leg. "What the heck is going on with you?"

"I have no idea. I bumped my leg on the coffee table yesterday."

"Something's not right. You shouldn't have a bruise that big for just bumping your leg. And what about your tricep? That one's even bigger."

I shrugged. "I didn't even know they were there."

"You need to get checked out, just to be safe."

"Can I at least get a new phone number first?"

"That I will allow. And I would even be okay stopping at In-N-Out Burger."

I smiled. "Nothing but the best for my baby brother."

"Hey—I'm actually thinking about you. I'm sure those bruises have something to do with a burger deficiency."

I laughed and glanced at my shin again before sliding my pant leg back down.

It was odd, but I wasn't going to worry about it.

A bruise wasn't going to kill me.

CHAPTER FOUR

ADAM

"Ford Charters and Excursions . . . this is Adam."

"Hi, Adam. It's Jonathon Masters."

"Hey, Jonathon!" I wasn't doing a good job of trying to hold the phone between my ear and shoulder. "Hang on—I'm adding sugar to my coffee and I don't want to drop you in the mug."

"I appreciate that—I'm wearing my favorite shirt." He chuckled.

I laughed and set the phone down on the counter, adding a teaspoon of sugar and stirring, eager to talk with one of my favorite clients.

Jonathon was CEO of one of the biggest Biotech companies in San Diego and a titan in the industry. As a private pilot, I'd been flying him back and forth across the United States for over ten years. We'd been to thirty-nine states, and I liked to joke with him that the other eleven states were hoping for a visit from him soon.

Jonathon was a joy to have as a client—the perfect client—because he always booked far in advance and he never canceled. Not one time in ten years of bookings.

I sat down at my desk and took a sip of my coffee. "Okay . . . I'm back. How are things?"

"Well . . . I will need to cancel our upcoming trip," Jonathon said.

There went that perfect record.

"Is everything okay?" I was a little in shock.

"My West Coast VP gave his two-week notice this morning. He's leaving to start his own company. I'm happy for him, but that means I need to focus on finding his replacement before the start of the next quarter, if possible. Sorry about this."

"Hey—don't be. Things happen."

"Well, the boss pointed out to me this morning this happened for a reason."

"Why is that?" I knew the boss he was referring to was his wife.

"She claims it was so I wouldn't miss my granddaughter's dance recital." He chuckled. "I've been in the doghouse for planning the trip in the first place, so this is a good thing. Priorities, you know? We have to keep our women happy."

I knew exactly what he meant.

I had been married to the love of my life, my soulmate, for twenty-three years before she died. I had always made it a mission to make her the happiest woman—the happiest wife—on the planet.

When she was happy, I was happy.

I glanced over at the photo of Mary on my desk and smiled.

"You there, Adam?" Jonathon asked.

"I'm here. No worries at all about the cancellation. Are we still on for the trip in October?"

"Absolutely. I should have the new VP in place by then, so we can leave it the way it is."

"Sounds good."

After disconnecting the call, I opened my laptop and deleted Jonathon's trip from my schedule, which automatically updated the online calendar on my business website.

I took another sip of my coffee, studying the schedule. I was leaving tomorrow to fly a client to Boise, and there were three other trips scheduled over the next two weeks: Chicago, Detroit, and Seattle. Then there was the gaping hole Jonathon had just left.

His cancellation was a financial hit since it was an eight-city flight itinerary that would've lasted almost three weeks. It was by far my biggest booking of the year. The chances of filling that entire slot now would be slim to none.

Running my own company as a pilot-for-hire was tricky, since there wasn't a guaranteed full-time salary. What it allowed me was flexibility and the opportunity, at least theoretically, to take time off. I made more money than most pilots, but I needed to plan well. I liked the calendar well-balanced to make sure I would be okay financially when things like this happened or when I wanted to take an extended vacation.

The biggest reason this cancellation was a disappointment was because it meant I would not be working on July 14th, the two-year anniversary of Mary's death. I'd accepted her death, but that didn't mean I wanted to sit around all day thinking about her not being around anymore.

Working was the best solution—the best distraction—but that looked like it wasn't going to happen.

Like Jonathon's wife, I believed this happened for a reason. Now, I just needed to wait to find out what that reason was. I also needed to let Orlando know about the change of plans. Orlando was my first officer on every trip. He was also my best friend.

I tapped Orlando's phone number on my phone and drank the rest of my coffee in one giant gulp.

"Adam!" He answered my call on the first ring, as usual. "It's a beautiful day."

I chuckled. "Yes. I knew that."

He was by far the most positive person I knew.

"Don't you forget it. Tell me something good today."

"Jonathon Masters canceled the big booking."

"Okay, okay . . . not the end of the world."

That was one thing I loved about Orlando. What most people would consider inconveniences or setbacks didn't faze Orlando in the least. He was a go-with-the-flow kind of guy. I was okay with plans changing because changes made life interesting. There is nothing worse than a boring routine life. Orlando taught me that and it made my life a lot less stressful when I was able to wrap my brain around it.

"That means we can get in a few rounds of golf, right?" Orlando asked. "And don't worry, we'll schedule one of them on the fourteenth to keep your mind off Mary."

He knew me well.

"Let's wait and see what happens first," I said. "I doubt

we'll be able to fill the entire gap, but maybe we'll get lucky and have someone book a flight or two."

"I bet we will," Orlando said. "Hey—did you hear some woman bought the winning lottery ticket at the Stater Brothers by your house?"

"No. I had no idea."

"Yes, sir. Just saw it on the news . . . Just think—you could've been squishing avocados right next to her in the produce department on any given day and didn't even know it was her."

"I don't squish avocados."

"Then how do you check if they're ripe?"

"I squeeze them. Gently."

"Squish. Squeeze. Squash. Same thing."

Orlando made me laugh often, which was also a good thing.

"But five hundred million big ones! Can you imagine having that much money?"

"No."

"Hey—maybe she's single." Orlando had a little too much enthusiasm. "And you know what? I can picture you with a sugar mama." He laughed.

"That would be a big fat no. I'm not driven by money."

"You may not be driven by it, but the money could fall into your lap."

"It's not going to fall into my lap. And even if it did, money can't buy me or you or anyone else happiness. Health is more important than money."

"Says the man who didn't have his colonoscopy when he was supposed to."

I sighed. "What's the rush? I just turned fifty."

"Ten months ago!"

It was true, so I couldn't argue with him. But I couldn't be called a procrastinator because that would mean I was putting it off until tomorrow or the future, which wasn't the case at all.

I had no plans on going into any hospital or any doctor's office.

And that included today, tomorrow, the day after, and the rest of my life.

Why should I?

Every time I went into a hospital someone died.

First my grandparents. Then my mom and dad together. Then Mary.

Just thinking about it gave me anxiety.

Orlando liked to tell me often that I suffered from nosocomephobia—the fear of hospitals. Richard Nixon was known to have had it and was certain if he went into the hospital, he'd never come out.

I felt the same way.

So, the best thing I could do was take care of myself, so I never had to enter a hospital again.

It was as simple as that.

That's why I went to the gym.

That's why I walked every day.

That's why I surfed.

I may not have been the oldest surfer out there catching waves, but I planned to be some day. I considered myself to be in optimum shape for a fifty-year-old man and I planned on keeping it that way until I turn a hundred years old and died peacefully in my sleep.

In fact . . .

"I'm heading to the gym," I said. "Meet me there."

"Fine, but just because you look good on the outside doesn't mean everything is in working order on the inside. You need preventive care, Mr. Nosocomephobia."

Here we go again.

Orlando could try all he wanted, but I would not change my mind.

Hospitals and doctors equaled death.

And I wasn't having any of that.

CHAPTER FIVE

Two Weeks Later . . .

LIZ

To die, or not to die, that is the question.

I waited with Josh in the examination room at the hospital to find out the results of my bone marrow tests. More accurately—I was waiting to see if I was going to live or die.

Tom Petty wrote a song where he sang about the waiting being the hardest part.

He wasn't lying.

The bruises from two weeks ago were gone now, but that didn't mean a thing. I was warned there was a good chance I had a rare bone marrow disease. They had even tested Josh, but found out he wasn't a match for me, in case I needed a transplant.

I admit I found it difficult not to think about it constantly. Yoga and meditation and wine helped, but they didn't last long. Soon my mind was right back on the one question that had been bouncing around inside my head for the last two weeks.

Am I going to die?

Not a fun question.

I'd rather have obsessed over the dessert menu at Maggiano's. No such luck.

And why was it taking them so long to get the test results from the lab?

There's a chance you might die! We'll let you know in a couple of weeks. Take care!

Don't get me wrong—I wasn't afraid to die.

I just wanted to know if it was going to happen or not, so I could do some things.

Some people would argue I should "do" more men since I wouldn't have a chance when I'm dead. Not a bad point at all, but I think I would have felt too guilty. What if one of them fell in love with me? What would I say to him?

Josh pulled me in for a hug. "You're tough. You can handle what life throws your way."

I had always been able to handle bumps in the road, but this bump had my expiration date written on it.

I stared at the door, wishing it would open. I was supposed to meet with a new hematologist, since the one I had originally seen went on maternity leave.

Dr. Singh had been my primary doctor for the last thirty years, and I trusted him more than anyone. I had asked him to be there for the results with the hematologist, and he hadn't hesitated to agree. He was down-to-earth, optimistic, and compassionate. He never beat around the bush with my health. I've always wanted straight answers, and he had always given them.

"Sorry to keep you waiting." Dr. Singh entered with another doctor I assumed was the hematologist. "This is an old colleague, Dr. Arya, who's a severe aplastic anemia specialist at Johns Hopkins. I was lucky he was in town speaking at a medical conference. He's one of the best."

"Nice to meet you both," Dr. Arya said.

"You, too." I sat up taller on the examination table. "So, I have the disease?"

Dr. Arya took a step toward me. "Yes, but your case is quite unique because you aren't exhibiting the typical headaches, flu-like symptoms, or even red spots on the skin. It seems you have a rare fusion of the disease, something we've never seen before."

"How bad is it?" I held up my hand. "Don't answer that. I would just like to know if I'm going to live or not."

"You need to find a bone marrow donor," Dr. Arya said.

"We already put you on the donor list," Dr. Singh said.

"So, I need to find a donor and that's it?" I asked, even though the look on Dr. Arya's face told me it would not be that simple.

"It's more complex than matching blood types," Dr. Arya said. "We're matching HLA tissue type. These are the proteins, or what we call markers. Your immune system uses these markers to determine which cells belong in your body. The match from the donor doesn't have to be exact, but it needs to be close to yours."

"And how likely is it she'll be able to find someone who matches?" Josh asked.

"Honestly, it won't be easy, since you're her only family and you're not a match. But we need someone who's close."

"What are my odds?" I asked, sure I knew the answer.

"Good question," Dr. Arya answered, thinking about it. "Your bone marrow tissue is not common, plus cure rates decline significantly after the age of forty. I wouldn't be surprised if your odds are around one-in-a-million."

I stared at him.

"If anyone can do it, you can," Josh said.

"Sure," I said. "I just need to win the lottery again. Easy peasy." I took in a deep breath, processing the info. "Okay, the other question I have is, if I don't find a match, how long do I have?"

Dr. Singh opened his mouth to answer and—

"You'll find a match," Josh said. "Don't you dare give up so easily."

"I'm not giving up."

Josh walked toward the poster on the wall of the human body and swung around. "Maybe you can find some alternative medicine or some ancient rainforest crap that'll cure you."

Dr. Singh cleared his throat. "I'm all for exploring alternative medicine options, but just be careful because there are a lot of scams out there."

"I'm just saying she shouldn't give up," Josh said.

I sighed. "I told you—I'm not giving up. I like to deal in facts. I need to know what I'm working with here, that's all." I turned back to Dr. Singh. "How long?"

"It's hard to tell since your case is so different from anything we've ever seen." Dr. Singh turned to Dr. Arya. "What would you say?"

"Since chemo and radiation are not even a possibility, it will progress rapidly," Dr. Arya said. "I would guess three months, if you're lucky."

Lucky to live three months?

That didn't sound like luck at all.

I shook my head in disbelief.

Not because of my diagnosis, but because of my reaction to the diagnosis.

It was the same as my reaction to winning the lottery.

It was like my mind was blank.

No emotion.

Was I already dead on the inside, just waiting for the outside to catch up?

I avoided looking at Josh after his eyes got glossy.

"What am I supposed to do in the next three months?" I asked. "Just wait?"

"Yes." Dr. Arya shrugged. "There's not much more you can do at this point. It's kind of out of our hands. You need to wait."

The waiting is the hardest part.

I didn't like that answer one bit.

"Thank you, Dr. Arya," I gave him my best smile. "Do you mind if I have a chat with Dr. Singh privately?"

"Not at all," Dr. Arya said. "I'll be around for another hour, if you have questions. I'm sorry the prognosis wasn't more positive, but nothing is impossible. Luck can strike twice."

"Thank you," I said, wondering why the word luck was being tossed around like my Wednesday salad. I waited for him to leave the examination room.

I crossed my arms and glared at Dr. Singh. "Sanjay, talk to me."

He smiled since it was the first time I had called him by his first name.

Dr. Singh had always insisted I call him Sanjay since we'd known each other for so long, but I'd never felt comfortable doing so in a professional environment.

Until now.

Maybe my horizons were being broadened because death was suddenly staring me in the face.

Dr. Singh set my medical folder on the counter. "Sorry about that. He's technical, but he's the best. What would you like to know?"

"What would you do if you were in my position?" I asked.

"I'm obligated to tell you exactly what the hospital and Dr. Arya would tell you. Rest. Avoid strenuous activities. Protect yourself from germs and wash your hands often. And don't stop believing you will have a bone marrow donor match."

"And what would you tell me as a friend?"

Dr. Singh scratched the side of his face and nodded. He walked over to the doorway, peeked outside, and closed the door all the way. "As a friend I would tell you something different." He leaned against the examination table next to me, smiling, his beautiful brown eyes so full of compassion and love. "I would tell you to eat chicken tikka masala and make a bucket list."

That made me laugh, picturing myself as Morgan Freeman

or Jack Nicholson eating chicken tikka masala in some Indian restaurant.

"If you expect me to believe that chicken tikka masala has healing properties—"

He shook his head. "Not at all. It just tastes very, very good." He winked.

I laughed again.

Why was I laughing when there was a good chance I was going to die?

Maybe I was in denial.

Josh's stomach rumbled. "Looks like I will need some, too."

"Okay." I shook my head at my brother. "We're going to eat chicken tikka masala as soon as we get out of here."

"Good." Dr. Singh smiled. "Then make a bucket list of all the things you've wanted to do. Of all the places you've ever wanted to visit. Go. See them all. And eat all the unhealthy foods you've wanted to try in your life, but never did."

"I don't have a problem with that. What else?"

He thought about it. "Know that you're now in the position to do many things with the money you have at your disposal. Do good. It will be good for your heart and soul."

I loved the way his mind worked. "Okay. Anything else?"

He nodded. "Believe in miracles."

Thirty minutes later, Josh and I were eating chicken tikka masala at Royal India, my mind on what Dr. Singh had said about believing in miracles.

I believed in them.

I also believed things happened for a reason, so I guess that meant I was supposed to get this disease. But why?

How many other people in this restaurant had a life-threatening disease? I glanced around, feeling silly for thinking I could spot them. That's when I noticed people were looking at me, pointing, and whispering.

They knew who I was.

The only reason they knew is because my name and picture had been plastered all over the news after the lottery office released my name out into the world. It didn't take long before people had gone onto Facebook and downloaded my picture.

Even though I had been staying at Josh's house to avoid the constant knocks on the door and visits from Snoop Dolly Dog, I still encountered people asking me for money just about every day since the day I had won.

Josh grabbed a piece of garlic naan from the basket and glanced up at me. "How are you doing?"

I shrugged. "I'm okay."

"Okay is such a horrible word. It needs to be removed from the English language. I will rephrase my question because I want to know how you're feeling about things overall. I want to know if you have hope. Because I don't want you to give up."

"I'm not going to."

"Good." Josh took a sip of his drink. "Then answer this . . . are you going to take Dr. Singh's advice?"

I tore off a piece of naan, dipped it in the masala sauce, and stuck it in my mouth. "I'm doing it right now."

Josh smiled. "The second part. The bucket list."

"Of course, I'm going to do it."

"Good." Josh stood and held up his index finger. "Just a second."

Josh walked over to the front reception area near the front door of the restaurant. After he exchanged a few words with the manager, Josh returned with a piece of paper and a pen.

He sat back down, pushing his plate toward the center of the table to give himself some room. "Okay. Time to make that bucket list."

I looked around the restaurant at the other people eating and looked back at Josh. "Now?"

"Yes. Now. Unless you want to wait three months. It's up to you."

"You think that's funny?"

"Actually, I do. I'm hilarious. Admit it."

"You're mildly amusing."

He chuckled. "I'll take it." He clicked the top of the pen a few times. "Okay, a bucket list of all the things you've wanted to do. What do you want to start with? Bungee jumping? Skydiving?"

"Did you forget how old I am?"

"Fine," Josh said, not looking happy that we were off to a bad start with the list. "Give me something. Anything."

I thought about it. "I've always wanted to spend the night in a castle."

Josh nodded. "Okay—that's a start. Very cool. We can stick that on your list of the places you've wanted to visit since the castle will most likely be in Europe. What was the other list Dr. Singh mentioned?"

"All the unhealthy foods I've wanted to try, but that list is easy, so let's focus on places I want to visit." I sat there deep in thought and shook my head.

"What?" Josh asked, twirling the pen between his fingers.

"I don't know . . . It's kind of sad that I've been teaching history for over twenty-five years, but haven't gone to any of the amazing places I've taught about in my classes."

"You've been busy."

"I've been putting it off." I thought about it a little more. "I guess I always figured I would travel when I retired. Not sure why I made the decision that I would have to wait until I stopped working to have fun."

"It's not unusual. What's more unusual is you choosing to work over your summer vacations when most people use that time to recharge and disconnect from their jobs. But enough of that. You can't change the past. Tell me where you want to go."

"This will be easy . . . London, Rome, New York to see some Broadway shows, Santorini, Greece. The Taj Mahal—"

"Hang on," Josh said, busy writing. "Okay, keep going."

"The pyramids in Egypt, Machu Picchu, Paris, and Russia. The northern lights in Norway has to be near the top of the list. An African safari. Oh! I need to walk on top of the Great Wall of China."

Josh sat there with a smile, which is just what I would expect from him. The last thing I needed was pity and sympathy. That would only bring me down and get me into negativity. I was certain the only things that would get me through this were positive thoughts and constant reinforcement that I will enjoy the time I have left. That old saying "live like it's your last day" applies perfectly and that will be how I live every single day, no matter how many I have left.

I pointed to Josh's face. "Why are you getting a kick out of this?"

"I'm excited for you, all these incredible places you'll get to see. You know I would go with you in a heartbeat if I didn't have to be in court."

"I know."

Josh was in the middle of a high-profile case and was a key witness, so I assumed he wouldn't be able to go since he said the case could last weeks. He also just started his detective training. It would be foolish of him to quit and selfish of me to ask.

"I'll be with you in spirit." Josh reached across the table and squeezed my hand. "Just make sure you take plenty of pictures. And add the international calling plan to your phone, so we can talk and text while you're gone."

"I will." I glanced down at my bucket list. "I need to narrow this down. People spend a lifetime going to all these places, but I only want to be gone around three weeks, so I can spend as much time as possible with you when I get back."

Josh chuckled. "All these places in three weeks? Impossible."

"That's why I'm going to make the list smaller." I pointed to Josh's plate. "Eat. You haven't finished."

A woman outside stopped in front of the window and waved. Then she walked away.

"Do you know her?" Josh asked.

"No."

"She must have recognized you from the news. There will be plenty more like her." He pointed to my head. "You should cut your hair and dye it a different color."

"Like the FBI witness protection program?" I laughed. "No way. This is my hair color for life."

"Come on, it's not going to kill you." Josh froze. "Sorry. Poor choice of words."

I smiled. "Don't worry about it."

"But you need to think about the logistics of this trip, too. It would be easier to charter a plane instead of flying commercial and dealing with scheduling, security, layovers, and people bugging you. Especially reporters, because you're bound to run into them. It would be just you, the pilot, and the crew."

"Do I look like a Kennedy to you?"

"No, but you have enough money to hang with them. And I'm serious about this. I'm sure there are plenty of pilots who would be happy to fly you around the world. In fact, hang on." Josh pulled out his phone and tapped a few things, shaking his head. "No." He scrolled more. "Not this either." Still scrolling. "Nope." A few seconds later, he turned his phone toward me to show me the screen. "Okay, here's a pilot for hire in San Diego, and no, I didn't pick him because he is good-looking, even though he is. Anyway, he's got perfect reviews, over a hundred. Adam Ford. Lots of experience. He's got an online calendar." He scrolled through a few things. "Looks like he's got the time for you this month, if this calendar is up-to-date. Easy peasy, as you would say. I'll send you the link to his website."

"That's not necessary."

"Too late." His smile got bigger and cockier. "Check your email when you get home and call him." He showed me the pilot's picture on his phone. "Did I mention he's a good-looking guy? I think I did. Too bad he's straight."

"How can you tell?"

"Believe me—I know."

I leaned in to get a better look.

His brown eyes were gorgeous. He had a full head of black hair, but with some white sprinkled in, especially around the ears and temples.

Yeah—he was good-looking.

I looked up at Josh, who was smiling.

I glanced at the picture one more time, clearing my throat. "How much experience does he have flying?"

"Nice try. I saw that."

"What?"

Josh pointed to my face. "You did a double-take. You checked him out twice."

"I did not."

"Yes, you did. Hey, nothing to be embarrassed about. Maybe you'll get lucky."

I crossed my arms. "Are you serious?"

"Why not? You said you wouldn't give up."

"I said I wasn't going to give up on living."

"Well, living includes dating, does it not?"

"Sure—we'll go out on a date and talk about the first thing that pops into my head. Death!" I grimaced and shook my head. "It's kind of a conversation killer, don't you think? Plus, he's probably married and with a family, and even if he wasn't, it doesn't matter. I'm not looking to meet a man."

"That's exactly what I was hoping you would say." Josh grinned.

I glared at my brother, more confused than ever. "What are you talking about?"

"That's usually when you're most likely to meet a man—when you're not looking."

Josh was right.

That's exactly how I'd met my two husbands.

But it wasn't going to happen this time. I would go on the trip of a lifetime, but would not be seeing, dating, or sleeping with any men. Even with someone as handsome as Adam Ford.

CHAPTER SIX

LIZ

I sat in my car in the driveway of my house, waiting for the mail to be delivered. This had been my routine every day this week. I would stop by and see if the check from the lottery office was in the mail, then head right back to Josh's place. Hopefully, today would be the day.

Francisco, the mailman, was always organized and always on schedule. And since he'd never missed a day of work in his life, I was confident he would deliver the mail right around ten minutes after two, like he did every day.

It was 2:09 pm.

One more minute.

If I could just avoid seeing Snoop Dolly Dog, things would be perfect, since she kept asking me what I'm going to do with all the money.

Surprisingly, she has never asked for any.

It had been a great idea staying with Josh because his

three-bedroom townhouse was located in a gated community with a security guard at the entrance. Not a soul knew I was there. Even if they had known, they wouldn't have knocked on the door because they knew Josh was a cop. It sure came in handy having a cop for a brother. I could even make up for missing my evening walks by using his treadmill.

Francisco arrived right on schedule, but this time he walked up my driveway with my mail instead of putting it in my box.

I lowered my window, surprised. "Hi, Francisco."

"Hello, Liz. I know you were expecting this, so I thought I would just give it to you." He winked and handed me the envelope from the state controller's office. "Enjoy your day."

"Thank you. You, too."

My hands shook as I stared at the envelope.

This was it.

The check was inside.

The check.

$200,000,000.00.

How were they going to fit all those zeroes on there?

I raised the window back up, locked my door, and stuck my finger under the flap of the envelope, carefully tearing it open.

I pulled out the check and stared at it, shocked at what I saw.

The check was ruined!

How could they have done such a thing?

I stared at the amount: $200,000,001.35.

"Unbelievable."

They messed up a perfectly good even number and a

perfectly good check by having that extra dollar and thirty-five cents there.

Why?

I would have been perfectly fine with $200,000,000.00. They could have kept the dollar thirty-five. It would have looked so much better on paper.

I shook my head and took out my phone to snap a few photos of the check. I drove directly to my credit union to deposit the check into my account. I had read online from multiple sources that I shouldn't keep all the money in the same account, so I would need to open more bank accounts soon and split the money between them.

But right now, there was only one thing on my mind.

The bucket list.

I went back to Josh's place and researched private jet chartering and pilots for hire. I called the first company with excellent reviews.

"Chaz Charters—I'm Chaz," the man answered. "How can I help you?"

"Hello, I'm inquiring about chartering a private jet."

"That's what we do. What's the date and destination?"

"I'm available as early as tomorrow. The destination would first be Peru. After that—"

"Tomorrow? Peru?"

"Well, yes, for starters."

"For starters . . ."

There was silence on the other end of the phone.

"Are you there?" I asked.

"Yeah. I'm here. How many people?"

"Just me."

"Just you . . ."

"Uh, is there a problem?"

"We shall see. You said you wanted to go someplace else after Peru?"

"Yes. Greece. France. Germany. Norway. Africa,"

More silence.

"Hello?"

"Yup. Still here. Is this a joke?"

"Pardon me?"

"You want to go to all these places? Have you ever chartered a plane before?"

"No. It's my first time."

"Most people who use our services for last-minute trips go domestically. Trips like yours are usually booked months in advance. And are you aware of what a trip like this would cost?"

What kind of question was that? It was almost as if he was trying to talk me out of it. Any company should be happy to get last-minute business they weren't expecting. I didn't know how to respond.

"And you're aware all jets and baggage are inspected, and that you still have to pass through security in both directions?" he added.

"Of course."

"Some people think private jets can skip all that. You'd be surprised what they try to take across the border from one country into another. I once had a client who tried to smuggle cockatoos from Australia into the US. Ha! Can you believe that? I almost lost my license. I'm just saying, in case you think I'm playing."

"Look, I should just—"

"One moment, please."

I could hear him tapping on a keyboard.

"Okay," Chaz said. "Just checked and we have nothing available tomorrow. One moment."

More tapping on a keyboard.

"Sorry. All booked up for the entire month."

I shook my head and said goodbye, wondering why he didn't know his schedule was full this month before we started our conversation. I also wondered why he was so skeptical.

What a waste of time.

And time wasn't on my side.

I called the next company and cut to the chase, after they answered the phone.

"Do you have any jets and pilots available tomorrow to fly me around the world?"

The man laughed. "You're kidding, right? Is this Margaret?"

"No, this is Liz."

"Right. You're hilarious, Margaret. I recognized your voice immediately. Hilarious."

After finally convincing the man I wasn't Margaret, he told me his company didn't have availability the next couple of months and said goodbye.

The next five calls weren't any better.

Nobody had availability.

Why was it so hard to charter a plane internationally?

Maybe I should just buy the darn plane.

I took a break and checked my email, deleting the first ten emails from strangers who were asking for money. I eyed the next email at the top of my inbox, the one Josh had sent me from the Indian restaurant.

Subject: Hunky pilot's website.

I opened the email and clicked on the link.

A new window popped open, taking me to Adam Ford's website.

There was a picture of a jet on the home page, with a bullet point list of his experience, which included being a pilot for both American Airlines and Southwest Airlines before he became a private pilot.

On the gallery page, I scrolled through pictures of Adam in various cockpits, on the tarmac in front of airplanes, and at some amazing destinations around the world. The one thing all the pictures had in common was his smile.

A gorgeous smile.

It was sincere, kind, and relaxed, like the man didn't have a care in the world.

Right.

Everybody had problems.

Some more than others.

Still, there was something soothing and comforting about Adam. Add the impressive resume and his sparkly white teeth and I couldn't help dialing his phone number.

While I waited for him to answer the phone, I clicked the link on his website that took me right to his Facebook page.

There was a photo of him shirtless on some tropical island.

"Ford Charters and Excursions, this is Adam."

"Hi, Adam." I tried to focus but couldn't pry my eyes off the photo. "Uh . . . my name is Liz, and I, uh, wanted to check on your availability."

"Of course. I'd be happy to help you. I just need the date and the destination."

"Well, this may sound weird based on the reactions of the last few people I talked to, but I was hoping to leave this week and be away for a few weeks. As for the destinations, I'd like to go to Machu Picchu in Peru, Africa, Germany, Greece, Norway, and France."

I braced myself for Adam's laughter or for the man to give me a lecture on why it was crazy to do something so last-minute.

Or maybe he would ask me if I was planning on trafficking drugs or human organs.

"Wow," Adam said. "This is an amazing itinerary—sounds like the trip of a lifetime."

"It's my bucket list."

"It sounds incredible. How many people will be traveling with you?"

I hesitated. "It's just me."

"Okay . . ."

There it was—the silence on the other end of the phone I had been waiting for. Maybe I should hang up now. He probably thought I was a crank-caller or someone who had completely lost her marbles. Maybe I had.

"Sorry for the delay," Adam said. "I'm actually available since I had a cancellation, but I was checking the system to make sure there's a long-distance aircraft available. It looks like the smallest jet I have available for this type of trip is a Gulfstream G-Six-Fifty that seats ten people. None of the other smaller aircraft that are available can make it across the Atlantic. Will that be okay?"

"Yes." I was surprised he was taking me seriously and wasn't asking me why I was traveling alone. "I'm okay with that. Are they your jets?"

Adam chuckled. "No, no. Not even close. I charge a thousand dollars a day for my services, and the aircraft that I mentioned costs almost seventy million dollars. I think I would need to work every day for about three hundred years to afford a jet like that." He laughed again. His laugh was deep and hearty, soothing even.

"There's a local aviation company I work with," Adam continued. "You pay the rental fee for the jet, plus fuel costs, and some other fees including mine. I can outline everything for you, so you can see exactly what a trip like this entails before you decide. I'll just need a little more info to send you a quote. You said you wanted to leave this week?"

"Yes. In the next couple of days, if possible."

"Well, I would need four days to get overflight and landing permits for Cusco, Peru. That's where we would fly to get you to Machu Picchu. It's sometimes possible to get them in three days. Would that still work for you?"

"Of course." I was surprised none of the other companies had mentioned that. This guy seemed like he knew what he was doing, which was a good sign.

I heard Adam's fingers tapping away on his keyboard.

"Okay, I have some good news and I have some good news."

I laughed. "Isn't the second part supposed to be the bad news?"

"No bad news at all here. The good news is that I'm available, eager, and ready to fly you wherever you want to go. The jet is available, and we can leave in three days if I can get the signed contract, payment, and itinerary sometime this evening. That's assuming you have your documentation and passport in order, but keep in mind I can't reserve the jet until I have everything from you."

I stared at the phone.

This was going to happen.

I chewed on a fingernail, certain I couldn't back out now.

Josh would kill me if I did.

I shook my head at the thought.

Josh killing me before I die of the disease.

Okay, maybe that wasn't so funny.

"Liz?"

"Yes—sorry, I'm here."

"Can you send me your itinerary?" Adam asked. "I'll need to make sure there aren't any other airports that require overflight and landing permits before I can send you the quote. I'll also go over the itinerary carefully to make sure it will work, logistically."

"I spent most of last night working on it and it is ready to go, so you don't have to worry about that. I can send you the Excel spreadsheet, so you can see for yourself."

"You got it, but please keep in mind I still need to approve it. There are logistics pertaining to airports and flying we need to keep in mind when putting together the itinerary."

I had done plenty of research, so I was sure the itinerary would be fine. I was proud of the thought and detail I had put into it. I had no doubts Adam would be impressed. Maybe I had missed my calling as a travel agent.

"Can I email you the itinerary and stop by with a check to take care of the rest in person?"

"Sounds perfect," Adam said.

There was no reason to wait and see if he would give me a good price. There had to be a going rate for something like this. Plus, money wasn't an issue anymore and time was more valuable. I needed to book the trip and pack.

Go figure. It looked like Josh had found me a pilot.

Adam sounded like a down-to-earth man, too. The last thing I needed was a high-strung person to spend the next few weeks with.

I emailed Adam my itinerary and stared at another photo of him on Facebook, swimming with dolphins. What a life he'd had flying around the world. And now it was my turn.

This was really going to happen.

CHAPTER SEVEN

LIZ

Forty-five minutes later, I walked into Adam Ford's office, located in a small building across the street from Montgomery-Gibbs Executive Airport in San Diego.

Adam was on the phone with his eyes glued to his laptop monitor. He turned to look at me, and did a double take, just like I had done when I had seen a photo of him for the first time.

What was that about?

He smiled and gestured for me to take a seat in the empty chair on the other side of his desk.

"That's right," Adam said to the person he was talking to on the phone. "Three weeks."

I took a seat and waited for him to finish his phone call, glancing at his cherrywood desk directly in front of me.

There wasn't a speck of dust on it.

Impressive.

Everything was neatly stacked, files directly on top of the other.

Equally impressive.

A pen sat next to a notepad to his right. A coffee mug on top of a coaster. Lots of elbow room for working on his laptop. He was organized. He was clean.

Adam was not a normal man.

To my right there was a small kitchen area tucked in the corner with a microwave, mini-refrigerator, coffeemaker, and electric tea kettle.

A flat-screen television hung on the wall directly behind him.

Next to it was a large framed image of the Taj Mahal in India.

"Sounds great," Adam said to the other person on the phone. He tapped a couple of keys on his laptop. A few seconds later the printer warmed up and spit out a couple of pages. He grabbed them both and sat back down, the phone still to his ear. "I can let you know in just a little bit."

My phone vibrated, and I pulled it from my purse. It was a text from Josh.

Josh: Are you still alive?

Liz: Hilarious. I'm meeting with a pilot.

Josh: The hunky one?

Liz: He's not hunky.

Josh: Liar!

. . .

I had no intention of admitting to my brother that Adam was attractive. The photos on his website didn't do him justice.

I tucked the phone back in my purse after Adam got off the phone.

"Sorry about that," he said. "You're obviously Liz."

"That's me—yes."

He stood and extended his hand across the desk. "I'm Adam Ford as you probably already figured out. A pleasure to meet you."

I shook his hand. "You, too."

We locked gazes and time stood still. It was the same feeling I had after my second glass of wine. I was relaxed and didn't have a care in the world, which made little sense since there was a good chance I was going to die pretty soon.

I couldn't take my eyes off him.

Was I paralyzed?

Dr. Singh failed to mention that symptom.

And what about my voice? Words were failing to come out of my mouth.

Why was Adam looking at me like that?

A warm, tingly feeling spread through my body. Something was familiar here. Had we met before? Maybe in a past life?

I stared at Adam, sure I knew what was going on.

He had hypnotized me.

It had to be the only logical explanation for why I had no interest in letting go of his hand. It was like we were playing a game of chicken to see who would let go first. Neither of us were making a move to end this handshake madness, and my palm was getting sweaty.

I cleared my throat and finally pulled my hand away,

wondering what the heck had happened there. I wasn't sure, but I needed to say something.

I pointed to the picture of the Taj Mahal. "Have you, uh, been there?"

He nodded. "Yeah. It's even more majestic in person. I think it's one of the most romantic buildings in the world. Do you know the story?"

"I do." The blood seemed to be returning to my brain. "I know the story well."

It was romantic, but what was surprising was that a man thought so as well.

"I love that the emperor built it to honor his wife," Adam continued.

"He had *more* than one wife," I teased.

Adam chuckled. "I guess when you put it that way it may not seem so romantic, but at least he wasn't married to all of them at the same time."

"Good point."

"And, yes, he was married three times, but the third time was a charm, since he considered her to be his first true love."

It was fascinating that the emperor hadn't met his soulmate until his third marriage. I had already been married twice, but the third time wouldn't be a charm for me, I knew that much. There would not be a third time, anyway.

"They had fourteen children together," I said.

"Yikes." Adam stared at me. "I didn't know that part."

"I wish I could teach things like this in my high school history class. It's romantic, but also a little sad, too. I had the Taj Mahal on my bucket list for a visit on the second Friday of this trip but removed it after my brother said I had too many places in such a short time span."

"I agree with your brother. And if it makes you feel any better, the Taj Mahal is closed on Fridays for prayers, so you wouldn't have been able to go on that day, anyway. One day isn't enough for India, or anywhere else. Speaking of which, your itinerary needed work, so I had to move things around."

I jerked my head back. "How is that possible? I did a lot of research before putting it together."

Adam grimaced. "Sorry. But don't worry, I fixed it."

Fixed it?

It didn't need fixing.

Adam inspected the documents he had printed earlier and glanced up at me. "Have you done much traveling?"

"Not much." I tried to peek at the two pages, but they were impossible to read since they were upside down. "I always thought I'd travel the world when I retired."

"Some people never make it to retirement."

"Like my parents . . ."

Adam blinked twice. "Sorry. My parents didn't make it, either."

We stared at each other for another long beat; the silence seemed to be our way of understanding and sympathizing with the other person.

Connecting.

Oh no.

Was he hypnotizing me again? I couldn't look away. What was with this man?

Adam finally broke the spell. "So, what made you change your mind?"

"About what?"

"About waiting for retirement to travel."

That subject was off limits.

I would not bring anybody down with my condition or my diagnosis. Sympathy was okay when it came to what happened to my parents, but as for me, I didn't need it and it wasn't going to cure me or make me feel better.

I shrugged. "There's no time like the present, right?"

Adam grinned. "That's a good attitude to have, although I should show you this." He lifted his coffee mug off the coaster and turned it around, so I could read the quote printed on it.

"Time is an illusion."
Albert Einstein

"Time is an illusion." I read it a couple more times in my head, trying to decipher Einstein's message. "So, I'm imagining time? Is that what Einstein meant?"

"Honestly, I'm not sure what he was trying to say. A client gave me the mug." Adam chuckled. "But if I were to guess, I'd bet Einstein was telling us that time can be anything we want it to be. It's what we make of the time that counts."

"Time is precious?"

"For the time being." Adam winked. "And don't forget time flies when you're with a pilot."

"A pilot pun?" I laughed and crossed my arms. "Now you're just killing time."

Adam laughed again.

I loved his laugh, and that he was comfortable enough in his own skin to joke around with a complete stranger.

"Okay, okay." Adam turned the two pieces of paper around so I could finally see them right-side-up. "I whipped this together. Tell me what you think. I had to make a few minor tweaks."

I scooted forward in my chair and stared at the pages for a few moments, popping back and forth from one page to the other.

It was an itinerary of my trip, but it looked nothing at all like the itinerary I'd spent so much time working on.

A few minor tweaks?

It was a complete overhaul.

It was like he tossed mine out the window and started again from scratch.

I cocked my head to the side. "What happened to my itinerary?"

Adam crinkled his nose. "Sorry, I had to throw it out. It needed work."

He threw away my itinerary?

That was much worse than tossing it out the window.

This man was a monster!

Adam cleared his throat. "Okay, I was married fewer times than that emperor of India, but I have enough experience from my one marriage to recognize that look on your face and know what it means. You need to trust me. I've been doing this a long time. Let me explain everything to you over a cup of tea. Some calming chamomile maybe?"

He obviously noticed I was tense.

A cup of chamomile sounded wonderful.

"Tea sounds great. Thank you."

"My pleasure, honey." He turned on the electric tea kettle and pulled a tea bag from the box on the shelf.

I cranked my head in Adam's direction, certain I pulled a muscle in my neck.

Did he say what I think he said?

He called me honey?

Noooooo.

I had to be imagining it.

I mean it sounded sexy when it came out of his mouth, but that didn't make it right. In fact, it was wrong, wrong, wrong to address someone you had just met that way. Sure, there was a waitress at my favorite diner who called all the men "Sugar" before, during, and after she served them, but this was different. I was here on business for an important trip, not eating waffles with cheesy scrambled eggs.

"Liz?" Adam leaned forward, studying me.

I stared right back at him, a little dazed and confused. "Huh?"

He held up a bottle of honey.

I continued to stare at him.

"For your tea? Would you like some?"

Oh . . .

Of course.

I felt my face heat up. "Honey sounds great. Thanks so much."

"Of course," Adam said, smiling and whistling.

I caught myself smiling, thinking of my dad and how he used to whistle while he worked in the garden or cooked on the barbecue. He had told me many times if he focused on the tune he was whistling it was impossible to have any bad thoughts at the same time. He whistled because it relaxed him and gave him positive energy. My mom said it was my dad's version of a mating call, and he only whistled when he was horny. Luckily, she had told me when I was an adult and not a teenager, or I would've been scarred for life.

My phone vibrated again.

Josh: Maybe you'll be joining the Mile-High Club with this guy.

"Bite me," would have been the perfect reply to my brother, but Adam approached with the tea, so I quickly slipped the phone back into my purse before he could see the ridiculous message. Even if I had wanted to join the Mile-High Club, I wouldn't have done it with the pilot because who would fly the plane while we were going at it? Safety always came first.

"Here you go." Adam handed me the tea.

"Thank you."

He grabbed the remote from his desk and pointed it at the flat panel television on the wall. A map of the world popped up on the screen and all the places I wanted to go to on this trip had a smiley face next to them.

Maybe it was impressive, but the guy still had torn up my itinerary. Just because he was charming and good-looking didn't give him the right to mangle my work.

"There are several things your itinerary didn't take into account." Adam gestured to the places I wanted to travel to. "First is the order of your destinations and how the wind plays a huge factor. It's an important part of traveling, more on the technical side. Most people don't even know about it. The way you had your itinerary planned, you would've been flying twice as long to get to the same places."

"Twice as long?"

Adam nodded. "Yes. The other thing you forgot was the layovers for refueling. For instance, it's not possible for us to fly non-stop from San Diego to Africa. We would need to stop and refuel somewhere. That's why it was better to rework it, so time is on your side."

I sighed. "Time . . ."

If only time were on my side.

Right now, my life was a ticking time bomb.

I'm not sure why I assumed we would fly non-stop to every destination, but if we had to stop, we had to stop.

"Don't worry," Adam said. "I've been doing this for a long time, and that's why I came up with the perfect plan for you. And since I appreciate your business, I would be happy to help with any other part of your travel arrangements, if you need some advice."

"That would be great—thank you."

Adam showed me the itinerary he had put together for me. It looked good, actually, except he had the trip ending with two nights in Paris. I had planned on ending the trip with two nights in Norway to see the northern lights. That had to be changed.

"You look like you want to say something." Adam studied me.

"Everything looks good, but I need you to swap France and Norway."

Adam glanced back up at the monitor and eyed the last two stops, before turning back. "What's the problem with the way it is now?"

"I need to be in Paris on July fourteenth."

Something flickered in his eyes.

I wasn't sure if it was annoyance, surprise, or confusion, but it disappeared in a flash. Something was on his mind since he wasn't acknowledging my need to be in Paris on that date.

"What's happening in Paris?" he finally asked.

"Bastille Day," I said. "I've been teaching about the French Revolution for twenty-five years and promised myself that one day I would be there for the celebration. It's a huge event and the entire country celebrates with parades, fireworks at the Eiffel Tower, even dancing."

He nodded, thinking about it.

"Anyway—I've always wanted to be there for the celebration, so just swap France with Norway, and we'll be good to go. It'll be perfect to end the trip with northern lights because that will be one of the most spectacular things I'll see in my life, from what I hear."

"Well . . ." He glanced at the monitor again and hesitated. "Let me look into it, to make sure there aren't any issues."

"What issues?" I stared at him, waiting for a response. This wasn't rocket science. Okay, maybe it was close to rocket science because rockets fly and planes fly, but that shouldn't matter. This seemed like an easy fix, but Adam was hesitating.

"What about the hotel?" Adam asked, not willing to make this easy. "If this event is that big all the hotels will be sold out."

I shook my head. "I'll sleep on the street if I have to."

"Sleep on the street?"

"I'm kidding. My point is I'll find something, okay?"

"Okay, but keep in mind some things are changed on the fly, so to speak. That's the beauty of chartering a private jet. Commercial flights have absolutely no flexibility. There's nothing worse than rigidity."

Was he talking about me?

Was he calling me rigid or was he talking about the commercial airlines or both?

Sure, I've been known to be a little rigid, but I never saw it as a flaw.

I liked what I liked, and I enjoyed planning things exactly how I liked them.

Was there anything wrong with that?

No way.

Adam typed a few things before the printer started up again, printing two pages.

He grabbed my two pages, tore them into a few pieces, and pulled the newly printed documents from the printer.

Adam placed the two pages in front of me. "There you go. Ending with the northern lights in Norway. Just keep in mind weather and other factors may throw us off schedule or alter the plans, so it's always good to go in with an open mind and a willingness to improvise and be spontaneous."

Spontaneity was not a part of my vocabulary and I saw nothing wrong with that because I always knew what I was getting. I have been meticulously planning my life this way for years and have never had a problem.

Wow. I sure feel defensive at the moment.

And Adam was staring at me again.

Had he said something, and I missed it?

My thoughts had blocked out his voice completely.

"What was that?" I asked.

"The most important thing is the first destination. It sounds like you're okay with Machu Picchu first, correct?"

"Yes."

"Great. You will get to see everything you want to see, but

you need to book the train ride that goes from Cusco to Machu Picchu immediately. It sometimes can be booked up a year in advance, but some hotels have packages with seats reserved for clients, so try to get it through the hotel in Cusco, if you can. And if we need to tweak something along the way, we can just do a little tweak."

We had different ideas of what a tweak was.

"Trust me," Adam said, a sincere and confident tone to his voice. He grabbed another piece of paper from the stack on his desk and handed it to me. "This is the breakdown of the costs." He pointed out a few things. "Jet rental, pilot rental." He grinned. "Fuel, first officer—"

"What's that?"

"FAA requires at least two pilots on board for all flights. The first officer is my backup, although he will do some of the flying as well. His name is Orlando. He's one of the best in the business. Since it isn't like a commercial flight, we do everything, serve food, stow your suitcase, you name it."

I nodded. "I don't expect you to deal with my suitcase."

"All part of the job. There's even a budget for food. I need to know your meal preferences to place an order. As for hotels—"

"I'll take care of that," I said. "For the three of us."

"That's unnecessary."

"I insist. I'll also pay for your food."

"That's also not necessary."

"I insist again."

He chuckled. "Okay—thank you. I appreciate that." He pointed to the document. "If everything looks good, just sign and date the bottom, and I'll need to get the check from you."

Even though I had more than enough money to buy the

jet for myself, seeing that this trip would cost more than I'd made in the last ten years as a teacher was a shock to the system.

I signed and dated the document without reading the rest of the details and wrote a check for the full amount, handing them both to Adam.

"Perfect." Adam sat back down at his laptop and typed a few things. "And you are good to go. This will be fun."

I hoped it would be fun and a great distraction.

Adam had no idea why I was doing this, and he wouldn't find out.

There was one thing I wondered, though.

"This may sound like an odd question, but what do you typically do after you drop your clients off at their destinations?"

Adam shrugged. "It depends on where we're going and for how long. If it's a short trip, I read and grab a bite to eat. If it's a longer trip to some touristy spot, I usually do the same thing they do. Go out, see the sites, and people watch."

People watch?

It made sense he would go out and play the part of the tourist, but people-watching sounded weird.

"You'll be visiting Machu Picchu when we get to Peru? And doing a safari in Africa?"

"I wouldn't miss it for the world," Adam said. "I've been to many places around the globe, but coincidentally you chose a few destinations I have never been to. Peru, Africa, and northern lights in Norway."

It felt weird going separately considering we were going on the same excursions, and also considering he was the one flying me all over the world. I also felt like it would be rude if

I didn't ask him to join me. I just didn't want him to think I was interested in him or trying to hit on him. I wouldn't have been surprised if rich millionaire women tried to seduce him all the time. I mean, look at him. Still, I would not be one of those women, no matter how attractive he was.

Please don't take this the wrong way.

"You're more than welcome to join me on the excursions," I said.

He stared at me.

"I mean, since we're going to the same places, staying at the same hotels."

I could see his Adam's apple—no pun intended—move up and down from swallowing hard.

He was thinking about it.

"Are you sure?" Adam asked, analyzing me again.

"Of course. In fact, I insist. My treat."

Okay, maybe that was a little too much.

Now, I was sure he would think I was trying to hit on him. *I'm an idiot.*

I was just trying to be nice—that's all.

"As acquaintances," I blurted out. "I don't want you to think—"

"No!" Adam said, thankfully understanding I had no interest in hooking up or being a member of the Mile-High Club. "I wasn't even thinking that at all. I was just surprised. Pleasantly surprised. Most clients aren't that generous, that's all. Are you sure? I didn't mention it as a hint to get you to offer it. I promise."

Well, I couldn't take it back now. I felt like a fool for being forward and offering, but I would feel like an even bigger fool if I took it back.

It wasn't going to happen.

"Yes—I'm sure. I haven't done any hiking in a while, so just don't make me look bad on the way to Machu Picchu."

He chuckled. "I doubt I could ever make you look bad. You are—" His smile disappeared.

Why hadn't he finished his sentence?

And what had he meant by that?

Was that a compliment?

A come-on?

Who was hitting on whom?

Nobody should be hitting on anybody!

I had no idea why my mind went there.

"Sorry." Adam's eyes were darting back and forth around the room, like he was watching a fly in the middle of an epileptic seizure.

"Don't be sorry," I said. "You did *nothing* wrong. I mean I should be telling you I could never make *you* look bad."

Oh, God. Why did I say that?

He was attractive, and probably out of my league, but I didn't want him to know I thought so. I didn't want him to feel bad about sticking his foot in his mouth, but now I had gone and done the exact same thing.

"It doesn't matter how you look," I said, trying to recover, but not doing the best job. "You can look great or horrible or mediocre and it wouldn't affect me at all. I mean, don't get me wrong, I'm not saying you look horrible or mediocre."

I'm making it worse. What the hell was in that tea? Someone please shoot me or open the ceiling and airlift me out of here.

Now, there were two feet in my mouth, and I could barely breathe. "I'm going to shut up now. And I give you permission to tear up the contract or kick me out."

A grin grew slowly on his face and he chuckled. "I think we're good."

I blinked. "You're not offended by my rambling mouth?"

"Not at all. I find it endearing. Like I said—we're good."

I wondered why he enjoyed rambling mouths. "Good." I nodded.

Adam chuckled. "Glad we got that cleared up." He reached out his hand.

I stared at it, wondering if the same thing would happen again. It would be rude not to shake it. The only thing I could do was avoid eye contact, shake his hand quickly, and make a clean break.

I grabbed his hand and shook. "Avoid eye contact. Avoid eye contact."

"Oh," Adam said. "So sorry."

I pulled my hand away, confused. "Sorry for what? What happened?"

"Well, you told me to avoid eye contact, but it was too late. I was already looking at you."

I closed my eyes, mentally screaming at myself.

I had said that out loud?

"I didn't say avoid eye contact." I tried to come up with something that sounded similar. "I said *oh boy, my contact*." I pointed to the floor. "I lost a contact."

Adam glanced down and squatted. "I'll help you find it."

I waved him off. "Don't worry. They're disposables. I've got plenty. Okay—gotta run!"

I flew out the door, accidentally slamming it.

I opened it back up and peeked inside. "Sorry."

"No worries," Adam said.

This time, I closed the door like a normal person would

close a door and walked to my car. I was embarrassed beyond belief over what had happened in there.

At least I felt better about the trip. It was booked and ready to go.

And Josh was right—planning a trip like this using commercial airlines would've been a logistical nightmare. It was amazing how fast Adam was able to line up everything. Now, the only thing I would do was research hotels and excursions and book them for me, Adam, and Orlando, the first officer. I considered myself an expert when it came to research and was confident I could get everything done within a few hours if there were no distractions. I had confidence that things would go off without a hitch. As Adam said, he'd been doing this for years, so it looked like I'd hired the right man.

I was curious about Adam. I had seen a picture of a woman on his desk. A beautiful woman. Not a surprise since he was such a handsome man, but who was she? A sister? He wasn't wearing a ring. It couldn't have been his wife or girlfriend, or he would have said something when we had that are-we-good-yes-we-are-good debacle or the handshake that almost brought me to an orgasm.

I guess the part that worried me the most was why I was thinking about him at all in something other than a professional manner.

There was no way I would get involved with any man. There was a good chance I was going to die. It wouldn't be fair to him. Still, I just couldn't help myself when I got home.

I opened my laptop and went to Adam's website again. I scrolled through the pictures on his gallery page, stopping on the one of him with his shirt off on some tropical island.

Holy guacamole.

The more I looked the more I wanted to keep looking.

Geez, Louise—I need to get ahold of myself.

I slammed the laptop shut. I needed to keep my eye on the prize and focus on my bucket list and nothing else. Adam was quite possibly the most attractive man I had ever met, but nothing would happen between us.

Nothing.

Maybe I needed to keep chanting that like a mantra until I believed it.

CHAPTER EIGHT

LIZ

We were fifty-thousand feet in the air and it was the closest to heaven I had ever been. Not because of the altitude. Not because of where we were on the map, but because I was being pampered like royalty.

I could definitely get used to this.

I was enjoying my glass of champagne, and the assortment of cheeses from France and Spain. And the chocolate-dipped strawberries. I couldn't forget the macadamia nuts. Or the heated slippers. My wide, comfortable leather seat had the perfect amount of lumbar support and there were no people sneezing or coughing or spreading a million germs throughout the cabin.

It was just me.

I pulled out my phone to text Josh, as giddy as one should be in this scenario.

. . .

Liz: I'm in heaven.

Josh: That was fast. No line at the pearly gates?

Liz: No.

Josh: There are lots of idiots in the world and most of them were taking the elevator down to the bottom, obviously.

Liz: You have a job as a cop because of those idiots.

Josh: True, but I would rather be unemployed in an idiot-free world.

Liz: That's my sweet brother. I love you and wish you were here.

Josh: Me, too. I mean, I love myself, too.

I laughed and set my phone down. Closing my eyes, I wiggled my toes inside the slippers.

The leather under my skin was so soft and the airplane seat so comfortable. There was a reason they called it butter leather. I was melting in it.

"Liz—look out the right side of the plane," said the voice of God from the cockpit. "We're flying over Puerto Vallarta, Mexico."

Okay, Adam was more like a Greek God. There was something about that man's voice that was heavenly. Something about his hair that made me want to run my fingers through it.

I held up my half-empty glass, analyzing it. Maybe it was time to cut off my supply of champagne. Those thoughts needed to stop.

Glancing out the jet window to my right, I admired the Pacific Ocean and the Mexican coast.

It was gorgeous.

Like Adam.

Stop it!

But honestly, looks aside, it was already clear I had underestimated Adam. I had only been with him for a few hours today, but there was no doubt he was an expert in all things related to travel. And he was so kind and down-to-earth.

Did I mention he was a Greek God?

Adam was doing everything possible to make this a comfortable flying experience for me, from the moment I had gotten out of Josh's car at the airport.

Speaking of which—even the airport was something I had never experienced before. Josh could drive his car right up to the side of the jet on the tarmac and drop me off, along with my bag. He insisted on meeting Adam and Orlando in person before I took off, which he did. They seemed to hit it off immediately and the three of them exchanged business cards. Then Adam had placed my suitcase underneath the jet and had given me the full tour of the jet.

The First Officer Orlando was a tall, slim black man with a smooth, clean-shaven head and a Southern accent that I would guess was from Texas or Louisiana. The man was a hoot, too.

Orlando had several duties onboard. Foremost he was the second pilot, so he was ready to assist or take over for Adam. He was also my flight attendant, which I would not complain about, since he was almost as gorgeous as Adam.

Almost.

Both of them looked dapper in their white and navy-blue uniforms.

The jet had everything I could imagine and not imagine.

My own private HD television, Wi-Fi, and a big bathroom where I didn't have to twist my body into a pretzel to pee.

I rubbed the leather armrest, thinking it couldn't get much better than this. The seat even reclined into a bed, although I wouldn't be sleeping much on this trip.

I'll sleep when I'm dead.

Okay, that had been one of my go-to phrases in the past, but I had to admit it sounded weird, considering my health situation.

Then again, it didn't *feel* like I was dying at all. I know Dr. Singh had told me I wasn't showing the normal signs of the disease, but how was I supposed to know when it was my time to go?

I swiveled around to look at the inside of the jet again, ready to get my mind on something else. It was odd staring at the empty seats around me that would remain empty for the duration of the trip. It seemed like a waste. Maybe I could pick up a few hitchhikers along the way.

Just the thought made me laugh.

"Careful there." Orlando pointed to my face. "You're seated in the *no fun, no frills* section."

"I think you're mistaken," I said. "I've got frills to last a lifetime here."

"Okay. You got me there." He smiled. "Can I top off that champagne for you?"

I glanced at my glass. "I'm good. I'm getting a little tipsy, actually. And for me, tipsiness equals sleepiness."

"Now, don't you worry about that." Orlando pointed to my seat. "There's a blackout sleep mask in the compartment there if you're in the mood for a little nap. Just recline back and enjoy the luxury. That's the most comfortable airline seat in the world or my name isn't Orlando."

I smiled. "How did you get your name? Don't tell me— you were born in Orlando, Florida?"

He shook his head. "*Conceived* there during my parents' wedding anniversary trip to Disney World. They needed to take a break between Epcot and Magic Kingdom to make a little magic of their own, if you know what I mean." He winked.

"I do." I thought about it. "Do you have any brothers and sisters?"

"Yes, ma'am. Three brothers. Austin, Houston, and Dallas."

"You're kidding me."

"Not at all." He chuckled. "My parents got around Texas a bit. What about you? What would your name be if your parents named you after the place where you were conceived?"

I smirked. "Kitchen floor."

Orlando laughed and slapped his hip. "That's a classic! For that, you get more champagne." He stepped toward me with the bottle.

I waved him off. "Thanks, but I think I've hit my limit. In fact, you can take this, if you don't mind." I handed him my champagne glass.

"Don't mind at all. Just let me know when you're ready for some coffee or tea with scones. Relax for now."

"Will do. Thank you."

The truth was, I was more relaxed than ever. It was almost as if I had taken a sleeping pill. Must be from all the champagne I had. A little nap wasn't such a bad idea.

I reclined the seat even farther, grabbed the sleep mask

from the armrest compartment, and pulled it over my head. I adjusted the pillow Orlando had given me, closed my eyes, and sighed.

Yup. This was pure heaven.

LIZ

"Buenos días, Liz."

"Buenos días," I answered. "¿Como estás?"

"Muy bien. Gracias. ¿Y tú?"

"Muy bien. Gracias."

Don't be impressed.

There were about ten or twelve words that had stuck with me since my high school Spanish class. I'd already used up half of them.

Dreaming in Spanish was new to me, but I would be perfectly fine dreaming like this every day. It was amazing how fast that velvety Latin voice had turned my insides to mush. I could listen to him talk all day. I wanted more, but why couldn't I see his face? I'll take just the voice if that was the only thing available in my dreams, but I wanted the whole enchilada.

Enchilada!

One more word I knew.

Speaking of tasty, maybe if I focused hard, I could continue the dream right where I had left off and get him to make an appearance this time.

"Talk to me, my mysterious Latin lover." I was hoping to summon him like he was a spirit or a genie coming out of a bottle. "And I want to see your face."

"You'll have to remove your sleep mask to see me."

Mask? Who was I? Zorro?

What a weird continuation of a dream.

And what happened to his Spanish?

Not that his English was that bad, since the man sounded a lot like Adam.

But why would I be wearing a mask in my dreams?

Unless . . .

I rolled back to my right until I was flat on my back, listening to the surrounding sounds.

A plane was taking off.

It couldn't have been our plane taking off, since the only thing we could have been doing was landing in Peru at some point, so . . .

My sleepy brain was catching up.

I wasn't asleep at all, was I?

Which meant . . .

I swallowed hard and slowly pulled the sleep mask off my head, fearing the worst.

There he was standing right in front of me.

El Capitán Sexy Pants.

"Did you sleep well?" Adam asked, grinning.

I nodded, mortified.

"Good to hear. Well, welcome to Cusco, Peru. Customs are on the way and will board the aircraft to clear us. We've got a shuttle waiting to take us to the hotel after that."

I glanced out the window. "Gracias."

It was funny how fast my fantasy had turned into a nightmare.

Actually, it wasn't funny at all.

Talk to me, my mysterious Latin lover.

I can't believe those words came out of my mouth.

What was I thinking?

Hopefully, Adam would just forget it ever happened.

He walked back toward the cockpit, the grin never leaving his face.

Right . . .

He's going to tell everyone he knows.

CHAPTER NINE

ADAM

"Mysterious Latin lover?" Orlando repeated, when I told him what Liz had called me shortly after I had landed the aircraft. "You don't have a Latin bone in your body. Where did she get that from?"

"I have no idea." I pulled a pair of pants from my suitcase and laid them on the bed in our suite. "I thought she was talking in her sleep, but then she took her sleep mask off."

"Then what did she say?"

"Nothing. She just stared at me and her face turned bright red." I smiled and laid my fleece jacket on the bed. "It was cute, actually."

"Maybe she was talking on the phone."

"That's what I thought, but she didn't have her ear buds in."

"Well . . ." Orlando slapped me on the back. "She obviously likes you."

That wasn't even worth a response because Orlando was always telling me women liked me. In fact, he was always trying to set me up with them. I appreciated his intentions, and I was even open to meeting someone, but I preferred for it to happen naturally.

"She is beautiful, you know," Orlando continued. "Don't tell me you haven't noticed."

"Can't say I have," I lied.

The woman was stunning, actually. And we had some connection, I was sure. That handshake we'd had in my office had almost brought me to my knees.

"Right," Orlando said. "She's traveling alone, so most likely she's single and—"

"Not interested in me at all." I realized he would keep pushing this one. "And she's a client, remember? Anyway, let's finish up here. We need to meet her downstairs and I'm starving."

"Okay, Mr. Sexy Lover."

"Latin lover," I corrected him. "And I'm mysterious—not sexy. Get it right."

Orlando saluted me. "Aye aye, Captain."

I chuckled and pulled my toiletry bag from my suitcase and placed it on the counter to the right side of the bathroom sink.

The plan was to meet Liz for a cup of coca tea, which has been known to help tourists adjust to Cusco's elevation of 11,152 feet. Then the three of us would grab a bite to eat somewhere within walking distance. I had never tried Peruvian food before and was looking forward to a new culinary adventure.

When I came out of the bathroom, Orlando was standing by the window, staring out at the plaza below.

I walked over and stood beside him, watching the people, a mix of tourists and locals.

"This will be an amazing trip—I know it," Orlando said.

"I feel the same way," I said.

"And I can't believe she put us up in this hotel." He spun around and admired the room. "In a suite! Ooh-la-la."

Even though I would never use the expression *ooh-la-la*—even in France—I had to agree with Orlando that the Belmond Hotel Monasterio was not just any hotel, since it was a former monastery and national monument dating back to 1592. Built on Inca foundations and showcasing eighteenth century original colonial paintings on the stone walls, it had to be the most unique place I had ever stayed in.

I had to admit I was also quite surprised Liz put us up here. Typically, we were on our own with finding accommodations. We were perfectly fine with a three-star hotel or even a hostel, as long as the place was clean and quiet. But Liz insisted on paying for our hotels and meals at every destination. She'd spent hours researching every little detail and had chosen the five-star Hotel Monasterio for our first night in Peru. Who was I to complain?

It wasn't about the money we were saving or even that we were staying in a luxury hotel. It was about Liz's generosity and her not even thinking twice about it. She had also said we could join her on any excursion she went on and she would pay for them all, which was unheard of in this industry. In all my years as a pilot-for-hire, not one client had paid for any excursions or luxury hotel accommodations for me. I had received some decent tips, but that was about it. Liz was different, and that made her even more attractive than she already was.

"Liz is the one who's mysterious," Orlando said. "What's her story?"

"You know as much as I do," I answered. "She's a history teacher, and this trip is her bucket list. Well, modified bucket list. She had a few more places she wanted to visit but removed them from the list because of time constraints."

"It's impossible for a history teacher to afford all this. And why is such a beautiful woman traveling around the world all by herself? Something doesn't add up."

I nodded. "I agree."

Orlando's eyes lit up. "We need to Google her."

"No, we don't."

"Maybe she comes from royalty in a small European country, but took a job teaching to rebel against the crown and family expectations."

I blinked. "Where the heck did you get that from?"

"In a Hallmark movie, I think." He chuckled. "Maybe we'll learn something about Liz over dinner."

"Maybe . . ."

I was just as curious about her as Orlando was.

A few minutes later, we met Liz downstairs in the lobby. We walked through the cobblestone foyer and past a wall covered by Inca masks to the massive doors leading to the courtyard. After we grabbed complimentary coca tea, we walked through the symmetrical courtyard with our cups. We admired the flowerbeds lined on both sides of the walkway, leading directly to a towering three-hundred-year-old cedar tree. The graceful, illuminated stone arches behind the tree were a sight to see under the perfectly clear, starry sky.

"Wow." Liz stopped in front of the tree and stared up into the branches. "This is something." She took a sip of her tea. "Someone planted this tree over three hundred years ago."

I glanced around at the other people in the courtyard who were admiring the tree. I was curious about who they were and what part of the world they came from.

"What is it?" Liz said.

I shook my head. "Nothing. I was just looking around at the people."

"Be aware—he does that a lot." Orlando chuckled.

Liz hesitated. "What exactly are you looking for?"

"I'm not looking for anything," I answered. "I'm fascinated by the different cultures of the world. They're so amazing, don't you think?"

"I do."

"He likes to come up with their backstories," Orlando said. "Who they are. What they do for a living and things like that."

Great. She didn't need to know that part.

Liz turned and arched an eyebrow. "You do that?"

I couldn't believe Orlando told her. "Maybe."

"All the time," Orlando said. "He should write fiction novels with that wild imagination of his, although he nails it occasionally. He has a sixth sense about things. About people."

Liz nodded. "Interesting." She glanced around the courtyard, stopping at the Chinese couple who were chatting on the bench as they admired the cedar tree. "Well, Mr. Sixth Sense, tell me about them."

I turned and studied the Chinese couple for a few moments. "This is easy. They've been happily married for ten years. No children, although they're thinking of adopting. He's a well-known surgeon who volunteers his services in third-world countries several times a year."

"And what about her?"

"She designs wedding dresses."

Liz laughed. "Of course, she does! Don't tell me—that's Vera Wang?"

I shook my head. "Not at all. That woman is the next biggest thing in the fashion world. She's going to make Vera Wang look like an amateur. In fact, Vera Wang will be asking *her* for advice."

"Uh-huh. And you got that just from looking at them?"

I grinned. "What can I say? It's a gift."

Liz turned to Orlando. "You're right—he does have a wild imagination."

"I told you he's got that sixth sense," Orlando said.

Liz studied me but didn't respond.

"You don't look convinced." I gestured over to the couple. "Go ask them. You'll see."

"I'm not going to ask them and you know it. That's why you told me to ask them."

"The truth shall set you free," I said.

"No, it won't. It will cost me the price of embarrassment."

"Suit yourself. Anyway—I like people, that's it."

Liz was about to take another sip of her tea and paused. "Me too, but my fascination is more with people of the past than people of the present."

"That makes sense since you're a history teacher."

Orlando laughed. "You two are total opposites. Adam lives in the present while Liz lives in the past."

It was true.

Opposites attract.

I wasn't sure where that thought came from, but it needed to pack its bags and leave my brain on the next flight out of here.

"Where should we eat?" I asked.

Liz pulled out her phone. "I've researched the top restaurants within walking distance and narrowed it down to three. From those three I narrowed it down to one." She pointed to her phone. "This is where we'll be dining this evening. It's only a few blocks away, on the other side of Plaza de Armas."

"Which restaurant is it?" I asked.

"This one." She held her phone in my direction for me to see the screen.

I read the description of the restaurant. "It's a burger joint."

"I love burgers," Orlando said.

"Me too," Liz said. "And tourists obviously love the place with all the great reviews."

I shrugged. "It's a tourist trap. And hamburgers aren't traditional food from Peru. How about we find a place where the locals eat? That's the real Peruvian experience."

Liz glanced at the phone again. "Why? Tourist traps don't have good food?"

"It's possible, but not typical."

"Well, this place looks promising from what I can tell. I do my research well, so I know what I'll get ahead of time. I don't like surprises."

"Never?" Orlando asked.

"Never."

I chuckled. "What if someone surprises you with flowers?"

She hesitated. "Well, if someone got me flowers, I

probably deserved them, so it wouldn't be that much of a surprise, would it?"

Orlando laughed. "My goodness, I *love* this woman!"

"*Thank* you," Liz said.

"What if they were certain flowers you weren't expecting, like Peruvian lilies?" I asked.

Liz took another sip of her tea. "You made that up. There's no such thing."

"Maybe I did and maybe I didn't."

"I admit I do like lilies. Actually, they're my favorite flowers, but still, that's different."

I nodded. "It's different because it's a surprise you like."

"I prefer to know what's going on."

"Then it wouldn't be a surprise."

"Exactly," she smirked. "Just the way I like it."

I couldn't help laughing at that because I had seen Liz's type before. She was set in her ways. She liked her routines and rarely strayed outside of her comfort zone. She always preferred a sure thing over the unknown. I'm not saying those things are bad, but they're just much different from the way I operate.

"The bottom line is you're not a fan of spontaneity?" I asked.

"The word doesn't even exist in my vocabulary."

"Which word?"

Liz shook her finger at me. "Nice try."

"The heart of pleasure is spontaneity."

She crossed her arms. "By failing to prepare, you are preparing to fail."

"I'm not going to change your mind, am I?"

"Not even a little."

I chuckled. "That's what I thought."

I still believed there were a hundred better options than that restaurant, but I needed to take my own advice and do something I didn't want to do. Because you never know, right? Maybe I was the one who would be surprised.

Still, for some reason, I was motivated to try opening her eyes to the many possibilities she was missing by not being spontaneous.

"How about we do this?" I said, giving it one more shot. "We eat at your restaurant and if it's not as good as you expected, you let me pick the next place to eat."

She gave me a confident smile. "I'm okay with that."

"Really?"

"Really."

Man, I like this woman.

I gestured to her. "But you need to promise me you'll be honest about the food."

Liz nodded. "I promise. And you need to promise to stop with all the spontaneity stuff if this restaurant turns out to be as good as I believe it will be."

"You've got yourself a deal." I held out my hand.

She froze. "What are you doing?"

"Well, we just made a deal. Now, we need to shake on it, of course."

"Oh . . ." She finally reached for my hand and shook it, holding my gaze as the air between us sizzled.

The chemistry we had was undeniable, but unlike the marathon handshake in my office that had nearly brought me to my knees, this one disappointingly ended a little too quickly.

"Time to eat the best burger of your life." Liz turned and

walked confidently toward the restaurant like she knew something I didn't know.

"You're going to eat those words," I called out to her, laughing. "And lucky for you, they'll be much tastier than the burger!"

CHAPTER TEN

LIZ

I picked up my burger and ignored the grease dripping down the side of my pinky. I took another bite and forced a smile in Adam's direction, chewing until my jaw cramped up again. The burger apparently was made of used tractor tires and cooked in motor oil. No amount of extra mustard or ketchup would make it taste better or allow me to finish it.

It was horrible.

Adam was right about the restaurant being a place with sub-par food. It was my own fault. I was the one who picked the place and forced them to join me. My research had failed me and now I was wondering what type of restaurant Adam would've chosen and if it would have been any better. Probably. This restaurant wouldn't have been hard to beat.

It wasn't the best first impression of Peruvian food, but what's done is done.

Adam was watching me eat, most likely waiting for the opportunity to tell me he was right.

Setting the burger down, I wiped my hands. "Say it."

"Say what?" Adam asked.

"You know what."

"Actually, I don't." Adam pointed to my plate. "I'm just curious about your burger."

Right.

Just curious.

He wanted me to admit the place was horrible. I was trying to hide the disgusted look on my face but wasn't doing a good job.

I will take that information with me to the grave!

Seriously, how many references to death do I use on a daily basis?

I needed to learn some new expressions.

And I also needed to come clean.

I had promised to tell Adam the truth about the food and I wasn't going to lie.

"You win." I pushed the plate away from me. "I can't eat anymore of this, whatever it is. You can choose the next restaurant. Happy?" I crossed my arms, feeling defensive.

Adam surprisingly didn't gloat. "Well, I'm happy I get to choose the next place, but disappointed that you didn't enjoy your meal, even a little. I'm passionate about food and would never wish a bad meal upon anyone."

That was a nice thing to say.

"I like my ensalada con pollo." Orlando gestured to his chicken salad.

At least someone was satisfied.

"I'm impressed you both speak Spanish," I said, trying to

get the topic off the food and onto something a little more positive.

Orlando wiped his mouth with his napkin. "Don't be impressed with me. I know just enough Spanish to read menus and ask for directions, but Adam is fluent. Well, he's fluent in four languages, actually."

I cranked my head in Adam's direction. "Which ones?"

Adam set his beer down. "English, Spanish, Italian, and Mandarin Chinese."

"Mandarin?" I glanced over at Orlando.

"He's serious," he said. "Damn impressive if you asked me, since the only Chinese I know is kung pao chicken."

Adam laughed. "Most people would never expect it by looking at me. I had a Chinese client for several years and he would teach me five words a day when we traveled. I enjoyed it. One day I decided I wanted to learn the language on my own."

I nodded. "That's wonderful. I only speak English."

"Yes, but you do it well." He grinned.

The waiter approached with a few smaller menus in his hand. "Dessert for anyone?"

"Oh . . ." I glanced over at Adam and Orlando and shrugged.

If the meal was bad, what were the chances the dessert would be any better?

"I think we're going to venture out and find something," Adam said before speaking to the waiter in Spanish.

I loved his confidence and command of a language not native to him. It was sexy and mysterious, since I had no idea what they were talking about.

Don't you dare call him your mysterious Latin lover again.

The waiter replied to Adam in Spanish.

"Muchas gracias," Adam said.

"De nada." The waiter walked away with the menus.

"What's going on?" I asked.

"The waiter is bringing the check and we're leaving to go find dessert."

"I don't like—"

"Surprises," Adam said. "I know."

"Fine." I pulled out my phone. "I'll just do a little research for dessert places and check out the reviews."

Adam waved me off. "Uh-uh."

"What do you mean *uh-uh*?"

"Would it *kill you* to let me choose the dessert place?"

I blinked.

Why did he have to phrase it like that?

Was he going to start using death expressions as well?

"Yes, it could quite possibly kill me," I said. "And how would you deal with that?"

Adam thought about it. "Well, I guess I'd miss you, but I would say something sincere and heartfelt at your memorial. I would even bring some Peruvian lilies." He winked.

My heart skipped a beat.

We locked gazes, and for the briefest of moments I believed he would truly miss me. Or, maybe I hoped he would. What was it about this man? We disagreed on just about everything, but why was I enjoying his company so much?

"And a deal is a deal," Adam added. "You said I could choose the next place to eat."

"I said the next *meal* and dessert is not a meal."

He grinned. "It depends on how much you have. It could be."

I was starving since I barely touched my burger. Maybe I would just look when we got there and decide if I wanted to have dessert or not.

"Okay," I said after I paid the bill. "Lead the way."

Adam looked as shocked as I felt. "Seriously?"

"Seriously. But hurry before I change my mind."

He chuckled. "Okay, then. Follow me."

I walked alongside Adam toward the unknown dessert destination, as Orlando trailed right behind us. We stopped at the sixteenth century Cusco Cathedral and took a few selfies in front, before continuing down the main street. Two blocks later, I slowed near the front window of a business that caught my eye.

The Peruvian Healing Center.

It appeared to be a place for natural healing remedies. I stopped and looked in the window, thinking of what Dr. Singh had said.

I'm all for exploring alternative medicine options, but just be careful because there are a lot of scams out there.

"Do you want to go inside?" Adam asked.

"No, no," I lied, pointing to the large tree painted on the window in front of the building. "I was just admiring the beautiful tree. It reminds me of the one in the courtyard at the hotel."

"You're right. They're similar."

I forced a smile. "Carry on."

The healing place looked legit, but you never know. Maybe I would look at their reviews online back in the hotel room and decide if I wanted to come back when Adam and Orlando weren't with me.

We rounded the corner and entered a cobblestone street closed off to cars for an outdoor event. Amazing smells invaded my senses from the various street vendors with pop-up kiosks and food trucks on both sides. There must have been a thousand people there, many of them eating standing up, while others waited in line in front of the street vendors. The ambiance was electric, especially with the live music coming from the street musicians.

I pointed to the giant banner at the entrance that said *Postres del Cielo*. "What does it say?"

Adam grinned. "Desserts from heaven. It's a dessert festival, from what the waiter told me." He scanned the area. "Hmmmm. Let's see."

I followed his gaze. "Which place did the waiter recommend?"

"He didn't. We will let our noses and eyes choose."

"Seriously?"

Adam nodded. "He said all the desserts here were good. And all are traditional Peruvian sweets and specialties."

"It smells fabulous," Orlando said.

I looked around, fearing the worst. I wasn't going to be able to research these dessert places online to know which one had the best reviews.

Orlando and I followed Adam through the crowd, looking at the different desserts.

"Right there." Adam pointed to a food truck. "That's the one."

The sign on the side of the truck said *Picarones*.

"How do you know?" I asked.

He tapped his nose, grinning. "My nose knows. There's no way something that looks and smells this good could be bad. Come on—my treat."

I shook my head, not wanting to take a chance. "I'll pass but thank you."

Adam studied me for a moment. "Do you want something else?"

"That's okay. You go for it. I'll wait right here."

"Okay. Be right back."

Adam walked with Orlando toward the *Picarones* truck.

I felt a little pathetic passing on the dessert. Everything smelled heavenly, so Desserts from Heaven seemed to be a fitting name.

Dr. Singh's advice came into my thoughts.

Eat all the unhealthy foods you've wanted to try in your life, but never did.

Adam and Orlando returned with desserts in their hands and smiles on their faces.

Orlando was already digging into the dessert on his paper plate, enjoying every bite.

I was trying to figure out what he was eating. It looked like a fritter. No, more like a donut. But they'd topped it with syrup.

It looked good and smelled even better.

Adam had two of the desserts on his plate, not one.

He grabbed the first piece, taking a bite, chewing slowly. Glaze oozed down his chin and his moans were overlapping with Orlando's moans.

This was getting ridiculous. The sounds they made were actually bordering on obscene.

Because I had no willpower, I snuck another peek at Adam's dessert.

I licked my lips, wondering what it tasted like.

My stomach gurgled loudly.

Adam cleared his throat. "Here."

My eyes opened wider.

There was now a piece of the dessert inches from my face.

"Try it." Adam waved the delectable treat under my nose.

It looked incredible, but I shook my head.

"Come on. Live a little."

I stared at his grin for a moment, wanting to tell him I didn't want to live a little. I wanted to live a lot. I wanted to live forever.

He moved the dessert closer to my lips.

It smelled divine. I was caving in.

I was suddenly tempted to swallow the whole thing right there on the spot.

I licked my lips. "If I get sick, I will kill you."

Adam chuckled. "You won't get sick. I promise. Just a little bite."

I couldn't take it any longer. I leaned forward and nibbled from the piece in his hand.

His eyes never left mine, except for the moment when his gaze dropped to my mouth as I chewed. Adam's grin got bigger.

Now, I knew why they called them desserts from heaven. It was like a fritter or a donut, but there was something different about it besides the hint of cinnamon I was enjoying.

"What exactly is this?"

I couldn't believe I had to ask. I had always researched food and knew ahead of time all the ingredients, so I knew what I was getting myself into. Plus, I knew the calories, the fat, and the carbs. Everything.

"First, tell me if you love it," Adam said.

I shrugged.

Adam laughed. "A little?"

"Okay, I love it!"

"Ha! I knew it. And to answer your question, it's deep-fried just like a donut, but the difference is in the batter. It's made of sweet potato and squash. Then it's topped with cinnamon and a syrup made from raw sugar straight from the sugarcane."

"You don't want anymore, do you?" Adam asked. "I can eat the extra one I brought for you."

"I want it!" I tried to grab it from his plate.

Adam laughed. "Okay, okay. Settle down. Here . . ." He removed a second plate from under his and scooted one of the desserts onto it, handing it to me. "Here you go."

"Thank you." I took the plate from Adam and didn't hesitate, taking a big bite. Not a surprise, I moaned like Orlando and Adam had moaned earlier.

They both laughed, watching me devour the dessert and lick my fingers.

It was one of the most delicious sweets ever.

"Any regrets?" Adam asked, taking the empty plate from my hand, and tossing it in the trash.

"No. Not at all." I licked another finger. "Thank you."

"My pleasure."

"I think I'll head back to the hotel and do a little reading before bed. I want to have plenty of energy for tomorrow."

And by reading, I meant researching the Peruvian Healing

Center. If they opened early enough tomorrow, I would make a quick stop there before we left town for Machu Picchu.

"That's a good plan to head back," Adam said. "Tomorrow, the real adventure begins, but luckily we don't have to get up too early."

The plan was to take a private shuttle at noon from the front of the hotel to the train station, about thirty minutes away. We would have three hours on a train through the Sacred Valley, taking us to our next hotel at the base of the mountain below the ruins of Machu Picchu.

I was excited to see Machu Picchu, the first place on my bucket list.

Oddly, I was also excited to spend more time with Adam.

As long as there weren't any surprises, I would enjoy every minute.

CHAPTER ELEVEN

LIZ

Sitting on the toilet for three hours was not on my bucket list, but that's what I got for thinking that a volcano-water cleanse would cure me. The morning wasn't going well at all and I only had ten minutes until our shuttle left for Machu Picchu. There was no way I'd make it, based on the rumbling continuing down below.

"What was I thinking?" I mumbled to myself, my voice echoing in the tile bathroom.

After over an hour of research last night, I decided to visit the Peruvian Healing Center this morning and sign up for their cleanse. The volcano water was sourced from the Sabancaya volcano in the nearby Andes, and was supposed to have natural healing properties, so why not give it a shot, right?

The thing I didn't realize—and sure, I will take the blame since I couldn't understand everything the woman was telling me at the center—was that the eight glasses of volcano water would immediately erupt from my bottom.

Maybe that was the real reason they called it volcano water.

Somehow, I had come to the ridiculous conclusion that the water would go through me, do some clean-up work, and come back out in my pee, taking all the unwanted toxins and illnesses in my body with it.

Wrong.

How was I going to explain this to Adam when he called to ask why I wasn't in front of the hotel where the shuttle was? I expected his call any minute now. That's why I had my cell phone clutched in my hand, while the other hand was clutching my stomach.

The phone rang, right on cue.

I wiped the sweat from my forehead and answered the phone. "Hi, Adam."

"Hi, Liz. The shuttle is here. We're waiting out front. Are you on your way down?"

"Well, not exactly."

"Oh. Is everything okay?"

I tried to figure out how to tell him. "Uh . . . well . . . my stomach isn't feeling so well at the moment."

"I'm sorry to hear that. Do you need some help? I can come right up."

"No!" I'm sure I broke his eardrum. "I'll be fine. I need a little more time."

"Of course," Adam said. "Just tell me how much longer and I'll let the driver know."

"I'm not sure . . . two hours? Maybe three?"

"Okay—we'll just have to rework things. The shuttle

driver has a pickup at the train station in Ollantaytambo to bring someone back here to Cusco. He won't be able to wait around long. Plus, that means we'll miss the train to Aguas Calientes. Let me check if we can get on another train a little later. We'll have to tell the shuttle driver to go without us and try to arrange another shuttle whenever you're ready."

"They already have the payment, so please give the driver a tip, and I'll reimburse you."

"Will do." Adam sighed. "And I'm sorry I did this to you."

What was he talking about? He didn't make me drink volcano water. He didn't even know about it, and never would.

"You didn't do anything," I said.

"I shouldn't have pushed the dessert on you. It was my fault."

"I didn't get sick from the dessert."

"How do you know?" Adam asked.

"And how do you know it wasn't the burger?"

"Because you barely touched it. You inhaled the dessert."

"It wasn't your fault." I wasn't going to tell him the truth and I needed to get him off the phone. "Gotta run. I'll give you an update later."

"Okay. Let me know if you need anything."

"Will do." I disconnected the call.

He sounded a little suspicious there at the end of the call, but what could I do? There was no way I would tell him about my condition, and I especially would not tell him what was happening to my body because of the volcano water. I should be grateful this didn't happen on the shuttle on the way to Machu Picchu. That would have been a nightmare. I needed to wait this out. Hopefully, it wouldn't be too much longer, and we would be on our way.

~

Four hours later, the eruptions in my lower extremities had ended and my mouth was drier than a Southern California drought. I was also starving since everything in my system had been completely purged, but I didn't want to delay the trip any longer by taking the time to eat something. I would just drink water until we found some food later. Spring water, not volcano water.

I had finally made it onto the private shuttle with Adam and Orlando. I was actually feeling pretty good, and only had to deal with the occasional rumbling of my stomach. At least my seat was comfortable, and I had a big window to enjoy the view.

We were traveling through the heart of the Inca Empire in a place called the Sacred Valley of the Incas. Even though I had taught about this region in my history class, I had never seen mountains so tall and valleys so deep and lush green in person. We hadn't been traveling long, and I had already snapped at least a hundred pictures of the stunning landscape all around us.

"How are you doing back there, Orlando?" I asked. "Are you enjoying this just as much as I am?"

He was seated directly behind me and Adam in the third row of the shuttle van.

"I'm doing just fine, enjoying the scenery and snapping pictures, like you."

I took a picture of three alpacas eating grass in the pasture. "This is so amazing."

"Indeed," Orlando said.

Adam stared out the window. "Breathtaking."

"How come you're not taking any pictures?" I asked.

Adam turned. "I prefer to just soak it all in."

It was an interesting perspective, but I thought of something else. "How are you going to remember everything?"

"Are you telling me you won't share copies of the photos you took?" he smirked.

I laughed. "Ah, I see how you operate."

"You need to watch out for me. I'm full of tricks." He smiled mischievously.

We shared a laugh and turned our attention back to the landscape.

I pointed up ahead to the stone buildings nestled between the mountains. "What town is that?"

"It's called Pisac," our driver Javier said. "It's one of the most beautiful villages in the Sacred Valley, and the ruins here are some of the most important in all of Peru."

"What are those rows on the mountainside?"

"They're agricultural terraces, held in place by stone walls. Next to them are the baths and temples of the ceremonial center. There you will see some of the most exquisite stonework. It's a long hike to get up there." He drove past a soccer field and slowed down as we entered the village. Javier pointed out the window toward a plaza filled with people and booths. "That's the main plaza, known for the world-famous craft market you see. We are proud of our ceramics and tapestries."

"Do we have time to stop?" I asked.

"Look at you!" Orlando said. "It sounds like you're being spontaneous."

I laughed. "Not quite. I need to pee."

Orlando, Adam, and Javier laughed.

"But we can check out the market while we're here, if there's time."

Adam checked his watch. "We have a little time, but we need to be careful or we'll miss the train again."

The train would take us from Ollantaytambo to the base of Machu Picchu.

Javier pulled the van over. "I'll wait here with your things."

"Thanks," I said. "We won't be long."

After I used the public restroom, the three of us walked down the street back toward the main square. The market was filled with artisans selling textiles dyed in bright colors, silver, reproductions of archaeological pieces, musical instruments, paintings, ceramics, and many other things we wouldn't have time to see.

Orlando wasted no time buying a colorful Inca mask, while Adam settled for a bag of roasted chestnuts. I was thinking of buying a sweatshirt or jacket since it can get cool in the evenings but hadn't found anything yet. There was also the urgent need to get some food in my system. And even though I told myself I needed to drink water, I had left my water bottle in the van. I would have to drink something soon, because I was thirsty.

The beautiful smile of a girl caught my eye. Maybe around ten years old, she stood in front of one of the booths, holding up a jacket for me to see. Her chocolate brown eyes were so sweet and innocent that I couldn't help but gravitate in her direction.

I waved. "Hola."

"Hello." The girl smiled again. "We have alpaca jackets." She pointed to the woman sitting on the chair behind her. "My mother makes them."

"It's a beautiful jacket. How old are you?"

"Ten."

She was the cutest thing, and her English was impressive, considering we were in a small Peruvian village.

"Your English is fantastic."

"Thank you. We had an American teacher at our school. She taught me a lot when I was just a kid."

Just a kid.

I couldn't help smiling at that.

"I learned a lot from the Internet, too. I also like math and history."

I smiled. "That's wonderful. I teach history in the United States!"

The girl stared at me. "The United States doesn't have a lot of history."

I laughed. "You're so right. Most of the history I teach is of other countries—even Peru. Do you enjoy going to school?"

Just because I quit my teaching job didn't mean I didn't care about kids and their education. It was natural for me to be curious since I loved to see children enthusiastic about learning.

"Yes, but the school is closed." The girl's smile disappeared.

"But you must enjoy your summer vacation, right?"

"I guess. I'd rather be in school. I enjoy learning things."

Adam stepped forward and said something to the girl's mother in Spanish. I listened as they chatted for a minute. The woman pointed to the church tower behind us.

"Would you like to buy the jacket?" the girl asked. "I think it would look beautiful on you."

"Do you?"

She held out the jacket toward me. "I do."

Her sales skills were just as impressive as her English.

"I would love to buy it." It would be impossible to say no to the girl. She must sell a thousand jackets a day with that smile.

I tried on the jacket to make sure it fit and then paid. I said goodbye to the girl and her mother, and we continued down the aisle. I stopped when I saw the church tower the mother had pointed to.

"What was the mother saying about the church?"

"She was talking about the girl's school. It's right next door to the church."

"Ahhh. Well, they're doing something right at the school, I'll tell you that much. Can you believe her English? That was amazing."

Adam nodded. "It was impressive."

"I guarantee that nobody will keep her away from school. She's a bright young girl, and she seems motivated to learn."

"Well, it may not be up to her. Remember—the school closed."

"It's summer vacation! Kids should be allowed to have fun, and the teachers need a break to recharge."

He shook his head. "Her mother said they shut down the school because it had structural damage. The roof collapsed. They couldn't finish the school year."

I stopped and placed my hand on my chest, my heart rate picking up. "Please tell me nobody got hurt."

"No, no. It happened in the middle of the night and the school was empty. But it destroyed everything inside, including the computers. The girl hasn't been to school in three months."

I turned back and glanced at the girl, who was holding up

a jacket for another tourist. "What a shame." I glanced back toward the church tower, curious about the school.

I started walking in that direction.

"Where are you going?" Adam asked.

"To see the school."

He checked his watch. "We need to get back to the shuttle soon."

"This will only take a minute."

We passed between two stone buildings and made a right turn toward the church. That's when the school came into view and I stopped in my tracks.

"Wow." I stared at the heavily damaged school building. There was a temporary barrier around the school, but we could move a little closer. The roof had completely caved in and there was debris everywhere. The school looked like it had been hit by an earthquake. "This is horrible. I wonder how long it will be until they reopen."

"It could be up to a year or longer," a male voice said from behind them.

The three of us turned around.

A reverend stood there dressed in black and white. "Pardon me for interrupting—I'm Reverend Casillas."

We introduced ourselves, and I asked, "What happened?"

"There was a big storm a few months back. The rain wasn't draining properly from the roof, and it accumulated all the water. Eventually, the roof couldn't handle the pressure from the weight of the water, and it collapsed. It was an old roof and there had been plans to repair it for years, but it didn't happen in time. It's unfortunate."

"There isn't another school close by for these kids?" Adam asked.

The reverend shook his head. "Unfortunately, not in our village or anywhere close by. In fact, there were children who walked over an hour each way to get to this school because they didn't have a school near their homes."

"Why would it take so long to rebuild?"

"Money. Plus, the school building is a historical landmark. That means the government needs to be involved in the rebuilding process, and you know how the government works."

"What about a temporary location for the school until they can rebuild it?" Orlando asked.

"That's a great idea," I said.

The reverend nodded. "There's a vacant building a few blocks from here that could be used, but there are no textbooks and desks for the students, or school supplies for the teachers. We had just used all our resources to replace everything. The roof and the water destroyed it all."

"Wow." I turned back to the school, deep in thought.

I wanted to help.

There were children willing to walk an hour each way to go to school, but now there wasn't even a school available for them? How sad was that?

I suddenly felt lightheaded, and it had nothing to do with the school or the children.

My limbs were getting heavy.

The damaged school spun in circles right before my eyes.

"This is not good," I said.

"I agree," Reverend Casillas said.

"No—I mean I don't feel well. It's like I'm going to—"

Adam wrapped both of his arms around me and pulled me

close to keep me from falling. "I've got you. Are you okay? Liz? Talk to me."

I stared into his beautiful brown eyes. "I'm just dandy. How are you?" I felt like someone had drugged me. My energy was zapped. I just wanted to close my eyes.

"Liz?"

It was like Adam was speaking in slow motion and his voice echoed in my ears.

Now, he was spinning, too.

And that was the last thing I remembered.

CHAPTER TWELVE

LIZ

I was sprinting down the cobblestone street with long, world-class-runner strides. I was rather impressed with how fast I was running but couldn't understand why I couldn't feel my feet hitting the ground. It was the weirdest sensation, like I was hovering above the cobblestone. I don't ever remember being this fast. Something wasn't right. Especially since I hadn't had anything to eat since yesterday.

Was this a dream?

That had to be it because I had never sprinted a day in my life, now that I thought about it. I had always been more of a speed walker, really. Okay, that's not true. I'm just a normal walker. Josh always joked that I strolled, not walked. I guess I would sprint if there were an emergency, like if a bull was chasing me or something like that.

Maybe that was it.

Was I in the middle of running with the bulls? I thought that only happened in Spain.

Not wanting to take a chance, I turned to look behind me for bulls and bumped my head on something hard.

"Ouch," Adam said. "Hang in there, Liz—you're going to be fine."

I had no idea Adam was sprinting with me, but why was he running so close to me? He kept bumping into me, which was annoying, but it was sexy, considering he didn't seem to mind at all.

I could even smell his cologne—something manly with a hint of something fruity.

Speaking of fruit, the people all around me were going bananas, yelling hysterically in Spanish as they ran alongside us.

Maybe this was really happening. Was I drunk? No, that couldn't be it, either.

I couldn't see any bulls and I never get drunk, unless you count that one time I played beer pong in my college dorm the same day I took part in that hot dog eating contest. I only did it to impress Tom, who would go on to be my first husband, and subsequently, my first divorce. That should have been my first lesson in life.

Drinking beer leads to divorce.

But I digress . . .

My mind was going off in a million different directions at the moment and I was so thirsty. What was wrong with me? And why were there so many people staring at me? Had I forgotten to put on pants? I had no clue what they were saying since they were all speaking in Spanish, but I seemed to be the topic at hand since all eyes were on me. None of this made sense.

Reverend Casillas rushed past us. "Over there." He pointed to a building that said *Clínica.*

What was that in English? A clinic? Why were we in a hurry to get there?

Hang in there, Liz—you're going to be fine.

That's it. There was something wrong with me. Everything was still so hazy, but I didn't feel any pain anywhere. Was I dying, already? I had to see Machu Picchu first.

"Get the door," Adam said.

Was he talking to me?

"Got it." Orlando ran past Reverend Casillas toward the door.

Oh, okay. Adam wasn't talking to me, but it didn't matter. I could listen to him talk all day long.

What a sexy voice.

"Thank you," Adam said.

Oops. Looks like I said that out loud.

I needed to stop doing that.

I tilted my head up and saw Adam's beautiful face, creased forehead and all, locking eyes with me. There was slight amusement in his eyes surrounded by lines of worry. His square jawline had the hint of a salt and pepper five o'clock shadow.

What was going on here? Why was he carrying me? Not that I minded at all, because I don't remember the last time a man touched me, unless you count my doctor, which I wouldn't expect you to.

That's when my slow brain figured it out. I hadn't been running at all. Adam was the one who was running, and I was in his arms. Why was he carrying me? Where was he carrying me?

Oh, that's right. The clinic.

Orlando swung the door open and stepped back out of the way.

Adam carried me toward the building and halted in front of the doorframe, banging my legs against it.

"So sorry," Adam said. "Are you okay?"

I nodded and swallowed hard. "I'm thirsty."

"We'll get you something to drink."

Orlando waved us toward the lobby. "Come on—let's get her inside, Adam."

Adam glanced inside the building, suddenly losing the color in his face.

"Are you okay?" I asked.

He avoided eye contact with me. "Totally fine." He turned to Orlando. "You're going to have to take her in, buddy. Here."

"You can do it, Adam. It's just right inside. No big deal."

He hesitated and shook his head. "Sorry, I can't." He handed me off to Orlando. I looked back over Orlando's shoulder as he carried me inside the clinic. Adam stood on the other side of the closing door, his back to us, his head down, his shoulders slumped.

"Is he okay? What happened?"

Orlando crinkled his nose. "I don't think it's my place to say."

"Uh-oh." I squeezed Orlando's shoulder.

He was following the nurse down the hallway but stopped. "Are you okay?"

"I . . ."

The walls inside the clinic spun around me.

This wasn't good.

I was pretty sure I was going to pass out.

LIZ

I awoke to bright lights in my face and a beeping in my right ear. I blinked twice and swallowed. I didn't feel as thirsty as earlier, which was a good thing. I felt relaxed and content lying there for a while.

"There you are," Orlando said. "Welcome back."

I felt a squeeze on my right hand and turned, glancing down.

Orlando was holding my hand.

My gaze followed the hand up his arm, to his shoulder, to his smiling face.

So sweet.

"How do you feel?" He continued holding on to my hand.

I nodded. "Not bad. Relaxed."

"Well, your face has color again. You gave us quite the scare."

My head felt a little foggy. "What happened?"

"You passed out. Twice, actually. Once in front of the school and again after we brought you in here. You were dehydrated, but you're getting plenty of fluids now." He gestured to my other arm.

I turned to my other side and glanced down at the IV

going into my vein. "Oh . . ." I looked around the room. "Do I have to spend the night here?"

"No, no. Nothing like that. Once the doctor is convinced that you're properly hydrated and your vitals are good, he'll release you. He said what happened to you was common around here and most people are released within a few hours."

"Good to know. Where's Adam?"

"He's just outside."

"Outside . . ." I didn't understand what he was doing out there when I was in here. "Was he in the room earlier?"

"No. He's been outside the entire time."

"And he's not planning on coming in?"

"No."

I glanced at the door. "Was I dreaming or did Adam carry me to the door and pass me off to you?"

"You didn't dream it."

My brain finally was catching up. "You're not telling me everything, are you?"

"Nope."

I smiled at Orlando's odd behavior. It would be impossible to be mad at such a kind man who was by my side and holding my hand. I knew he was hiding something but was confident I could get it out of him.

It disappointed me that Adam wasn't there in the room with me. It also confused me. He had taken the time to carry me to the medical clinic, but why didn't he come inside?

I sat up, remembering something Orlando had said. "I asked you what happened to Adam when you carried me in, and you said it wasn't your place to say."

"That is correct."

"I think it is your place to say."

"Liz . . ."

"Okay, give me a hint. Tell me if I'm getting hot or cold."

Orlando let go of my hand and crossed his arms. "I'd rather not."

"Is he a germaphobe? Maybe he's afraid of picking up an illness from a patient here? That's it, right? Am I hot or cold?"

Orlando sighed. "I can't believe I'm doing this. Cold."

"Okay . . ." I stared up into the bright lights, deep in thought. "Got it. He's scared of needles and blood?"

"Cold."

I snapped my finger. "His wife used to be a doctor or a nurse, and he knew coming in here would bring back memories of their marriage he didn't want to deal with?"

He sighed. "You're warm."

I rubbed my hands together and almost yanked the IV from my arm. "Ouch."

Orlando stood. "I should get the doctor."

"I'm fine. Don't leave now because I'm enjoying this. I feel like Nancy Drew."

Orlando hesitated, but then sat.

"I was warm. Good. Now, I'm getting somewhere. So, his wife was a doctor or a nurse?"

"Cold."

I stared at Orlando. "Cold?"

"Yup."

"If his wife wasn't a doctor or nurse, that would mean that coming in here would bring back memories Adam didn't want to deal with."

"Correct."

I shook my head. "Uh-uh. You need to say hot or cold, if we're going to play the game right."

Orlando chuckled. "You're a kick, I'll give you that much, but Adam will kick my butt if I tell you."

"You can take him." I smiled. "I won't say a thing."

He studied me for a moment. "Promise?"

"Promise. What happened?"

"Nosocomephobia is what happened."

"Noso what?"

"Nosocomephobia. It's the fear of hospitals."

"Are you making this up?"

"No, ma'am."

I thought people were more afraid of going to the dentist, but the fear of hospitals? Why would he be afraid? The man was in amazing shape, so what did he have to worry about? It would make sense if someone like me were afraid of hospitals, based on my current diagnosis, but why would Adam be afraid?

I glanced back over at Orlando. He looked content with not giving up any more information.

I needed to know more.

"What gave him the phobia?" I asked. "I had no idea there was actually a fear of hospitals."

Orlando nodded. "It's more common than you think. As for how it happened to Adam, it may be easy to understand. Many of the people he loved died in hospitals."

"But lots of people die in hospitals."

"Yes, but the last five times Adam stepped foot inside a hospital, someone in his life died."

"Five times in a row?"

"Yes. First it was his grandparents—not at the same time. Then his mom died, followed closely by his dad. And then there was Mary. Basically, he associates hospitals and medical clinics with death. He doesn't admit to having nosocomephobia, but he and I both know he has it." He gestured to me. "Well, now you know as well. Please don't tell him I told you."

"I will take it to the grave with me."

A man with a white jacket walked in, carrying a clipboard. "Hello. I'm Dr. Rubio. How do you feel?"

"Darn good, actually," I said.

"Fluids with electrolytes usually do the trick."

"Sorry about this. I'm sure you have more important people to see and illnesses to tend to."

He shook his head. "Not at all. This is a typical day for me. The elevation for most of our villages and cities in Peru are some of the highest in the world. It can be a problem adjusting to the altitude for most tourists, not knowing to increase water intake, which leads to dehydration, among other problems." He flipped through a couple of pages on his clipboard. "I ran a blood test and noticed something odd I wanted to investigate. It's probably nothing, but I would like to have it analyzed further, just to be sure."

I shot up to a seated position, yanking my hands away from Orlando. "That's not necessary."

The doctor stared at me. "It's just a precaution."

"How are my vitals?"

"Vitals are good. It's just your—"

"I had a medical exam just a few weeks ago. I'm sure it was just a faulty blood test. It probably happens all the time."

"Actually, it doesn't."

"That's okay." I pulled the blanket off of me. "I'm good. We have things to do."

"What's the hurry?" Orlando said. "We already missed the

next train. You might as well let him do the follow-up blood test. Better to make sure everything is perfect before we take off since there are no medical clinics in Machu Picchu."

Another blood test was out of the question.

They all would know.

"That's quite all right," I said. "I'm ready to go."

Orlando grabbed my hand again and squeezed it. "It's just to be sure. It won't take long."

"Don't worry." I squeezed his hand back and decided to change the subject. "Where is Reverend Casillas? I have an idea I want to run by him."

"He had to go back to the church. He told us to keep him updated, but the doctor isn't finished with you."

I turned to Dr. Rubio. "Are you demanding I stay here?"

He shook his head. "Not at all. If you're feeling good, you are free to go. It's just—"

"Great. If someone can remove the IV, I'll pay, and we'll be on our way."

The doctor hesitated. "As you wish. I'll have the nurse come in to take care of it."

Orlando arched an eyebrow. "Now, who's hiding something?"

I avoided eye contact with him. "I have no idea what you're talking about."

CHAPTER THIRTEEN

LIZ

I thanked the doctor and his staff for everything and paid the bill in the reception area of the medical clinic. I stepped outside with Orlando, taking a deep breath and exhaling slowly.

"How do you feel?' Orlando asked.

"Good, actually. Strong. Like I had two or three shots of espresso." I looked down the street to the left and to the right. "Where's Adam?"

Orlando pointed. "Over there."

I followed the direction of his finger to a spot in front of a cafe. Adam was sitting on the curb, talking to a boy who had a soccer ball under one of his feet.

We walked in his direction.

"Adam!" Orlando said.

Adam looked in our direction and stood up, a smile of relief on his face. "How are you feeling?"

I smiled back at him. "I feel great. Like nothing ever happened."

"Good to hear." Adam winced, rubbing his lower back in a circular motion.

"You should get that checked out while we're here," Orlando said.

"What happened?" I asked.

Adam waved me off. "I tweaked my back a little. Nothing that a few stretches and a hot bath won't be able to heal. I'm fine."

Orlando scoffed. "I'm sorry, but credit should be given where credit is due. You carried Liz in your arms for almost a quarter mile. That's something!"

A quarter mile?

I assumed he carried me a block or so from around the corner.

"Especially for someone who's fifty years old," Orlando added.

"Oh . . ." I said.

Adam stepped closer. "What is it?" He grabbed my hand again. "Are you okay?"

I stared down at his hand squeezing mine. "Yeah—I'm okay. It's just . . . we're both fifty. I thought you were younger."

"I thought *you* were younger."

"What a coinkydink."

Adam stared at me. "A coinkydink? I didn't think anyone used that word anymore."

"*Love* the word," Orlando said.

"Thank you." I smiled. "Anyway, Dr. Rubio said to stay hydrated and that it would be a good idea to get food in my system."

Adam pointed to the kid with the soccer ball. "That boy said the cafe there had great food. That's good enough for me, unless you want to do five hours of research to determine if you should eat a sandwich there."

I placed my hands on my hips. "I'll have you know it would only take me *ten* minutes to determine if that place is any good. And you know what? You just watch this."

I turned, headed to the café, and entered, not looking back.

I showed him.

I can be spontaneous.

They entered the cafe right behind me.

Adam nodded his appreciation. "I'm impressed."

I bowed. "Thank you."

"Especially since this place is known for tacos *de lengua de vaca*."

"Sounds yummy. I can't wait."

Adam shrugged. "I had *no* idea you were into cow-tongue tacos."

I jumped back. "What?"

Adam laughed one of his hearty laughs. "I'm kidding. Relax."

Orlando shook his head. "That wasn't nice."

"Okay, sorry. To make it up to you, I'll treat."

"That is not even on the table for discussion," I said. "I'm treating."

After our delicious sandwiches, we headed down the cobblestone street in the church's direction to find Reverend Casillas.

Adam gestured over his shoulder at the cafe behind us. "How did you like the sandwich?"

"It was amazing."

He chuckled. "You were spontaneous again, and you found something you enjoyed, without any research. Imagine that."

"There's a difference between desperate and spontaneous."

"If you say so, but I'm rubbing off on you."

"Not even a little," I lied.

"By the way . . ." Adam grabbed my arm and pulled me to a stop. The smile from his face disappeared. "I'm sorry for what happened earlier."

I nudged him on the arm. "You mean for eating the last potato chip?"

That didn't get a laugh out of him.

He was being serious.

I cleared my throat. "You were saying?"

"I'm sorry for not being with you inside the clinic. I felt horrible."

I rubbed him on the side of the arm. "It's okay. Don't even worry about it. I totally understand."

Adam looked at me, then Orlando, then back at me. "How do you understand if you don't know the reason?"

"Well . . ."

Come on brain! You've got electrolytes and a sandwich in your system now! Think of the best lie you can think of!

"Liz?"

"I'm sure you had a good reason for not going in. That's all that matters." It was better to dance around the truth than tell a flat-out lie. "And it's not like it's your job to take care of me. Orlando was there, too. You don't need to be sorry. Okay? Now, let's go find Reverend Casillas."

"Wait just one minute." Adam pointed to Orlando. "He told you, didn't he?"

It was best if I didn't lie. "Yes, but it's not that big a deal. He didn't want to tell me. It was my fault. I can be persuasive."

"Liz!" Orlando said. "You promised you wouldn't tell!"

I pointed to Adam. "He found out!"

Adam pointed to Orlando. "And you promised *you* wouldn't tell."

Orlando pointed to me. "*She* found out!"

I glanced at Orlando.

Orlando glanced at me.

I glanced at Adam.

Orlando glanced at Adam. "Just look at us, three pathetic people who don't know how to keep secrets."

I laughed.

Orlando and Adam joined me, the three of us laughing together like we were drunk.

"Okay—we should get moving." Adam gestured to the church as we approached. "There's the reverend."

"You look much better!" Reverend Casillas said, handing a flyer to a man walking by.

I nodded. "I feel much better. I've got fluids and food in my system now."

"You need to be careful with the elevation here."

"Believe me—I've learned my lesson."

"Good. And don't forget to drink the coca tea to help you adjust to the elevation."

"I won't. I wanted to talk to you about something, if you have a minute."

"Of course."

I pointed to the school. "I feel horrible about what

happened to the building, and especially about the students missing their classes for the last few months. They're falling behind."

"I pray every day those kids will get the education they deserve. God has a plan, and we need to have patience to find out what it is."

"Maybe I'm part of that plan."

The reverend smiled. "Bless you, Liz. What did you have in mind?"

"You mentioned there was a vacant building a few blocks away."

"Yes, it is available for us to use, but remember that even if we were to use that space, we still don't have school supplies, desks, boards, and other things necessary to start running it. Everything was destroyed."

"I understand that. Can you show it to me anyway—the vacant building?"

"It would be my pleasure."

I turned to Adam and Orlando, thinking of our driver. "Can you call Javier and let him know we haven't forgotten about him?"

"I already did. He talked with his boss and said he could wait as long as necessary, but to let you know he was on the clock and you were being charged by the hour."

"I'm okay with that."

Adam checked his watch. "Looks like we missed another train."

"I'm okay with that too, but if you and Orlando want to go ahead—"

Adam shook his head. "No way. Count me in."

"Me, too," Orlando said.

Adam had been looking forward to seeing Machu Picchu. I felt bad he was stuck with me. Most likely we would have to spend the night in Pisac, but his response to helping with my plan seemed sincere. It was an ambitious plan, for sure. I was confident we could do it with the help of the Internet.

We followed Reverend Casillas around the corner.

He stopped in front of a large white stucco building with the brown tile roof. "This is it."

"It's a beautiful building." I pointed to the sign in the window that said *Se Vende*. "What does that say?"

"For sale," Adam said.

"The owner has been trying to sell it for over a year," Reverend Casillas said. "But he said we could use it until he sells it."

"Vacant for over a year?" I said.

"Is that because it's expensive?" Adam asked.

"Or it needs a lot of work." Orlando peeked through the window. "Then again—maybe not. This place looks immaculate."

"It *is* immaculate," Reverend Casillas said. "And it's a steal compared to real estate in the US. The real estate business has been slow in Peru the last few years. And understand that it's much harder to sell buildings in the smaller villages in our country when they're not in the main tourist areas, such as the streets closer to the market here in Pisac." He pointed to the building. "He's asking three hundred thousand Peruvian soles, which is right around ninety-thousand American dollars."

I scooted up next to Orlando and peeked through the window. "You're right. That is a steal, and it looks like it's in great shape. It'll need to be turned into a school, with classes and bathrooms."

Should I just buy the building? If I didn't, someone else could buy it and kick the children out of school after going through all the work of getting them in there. That would be the worst-case scenario. The best-case scenario was owning the building myself, so we wouldn't have to worry about that. It wouldn't even put a dent in my two hundred million dollars. Ordering the school supplies online would be a snap, and we could have them shipped overnight.

Then the children could come back to school soon.

It amazed me how clear my head was. Not long ago I was confused and lethargic, but suddenly thoughts and ideas were banging back and forth inside my brain like a pinball machine. Must have been those electrolytes and fluids they gave me at the clinic.

"You're mighty quiet," Adam said. "Don't pass out on us again, please."

I shook my head. "Twice in one day is more than enough. I'm just thinking."

"About what?"

"About helping the kids."

"It would be wonderful if you could," Reverend Casillas said. "What do you have in mind?"

"Let me think about this a moment."

The only option was to buy the building. And the crazy part was I didn't even know any of those kids! Well, except for the cute girl who'd sold me the jacket. That look on her face when she told me the school was closed did something to me. It planted a seed inside my heart—the same seed Dr. Singh had planted when he had told me to do something good with my fortune.

That's what was going to happen.

My heart rate picked up, and I giggled at the thought.

Orlando leaned toward me, grinning. "What's so funny?"

"I'm feeling a little giddy because I'm going to buy this building for the children."

"What?" Adam jerked his head in my direction.

"Why not? If the owner will sell it to me."

"The owner is a good friend of mine and *I'm sure* he would sell it to you," Reverend Casillas said. "I can give him a call."

"Then that just leaves the school supplies. I know this is a small town, but does Amazon deliver here?"

He grinned. "Amazon delivers everywhere."

"Great! Let's make this happen then."

"God bless you." Reverend Casillas stepped toward me and hugged me with teary eyes. "You're a saint."

"She is." Orlando stepped toward me and also hugged me. "My kind of lady." He stepped away and glanced at Adam, who was quiet, but smiling. "What's on your mind?"

"Nothing." Adam grinned.

I crossed my arms. "Spontaneity is on his mind, but I had *plenty* of time to think about this."

Adam chuckled. "When? Between passing out at the school and passing out at the clinic?"

"Are you going to analyze everything or are you going to help me get these kids back to school?"

Adam smirked. "Both. And by the way, you're amazing." He stepped toward me and hugged me. He pulled away and held my gaze for a moment.

My heart skipped a beat, again.

There was something in the way he looked at me. It wasn't a look you gave someone for just being generous. This was different. In the past, that look got me into trouble because I loved when a man looked at me that way. How could I describe it?

He looked like I was the only one he was thinking of.

Like he cared about me.

Like he wanted me.

After letting that sink in for a few moments, it hit me.

Uh-oh.

I was in serious trouble.

Because I was looking at him the same way.

CHAPTER FOURTEEN

Two Days Later . . .

LIZ

We had finally made it to Machu Picchu. Sitting on top of an alpaca blanket I had purchased from one of the local sellers near the entrance, I looked out into the distance and marveled at one of the new Seven Wonders of the World. I had been teaching my students about the well-preserved fifteenth century Inca ruins for years, but I couldn't believe I was finally here in person to see it with my own eyes. The pictures and videos I had shown in my classroom didn't do this place justice.

My gaze wandered from the three-sided stone building known as the Guardhouse over to the tourists taking countless selfies in front of the semicircular outer wall of the Temple of the Sun. I stared at Huayna Picchu, the looming green mountain on the other side of the ruins. Its peak disappeared into the mist, making me wonder if that's where the expression "you've got your head in the clouds" came from.

I was in awe.

"Looks like you found the perfect place to squat." Adam approached from below and was out of breath. He pointed to my blanket. "Do you have room for me?"

I nodded and scooted over on the blanket.

He sat down next to me and wrapped his arms around his knees. "Nobody would ever know you were being treated in the clinic two days ago. How did you get up here so fast?"

I smirked. "I flew."

Adam chuckled. "Of course, you did."

"And what about you? You nearly broke your back when you carried me for ten miles, and you didn't seem to have a problem getting up here yourself."

"I'm sure it was only a quarter mile maximum, and I told you, it was nothing. A hot bath, a little stretching in the hotel room, and some ibuprofen, and I'm as good as new."

We were both silent for a minute, taking in the magic and mystery of what was in front of us. I snapped a few photos of the ruins with my phone and a few more of the majestic Andes mountains surrounding us.

He pointed to my phone. "We have the exact same phone."

"Yeah?"

"Same model, color, everything."

"What a coinkydink."

Adam chuckled. "There you go with that word again."

"It's not such a bad word. Try saying it."

He shook his head. "Never."

We were silent again for a few minutes, taking in the view.

"Who would ever think of buying a school bus in Peru?"

I blinked. "I can't believe you're sitting in front of one of the most breathtaking panoramic views in the entire world and all you're thinking about is a school bus."

"Not true. I was also thinking about the person who bought the school bus."

I hesitated. "It was no big deal."

"It was a *huge* deal. I was already impressed you bought the building and all the supplies without blinking an eye, but the school bus just took it to another level. You haven't been thinking about that at all? About the kids?"

"Of course. That's why I did it."

Even sitting there in front of a place I thought everyone in the world should see before they died, my thoughts went back to the school and the kids, and the bus. And the little girl from the market. I wished I could be there when they told her she would be going back to school soon.

It was amazing how fast everything happened. Real estate transactions sometimes took forever in the United States. It helped I paid cash and had wired the money within an hour after signing the papers. And buying all the school supplies online was a breeze. They just had to build some inner walls to create the classrooms, and install more bathrooms, but that would all be done quickly, considering the amount of people working on it. I never thought I would be creating employment.

"And you're doing all this in a foreign country," Adam continued. "You're single-handedly changing the course of those kids' lives."

I was fortunate enough to have the resources to make it

happen, so why not? I had to admit the feeling of being able to help someone in need was exhilarating. It made me want to do more. Now, I could see why people volunteered or started their own philanthropic organizations.

Adam pointed to my water bottle. "Drink up. I don't want you passing out on me again."

"Afraid you'll have to carry me down the hill?"

He chuckled. "Not at all. Sounds like fun."

I laughed and playfully pushed him on the arm. "I've got something fun for you. Picture yourself living here in the fourteen hundreds. What do you think that would be like?"

"Without a Cheesecake Factory nearby? I wouldn't survive a day." He winked. "Sure, it's fascinating, but I'm more interested in that guy right there and what his life is like." Adam pointed to the anthropologist hanging off the cliff and clinging to the wall. The man was pulling away vegetation to reveal the white granite stone face of the ancient citadel. "I'm curious why he would risk his life for this place."

"It must be his passion."

"Yeah . . . makes sense. We all have different things that fulfill us."

"There's no doubt about that."

I was enjoying Adam's company more each day, but I needed to be careful and think with my head, not my heart.

Nothing would happen between us.

A man and woman hiked by us, and I cranked my head around to get a better look at them.

Adam leaned forward to look into my eyes. "What?"

I shrugged. "For some reason, they reminded me of my parents."

"You were close?"

"Very. They were the best parents a kid could ask for." I smiled.

"Do you have your mother's smile?"

The question surprised me.

I nodded since I had been told many times I had her smile.

"Then your mother had a drop-dead gorgeous smile," Adam said.

Okay, I see what he did there.

He complimented my mom, but what he was really doing was complimenting me.

Smooth.

Clever.

Charming.

I froze, realizing what was going on here.

I was enjoying it.

Stop it!

I stood to fold the blanket. "We should probably find Orlando."

"He's taking a dip in the natural hot springs. Here—let me help you." Adam grabbed the bottom end of the blanket and pulled it up so the edges aligned with the top part in my hands. Our fingers brushed each other, catching us both off guard.

He cleared his throat. "Do you mind me asking how they died?"

I folded the blanket two more times and tucked it under my arm. "My mom ended up in the hospital because of the flu, which turned into a severe case of pneumonia. She never recovered." I turned and headed back down the hill. "My father had a heart attack three months after that."

"I'm sorry."

"Thanks. He wasn't the same after she died. His heart was broken, so it wasn't a surprise." I stopped and turned to Adam. "What about your parents?"

"My parents . . ." He stopped and thought about it. "A drunk driver going in the wrong direction."

"No." I gasped, touching him on the shoulder with my hand.

"Yup. In the blink of an eye—they were gone."

"That's just wrong because it could've been prevented."

Adam nodded, but didn't speak.

"I'm so sorry." The urge to give him a hug was too much to ignore. I stepped closer, wrapping my arms around him, and pulling him close.

He wrapped his arms around me tighter.

It was something he must have needed.

Me, too.

Now, if I could just stop hugging him before it became awkward.

CHAPTER FIFTEEN

ADAM

Flying from Peru to Kenya required two stops and almost twenty hours in the air. We had already stopped over in Rio de Janeiro, Brazil and Johannesburg, South Africa and were on the last leg of the trip, just forty-five minutes from touching down in Nairobi, our destination for the next few days.

I had seen Liz a couple of times when Orlando had taken over the flying duties, but the last two times I went into the cabin to check on her, she had been sleeping. Why was she sleeping so much? Nobody needed to sleep that much. Okay, maybe it was the jet lag, but that didn't mean I had to like it.

It had been the first time since becoming a private pilot that I had no problem giving up the controls of the aircraft. That's saying a lot, considering how passionate I was about flying.

It was because of Liz.

It was hard not to notice the way she looked at me when

we talked. And the way she looked at me when she didn't think I was looking. She was interested, although occasionally she flipped a switch and the look of interest would be gone. That bugged the hell out of me, since I knew there was something going on between us. The thing I didn't understand was what was going on with her. Maybe she had some things going on in her life. A divorce, maybe? Who knew?

Orlando entered the cockpit and closed the door behind him.

"How is Liz doing?" I couldn't help asking.

Orlando slid into his seat and strapped himself in. "She's doing just as good as she was when you saw her two hours ago."

"She didn't say anything about the change of plans?"

Orlando shook his head. "Not a thing."

"Good."

Because of the extra time we had spent in Peru, I had told Liz we would have to skip one of the other places she had on her bucket list to get her home on time. I had suggested dropping Paris, but Liz told me there was no way she would miss the Bastille Day celebration. She preferred to skip Greece. I tried to change her mind by mentioning the white sandy beaches of Santorini and the history of Athens since she was a history teacher, but she had already made up her mind.

I could feel Orlando's eyes on me.

He knew I was attracted to her.

He knew I was conflicted because she was a client.

He knew it bugged me that he knew.

And because of that, I knew it would only be a matter of time before he began dispensing the dating advice. How could the man know so much about women when he had no interest in them?

Any second now . . .

"You need to ask her out," Orlando said, right on cue. "She's interested."

"Did she ask about me?" I immediately regretted asking.

"Yes. She thinks you're so cute and wants you to carry her books to school."

I set myself up for that one. "Never mind."

Orlando laughed. "Ask her out."

"You know I can't do that."

"Yes, you can. Just wait until after we get her back home when she's not a client anymore."

I shot a quick glance at him and eyed the engine oil pressure and hydraulic fluid contents gauge in front of me. It was time to descend into Nairobi.

"Did you hear me?" Orlando pestered.

"Yes. I heard you."

"And your response to my intelligent advice would be?"

"No comment."

"Well—you should think about it."

Orlando's advice wasn't bad at all. Maybe I could just wait until we got home and call her after she had a few days to settle back into her daily routine. The only problem was I would have to wait until we got home.

I hated waiting.

When I see something I like, I go for it.

"Or just ask her now," Orlando added. "What's the worst thing that could happen?"

"She could say no. She could fire me."

"She's not going to fire you. Then what would she do? Get

off the plane in the middle of Africa and Uber back to the US?"

I chuckled. "I'm not flying the last aircraft known to mankind. She could grab a commercial flight back home."

"She won't do that, either. Quit worrying."

Maybe Orlando was right. She probably wouldn't fire me, but it wasn't just about the job she hired me to do. No matter how she reacted, I didn't want to disappoint Liz.

Did I have the patience to wait until we got back home to ask her out or let her know I was interested in her? The urge to get closer to Liz was stronger with every passing minute. How was that going to happen when she was always sleeping?

What could I do? Bang on a drum every time she fell asleep?

I had no idea.

All I knew was I had to do something.

CHAPTER SIXTEEN

LIZ

Two loud bangs woke me up from my deep sleep. I sat up, my heart pounding, my mind disoriented. I rubbed my eyes, more confused than ever.

"Where am I?" I mumbled to myself.

I didn't have an answer, but I wasn't on the jet any longer, that was for sure.

I yawned and looked around the large room toward the en-suite bathroom, the ornate brick fireplace, and lastly at the posts on each corner of my king-size bed.

This couldn't have been a dream because the room seemed familiar.

The biggest mystery was where the banging was coming from.

There were two more bangs, but this time I saw movement just outside the window.

"That's right!" I might have been suffering from a little jet lag.

I remembered checking into our hotel last night. Well, it wasn't a hotel. Giraffe Manor was built in 1932 and modeled after a Scottish hunting lodge. It was more like a mansion in the African countryside with five-star cuisine. And I couldn't forget the giraffes. Lots of giraffes.

The amazing property had only twelve guest rooms set within one hundred and forty acres of indigenous forest in the Langata suburb of Nairobi. Yes, there were vibrant green gardens and quaint courtyards, but the best part of the property was the giraffes and the forest sanctuary. We were also just across the border from Tanzania and one Land Rover ride away from the next place on my bucket list, the Serengeti.

That's why I was there.

As for Giraffe Manor, the manager told us last night the giraffes would most likely come looking for treats in the early morning hours when the sun came up, poking their heads into open windows or banging on the balconies for a handout. That was obviously where the noise had come from. The giraffes were right on schedule.

I popped out of bed in my Easy Peasy T-shirt, making my way to the balcony. There was no need for a robe since it was summer and the temperature was pleasant, even so early in the morning.

I pulled open the curtains and unlatched the French doors, pulling them open to see two beautiful giraffe faces staring right back at me, the Ngong Hills behind them in the distance.

What a sight to see.

Take a picture.

I held up an index finger for the giraffes. "Wait."

Did I really just give the giraffes a command as if they were dogs and understood English?

I felt silly, but at least nobody saw me do it.

Running back inside, I grabbed my phone and returned to the balcony.

"Okay, hold it and smile." I shook my head, realizing I'd given the giraffes another command. "I know you don't understand me, but I hope you'll stay still"

I took a few photos and checked them to make sure they weren't blurry. I set the phone down on the table to admire them both. These two majestic creatures were part of the herd of Rothschild's giraffes on the property, the most endangered giraffes in the world.

They banged on the balcony again, waiting for their treats.

"Oops. Sorry. Hang on." I went back inside the room, grabbed the bucket of grass pellets the staff had left for me next to the fireplace, and headed back outside. I moved closer to the giraffes. "Breakfast is served."

The larger of the two giraffes slid his long neck over the balcony rail toward me.

"Hello there. You are so beautiful." I pulled a pellet from the bucket and held it out, watching as his incredibly long tongue swooped in and gently grabbed it from my hand. The other giraffe moved closer, ready for his turn. "And you're beautiful, too!" I pulled out another pellet and held it out.

When they finished chewing, I handed another pellet to each of them.

It was so peaceful this morning and the birds were already singing.

I especially loved the fact that there was so much privacy on my—

"Good morning, neighbor."

I froze, as the bucket of giraffe pellets dangled from my hand.

It was Adam, but he was nowhere in sight.

He had the room right next to mine, although his didn't have a balcony, but instead a large window. I didn't notice him when I came out. He must have been standing in front of the window or sitting on the ledge.

The problem was that he could see me standing there in my skimpy t-shirt that barely covered my southern hemisphere.

"Good morning." There was no way I was going to turn around.

Should I make a run for it back inside? I would look like an idiot if I did. I'm not ashamed of my body and we were both adults, but you think differently about bodies and skin when you're attracted to a person.

"It's a beautiful day, isn't it?" Adam said.

"Yes—it's a beautiful day."

"Did you sleep well? You seem to sleep a lot."

What was it with this man and all this communicating?

He wasn't normal.

And he was obviously referring to my sleeping on the jet. Dr. Singh had told me that fatigue could be one of my symptoms, but it also could've been jet lag. Either way, Adam noticed, which was sweet. I needed to be careful because I was developing feelings for the man.

"Liz, is everything okay? It's like you're avoiding looking at me."

"Don't be silly." I crossed my arms over my chest to make sure he couldn't see through my T-shirt and turned to face him and froze.

Wow.

Would you look at that?

Adam was casually sitting on the window ledge of his room.

Shirtless.

I forced a smile and kept my eyes glued to his, even though the urge to drop my gaze to his chest and abs was strong.

"Everything is great!" I said with too much enthusiasm through gritted teeth, using every ounce of energy I had to hold my head up high. "Yes—I slept well."

I usually had amazing willpower, but maybe it didn't apply in Africa. Especially when I remembered what Adam looked like without a shirt from the pictures on his website.

I had to look.

A little peek wouldn't hurt anyone, would it?

"The giraffes woke me up." I pointed to the giraffes to lure Adam's eyes in that direction while I quickly glanced down to admire his body.

Now, for a quick look-see.

Chest.

Abs.

Chest.

Abs.

Yummy.

Done!

I shot my gaze back up to his eyes and—

Uh-oh.

Adam was staring at me.

His bottom lip curled up into a smile.

Yup. He knew.

Busted.

I could never be a spy.

Neither could he, the way his gaze dropped to my chest.

It was a good thing I had my arms crossed, so he couldn't see much.

He grinned. "Easy?"

What was he talking about? Did he call me easy just because I was wearing a skimpy T-shirt? How dare he! I woke up, got straight out of bed, and came to the balcony. I didn't expect to see him or anyone else.

I hesitated. "What did you call me?"

"I didn't call you anything. I was just reading." He pointed to my T-shirt.

I looked down and blinked.

Oh.

Well, that explains a lot.

My T-shirt said "Easy Peasy" on the front, but my crossed arms were covering up the bottom word. Adam thought I was advertising to the world I was easy.

I wasn't easy.

Horrified was more accurate.

"No, no, no." I needed to clear this up as quickly as possible. "It says *easy peasy*. It's one of my favorite expressions, but you can't see the second word because my arms are in the way." I uncrossed my arms and dropped them to my sides so he could see both words. "See? Easy peasy."

His gaze dropped to my chest again and he swallowed hard. "Yeah . . . I can see that now."

Oh, my goodness.

The sun was coming up and hitting me square in the chest, so I wondered if he could see through my T-shirt. It was made of a super-soft, breathable sheer fabric that made it comfy to sleep in, but did it also reveal my girls in certain lighting conditions? Had I just invited Adam to check out my boobs? His reaction sure made it seem so.

I quickly crossed my arms again. "Anyway, I'm not easy. Not even close to easy. In fact, I'm difficult. *Very* difficult."

He chuckled but didn't respond.

I needed to stop talking because I was making it worse. Or maybe I needed to find a rhino stampede or the wildebeest migration and throw myself in front of it.

He grinned, not seeming to mind that I was acting like a dope. "You can be whatever you want to be, but you're delightful just the way you are."

He looked at me that way again.

Like I was desirable.

Why would he do such a thing? I had no makeup on and the worst case of bedhead known to mankind. I probably had sleepers in my eyes. My toenails weren't painted. I felt insecure and vulnerable. Plus, I was rambling like a fool.

And he liked that?

He liked me with all my flaws?

What kind of freak was this man?

Adam gestured back inside his room with his thumb. "Orlando should be done with his shower, so I need to take mine before I head down for breakfast. Will I see you there?"

I nodded. "Yup. Yup. I have to eat. I mean, I *want* to eat. Who doesn't like food?" I cleared my throat. "Anyway, see you there."

"Sounds good." Adam disappeared back inside his room.

I shook my head and wondered if I needed to go back to school to learn how to talk in complete sentences again. A three-time "Teacher of the Year" winner should not have had such problems expressing herself.

It was Adam's fault.

Him and that chest and those abs, not to mention his never-ending supply of charm.

How dare he?

I turned back to the two giraffes who stood there, staring at me, judging me.

"Don't look at me that way," I whispered to them. "I'll have you know that I usually have a much better command of the English language. I mean, do you have to deal with silly things like thoughts and feelings? I think not. You hang around all day eating food from the guests' hands, pooping wherever you want. Do you see me pooping wherever I want?"

Adam stuck his head back out the window. "Sorry, were you talking to me?"

Somebody kill me. Kill me now.

"No." I turned to go back in the room and—

"Wow!" Adam said, making me jump.

I stopped and turned back toward him, crossing my arms. "What?"

He gestured to my lower extremity and shook his head. "Your legs . . . I mean . . . wow."

Okay, so Adam was a leg man, as well? Nothing wrong with that.

I'm so glad I shaved.

My legs were my best feature, but I thought he was being a

little forward the way he was still staring at them. His mouth was hanging open, too.

It was good to know I still had it at the age of fifty, but enough was enough. "You're going to make me blush. Will you stop staring?"

"I can't help it. How did they get that way?"

"Well, I do yoga once a week, for starters. I also—"

"Sorry, that's not what I meant. Yes, you have fantastic legs, but I'm not talking about that." Adam pointed to my thighs. "Look. You have two massive bruises."

"What?" I looked down, studying them for a minute. Yeah, they were huge. Almost as big as the two bruises that had prompted Josh to take me to the doctor.

"You didn't know they were there?"

"No."

"Maybe we need to get you to another doctor," Adam said. "That's not normal. Orlando told me you refused to have more tests done at the clinic even though the doctor recommended them. This could be related."

"Don't be silly. I've gotten these bruises before. They're a symptom of—"

Whoops.

I had almost mentioned the disease.

Don't want to do that!

Adam cocked his head to the side. "A symptom of what?"

Think, think, think!

"Well, a symptom of . . . uh . . . *you* being clumsy. This happened when you banged my legs against the doorframe at the entrance of the clinic. Remember?"

"Hey—I remember and feel bad about that. I didn't think

that's where your legs hit the doorframe, plus I didn't bang you that hard."

I arched an eyebrow.

Adam chuckled. "Okay, poor choice of words, but let's not get off subject here. You should have those bruises checked out by a doctor. You could be hemorrhaging or have internal bleeding and not even know. A simple visit to the doctor won't kill you."

"Says the man who avoids doctors and hospitals at all costs."

"We're not talking about me."

"Now, we are, Mr. Nosocomephobia. Have you had the colonoscopy you're supposed to get at the age of fifty?"

"It's not the same."

"Why not?"

"Because . . ." Adam thought about it for a moment. "I'm a man and men are expected to be big babies and stubborn as hell. Women are strong and can handle just about anything thrown at them."

"Nice try."

Adam held my gaze. "The difference is I'm not showing any signs of something going on with my body." He pointed to my legs. "You are. Not to mention the two times you passed out, plus I didn't forget when you had something going on with your stomach in Cusco."

"It's the elevation. You heard what Reverend Casillas and Dr. Rubio said."

"I'm not so sure."

"Okay." I was ready to make a deal I knew he wouldn't agree to. "I'll tell you what. I'll go see a doctor about this if you promise to get a colonoscopy. What do you say?"

Adam hesitated. "I'm sorry, but I can't make that promise." He sighed. "You should still go, though. Do you know how I'd feel if you died on me?"

I did, and that's why I had to make sure nothing happened between us.

I placed my hands on my hips. "Would you quit worrying? Everything will be fine, and these bruises will go away in a few days. Easy peasy."

His gaze dropped to my chest again.

I can't believe I flashed him again, but at least it shut him up.

I crossed my arms and made a beeline for my room. "Gotta run!"

"We haven't finished!"

"Yes, we have!"

Closing the French doors behind me, I headed straight to the bathroom, turning on the main light. I turned on the makeup vanity mirror light as well, extended it from the wall, and pointed it toward my legs.

I dropped my head down to glance at the two bruises on my legs, gently running my fingers across them. The human body was a crazy, complex thing that sometimes made no sense at all. I wondered how long the bruises would last this time and when I would get more. I also wondered how I would explain it to Adam.

"Quit worrying so much." I stood up straight and looked at myself in the mirror.

Wait a minute.

I adjusted the makeup vanity mirror light, so it was shining on my chest, and leaned closer, analyzing my T-shirt from the front and the side.

"Wonderful."

It was just as I expected.

With direct light on my T-shirt, it was see-through.

I had given Adam a free peep show.

I sighed and clicked both lights off, walking over to the bed and sitting down.

My phone vibrated on the bedside table. It was a text from my brother.

Josh: It's mighty quiet over there. Are you still alive and kicking?

Liz: Yes. I'm fine. I miss you.

Josh: Miss you, too. Any word on a bone marrow donor match yet?

Liz: Nothing yet. No emails or calls.

Josh: It will happen.

Liz: You know what's weird? I haven't been thinking about it much.

Josh: Not weird at all. You're living in the moment, which is a good thing. That must mean you're enjoying your trip. Are you still in Peru?

Liz: No. I'm in Africa now. I'm going to jump in the shower before heading down for breakfast. Then we're going on a safari through the Serengeti! You won't believe what happened in Peru. I can fill you in when we get back from the safari in a couple of days since I have to get ready.

Josh: WAIT! Don't you dare leave me hanging like that. Give me a clue. Are you married? Pregnant? Oh wait, you're 50 and celibate. That can't be it.

Liz: Not funny.

Josh: How is hunky pilot man?

Liz: He's good. I saw him half-naked on the balcony.

Josh: Photo please.

Liz: Dream on.

Josh: What about Orlando? Hey, do you know if he is single?

Liz: How do you know about Orlando?

Josh: I met him and Adam when I dropped you off at the airport! Are you losing your memory?

Liz: Oh, that's right. And sorry, I don't know if he's single.

Josh: You still didn't tell me about Peru. Give me something before you go.

Liz: Okay, here's the Reader's Digest version: I bought a building and turned it into a school. Oh, and I bought a school bus to get the kids there.

Josh: Wow. I love this. I would say I'm surprised, but I know you. You make me proud, sis. Always have. Love you and don't forget to call me later.

Liz: Will do. Love you, too.

I set the phone back down on the bedside table and thought about what a wonderful brother I had. I was so lucky to have him in my life.

Two minutes later, I got in the shower and my thoughts went immediately to Adam.

I liked him a lot.

There was no doubting the attraction was real.

Adam was kind, considerate, funny, charming, and very attractive. Sure, I think it's good to be attracted to someone physically, but it's what's inside a person's heart and their actions that truly defines a person and shows me what they're made of.

He carried me in his arms for a quarter of a mile!

I'm usually a good judge of character and Adam was one of the good ones, I was sure. He's the kind of man who could be much less attractive, and I'd still be attracted to him, although you would never see me complaining if he's shirtless again.

I sighed, squeezing shower gel into the palm of my hand, and washing the bruises on my legs. Maybe I could make them magically disappear.

No such luck.

These were the cards the universe had dealt me.

I had to live with them.

I had to die with them.

Under different circumstances, Adam and I could have had something special. I missed being in love, missed having a man in my life.

I missed the intimacy.

I leaned my forehead against the shower tile, deep in thought about how life sometimes made little sense at all.

It took me a minute to realize I was crying.

It was the first time I had cried since I had won the lottery and gotten the diagnosis, but I couldn't be certain these were tears of sadness. Most likely, they were tears of a thousand emotions bottled up inside of me, finally ready to be released. I consider myself to be a strong woman, but everyone has their breaking point. I wasn't sure if this was my breaking point, but I needed to allow it to happen. I needed to listen to my body and my heart.

These also had to be tears of confusion. I wondered why I was twice divorced, why I had lost both of my parents, why I was the chosen one, or why anybody had to be the chosen one to contract a deadly disease.

I finished crying and got out of the shower to get dressed.

I stared at myself in the mirror as I applied sunscreen to my face. I would wait until the redness from my eyes went away before heading downstairs for breakfast. Surprisingly, I felt much better after the cry.

"Things will be fine," I said to myself. "It ain't over until it's over."

I still had time to have fun.

I still had time to do more good deeds with my fortune.

I still had time to enjoy Adam's company before we said goodbye.

CHAPTER SEVENTEEN

ADAM

Orlando looked up from tying his shoes as he sat on the edge of the bed. "We need to be downstairs in five minutes to meet Liz and the driver. Are you almost ready?"

"Almost." I rubbed the last bit of sunscreen on my forehead and closed the cap on the bottle. "Hey, did you notice how quiet Liz was during breakfast?"

"I noticed. I was going to ask you what you did."

"I did nothing."

Orlando crossed his arms. "Right."

"Seriously. I would never do anything to hurt her. There's a huge attraction between us, but it's more than that."

Orlando snorted. "Tell me something I don't know. You're going to ask her out then?"

I thought about it and had a better solution. "Maybe we should just skip straight to marriage."

"Without a date? Baby steps, buddy. You don't want to scare the woman away."

"Okay—I'm only half kidding. But you know how some people say the moment they meet someone they know they want to marry that person? Well, maybe it wasn't instant. It was darn close, though. There was something going on the moment she walked into my office. I can't get her off my mind. I'm sure it's mutual, but something is stopping her from exploring her feelings. There's so much mystery surrounding her. Even though I feel as if I have known her forever, there's this side of her I don't know at all."

"How do you explain her behavior during breakfast then? Unless you did or said something to annoy her, which I'm guessing you did."

"Me? I'm as innocent as they come."

Orlando arched an eyebrow. "You?"

"Okay, okay, I may have pushed her a little to go get checked out by a doctor. She had two bruises on her legs that looked scary. Have you seen them?"

"No, but why would she go see a doctor? Everybody gets bruises."

"You wouldn't believe the size. They were massive. Anyway, I was worried about her."

"And what did she say?"

"She said they were no big deal. She'd had bruises like that before."

Orlando grabbed his wallet and phone from the bedside table, sliding them both into his pants pocket. "Well then, if she says it's no big deal it must be no big deal."

"But her eyes and her body language are telling different

stories." I grabbed the room key and stuck it in my pocket. "I don't know if I buy it."

"What? Are you saying she was lying to you?"

"No, not exactly. Maybe. Or maybe she was just withholding information. Remember, she got sick in Cusco. She passed out twice in Pisac. Now, the two freakish bruises. You told me she seemed jumpy and said no when the doctor asked to do more blood tests. Why would someone go against the doctor's advice? Who would do that?"

"You!" Orlando pointed at me. "You're jumpy whenever I mention a doctor to you."

"That's different."

"No, it isn't."

"She needs to see a doctor."

"So do you, but you won't listen. In fact, I don't think there's anyone on this earth who can get you to go. Am I right?"

"The only people who could have guilted me into going were my parents and they're no longer around."

"Well then, you found your answer."

I was confused. "Spell it out for me. I'm a little slow this morning."

Orlando sighed and headed toward the door, stopping and turning. "If she's just as stubborn as you, then the only one who can convince her to go to the doctor would also be a family member, in this case it would be her brother, Josh."

I snapped my fingers and pointed at Orlando. "You're right. You're brilliant."

"I know. Can we go now?"

"Just a second. I need to call Josh."

"Now?"

"Yes, now. It'll just take a second." I opened my wallet and pulled out the business card he gave me when we met at the airport. I dialed his phone number, but it went straight to voicemail. I disconnected the call, slipping the phone back in my pocket.

"Not there?" Orlando asked.

"It went straight to voicemail."

"He could be sleeping."

"He's ten hours behind us—it's not late in San Diego. I'll try him again later. We'd better get going."

We grabbed our backpacks and went downstairs. The driver and Liz were standing in front of the main building near the Land Rover we would take on our road trip to the Serengeti.

Liz looked cute in her white blouse and khaki-colored shorts that were long enough to cover the bruises on her thighs.

"There they are." Liz pointed to us. "Let's get going, guys! There are some beautiful animals to see."

"Let's do it." I extended my hand. "Hi—I'm Adam and this is Orlando."

"It is a pleasure to meet you both." The driver shook both of our hands. "My name is Chitundu and I will be your driver and tour guide for the day. You will see many beautiful things on the way to your lodge in the Serengeti. Shall we go?"

"Sounds great." I stepped toward the Land Rover and stopped. "Any preferences on the seating? Liz, how about you take the front seat?"

"It doesn't matter," Liz said. "If one of you want to ride in front, I'm fine with that."

"I'll take the front seat." Orlando winked at me and

clapped me on the shoulder as he passed me. He went around the front of the Land Rover to get in the front seat.

Just as I suspected.

This was a set-up.

What was he up to? Did he think something would happen between me and Liz in the back seat? I wouldn't be surprised if she was quiet for the entire ride, although I don't think my caring about her wellbeing was a valid reason to be mad at me.

Liz and I got in the back seat, both reaching for our seat belts, and bumping hands when we tried to fasten them into the same buckle in the middle.

"Sorry," Liz said. "Is that your hole or my hole?"

"Excuse me?" Orlando said. "I would like to know what's going on back there."

"*Nothing* is going on back here." I laughed, turning to Liz. "Now, who's the one with the poor choice of words?"

She fastened her seatbelt and held up her hand. "That would be me. It's just, I couldn't remember for the life of me what that darn thing was called."

"It's called a buckle."

She pointed. "That. Exactly. Well, buckle up, buttercup."

I laughed again. "Right." I fastened my seatbelt, as Chitundu pulled out of the property and onto the main road.

Liz turned away from me to look out the window, but I could see the smirk on her face. It was good to know she wasn't still mad at me over the doctor thing on the balcony.

I glanced down at her fantastic legs. I couldn't see the bruises, which wasn't a surprise. That T-shirt she had worn this morning was short.

Really short.

I wasn't complaining.

I needed to get my eyes off her legs before she—

Oops.

Too late.

Liz looked over and crossed her arms. "Can I help you with something?"

"Not at all. Thanks for asking." I pointed out the window. "Look, a weird bird."

Liz followed the direction of my hand. "I don't see any."

I tried to keep a straight face. "Hmm. I guess it's gone."

Chitundu drove us down the main road bordering Nairobi National Park, away from the city and toward the Tanzanian border and the Serengeti. We would spend most of the day driving, with the occasional stop for bathroom breaks and food and sights.

A few minutes later, Liz lowered her window and pointed off in the distance toward the foothills. "Look. Elephants."

"Wow," Orlando said.

Liz pointed again. "And rhinos over there! I didn't think we'd be seeing animals in the wild until we crossed the border into Tanzania."

"Those animals are not in the wild," Chitundu said. "That property is part of the Sheldrick Wildlife Trust. It's an orphanage for elephants and rhinos."

"An orphanage?"

"Yes. It's the most successful rehabilitation program for those animals in the world. In fact, you can even adopt an elephant there, although I must tell you, you cannot take it home." He chuckled. "I'm sure you know the adoption is more of a financial gesture of kindness to help with medical expenses, food, and getting the animals back in the wild where they belong."

"It sounds like a wonderful organization."

"It is."

Liz continued to stare out the window, even after the elephants and rhinos disappeared out of view. "I would like to adopt an elephant."

"Great idea." Orlando waved his hand. "Count me in."

"Me, three!" I said.

"This is wonderful!" Chitundu glanced over at Orlando in the passenger seat, and at me and Liz in the rearview mirror. "You all have beautiful and kind hearts."

"I was just following Liz's example," I said.

Liz glanced over and gave me a smile.

I smiled back at her.

She blushed before looking up at Chitundu. "Can we stop there on the way back?"

Chitundu nodded. "I will make sure of it."

He continued driving, proudly talking about some points of interest we passed on the road, a cheese farm, a tea farm, even a castle which was surprising to see in Kenya. He showed us where they filmed part of the movie *Out of Africa* with Robert Redford and Meryl Streep.

A minute later, Chitundu lowered his window again. "Do you see those cherries over there?"

"Yes," we all answered together.

"Ha!" He chuckled. "They are not cherries!"

"What are they?" Liz and I asked at the same time.

We gave each other surprised looks and turned our attention back to Chitundu.

"That is a coffee farm, my friends! Kenya has thousands."

Liz shook her head. "I can't believe those are coffee plants."

"Yes!" Chitundu said. "The coffee bean is actually the seed of the coffee plant, and it is located inside that fruit which is often referred to as a cherry."

"Wow," I said. "I had no idea."

Chitundu smiled. "We are proud of our coffee. It is so good it travels the world."

"I've seen it at Starbucks and Peet's."

"Ahhh, but nothing is better than trying it in the country of origin. It doesn't get fresher than that, my friends."

"Well, now you've got me in the mood for a cup!"

"Me too," I said.

"Well then, I know the perfect place to stop, a quaint cafe with the best coffee in the world." Chitundu slowed the Land Rover. "Goodness, this is not good."

I sat forward in my seat. "What is it?"

"There is a lion loose, on the wrong side of the park fence."

I looked out my window. "I see it. Wow."

The lion seemed to be preoccupied with something near a dead tree stump. It had a yellowish, brown fur with a tuft on the end of its tail.

"Where is it?" Liz tried to lean in my direction to get a better look out my window, but the seat belt stopped her.

Chitundu looked in the rearview mirror. "I need to pull over and call the KWS. That is the Kenya Wildlife Service. They manage the animals for the Kenyan people." Chitundu pulled off to the shoulder. "Please do not get out of the car." He gestured to the glove compartment. "Do you mind taking my phone out?"

"I don't mind at all." Orlando opened the glove compartment and grabbed Chitundu's phone.

Liz moved closer, trying to look out my window. "I still don't see it."

"Switch places with me." I sat back in my seat and reached over to unfasten my seat belt.

"Thanks." Liz undid her seatbelt and scooted to the edge of her seat. She stood as much as she could inside the Land Rover, grabbed the back of Chitundu's headrest for balance and slid her butt over my legs, as I moved over to where she was.

It shouldn't have been difficult, but Liz hit her head on the ceiling, stepped on my foot, and fell back toward me.

I instinctively grabbed her waist to keep her from falling. To my surprise, her momentum caused her butt to end up in my lap and her shoulders in my arms.

"Are you okay?" I asked.

She rubbed the top of her head. "Yeah."

My heart rate picked up when I felt heat emanating from her body.

And she smelled divine—like a meadow in full-bloom spring.

Her exposed neck was inches from my mouth.

I had the sudden urge to kiss it gently.

Down, boy. That's a good way to get slapped.

Liz placed her hand on my leg to move over and pulled it away quickly. "Sorry." She turned toward me, and our faces were inches apart.

I swallowed hard and couldn't help looking down at her lips.

So kissable.

She glanced down at my lips and looked away, finally sliding over.

"Can you see the lion now?" I asked.

That had to be the dumbest question.

I was nervous, and that was the only thing I could think of.

Of course, she can see it!

Liz nodded. "Yes. It's so beautiful. I hope it doesn't get hit by a car."

"That is what I am hoping to prevent." Chitundu held the phone to his ear. "Or a tourist can get badly injured trying to move closer for a picture." He held up an index finger. "Excuse me."

Chitundu spoke on the phone to someone in another language I'm guessing was Swahili. A minute later he disconnected the call. "They're on their way. Occasionally, this can occur. That's what happens when you have a national park so close to civilization." He sighed. "Please fasten your seat belts. They have instructed me to leave the area immediately, so that is what I will do. I always obey the law and keep my guests safe or I can lose my license." He pointed to the license with his name and picture on it attached to the dashboard.

"What does Chitundu mean?" I asked.

"It means bird nest." Chitundu smiled proudly. "I was born underneath a speckled pigeon nest in an acacia tree just in front of our home. I am thankful my parents did not name me Acacia."

I laughed, along with Orlando and Liz.

"How long have you been a tour guide and driver?" Liz asked.

"Seventeen years." Chitundu pulled back onto the road. "My mother said she could tell before I was born that I loved the outdoors so much because I only kicked inside her tummy when we were inside the house. She also said it was destiny I became a tour guide and I think she was right."

An hour later, we stopped for coffee in a small town, and it surprised me how many buildings had signs written in English. The coffee was amazing, but we took it to go, since we needed to travel all day to get to the Four Seasons Safari Lodge in the Serengeti. Chitundu had also mentioned that the cafe was the last place we would have a strong cell signal, so he recommended making any calls before we headed out since it could be spotty the farther out we traveled. I stepped outside to sneak another call to Josh. It went straight to his voicemail.

As Chitundu continued to drive farther and farther away from the big city and civilization, the landscape transformed. The modern buildings had completely disappeared, making way for wide plains and hills. The houses we could see from the road were made of grass and mud, just like those I had seen in the movies and many National Geographic documentaries. The roads became bumpier and even more narrow.

"We're about six kilometers from the first Maasai village you will encounter on this journey," Chitundu said. "That is a little less than four miles from here."

We passed a woman in a blue and red sarong on the side of the road, walking with a giant jug on top of her head and a baby on her back. We passed five more women, all carrying jugs on tops of their heads.

"What are they carrying?" I asked.

Chitundu glanced at me in his rearview mirror and got his eyes back on the road. "They are carrying water. Some are lucky to have a donkey to carry the water for them. Most do not have that luxury."

We passed another woman, and another, both also carrying water on their heads.

"That can't be comfortable." Liz watched as we passed another woman carrying a jug. "I can't imagine the stress that puts on the neck, shoulders, and back. How far do they have to go?"

"They are walking to the village we will pass through."

"What?" Liz practically yelled. "The one four miles away?"

"I'm afraid so. The village has a natural spring, but the water is contaminated and not usable, so they need to go to the next closest clean water source which is quite a distance away. However, it is necessary to have the water for drinking, cooking, washing, and bathing. They make the journey on foot regularly. Sometimes multiple times daily."

"Where are the men?"

"The men are also working, taking care of the land, tending to cattle, and protecting the community. Everybody works and everybody cares for the village."

We passed another woman walking with a jug on her head.

Liz shook her head. "If it were a short distance, that would be different. Four miles is ridiculous. It's not right. I want to fix this."

I turned to Liz. "What are you going to do? Buy another bus?"

"No. It needs to be more than that." Liz shrugged. "I need to figure out a way for them to have clean water without having to walk miles to get it. I want to make their lives easier. Everybody deserves that, no matter what part of the world you live in. We all need water to survive."

I marveled at what a wonderful woman Liz was.

Not long ago she'd had to plan everything in advance and research for hours before deciding on something. This time she'd just decided without taking much time to think about it. She was transforming right before my eyes. She was on a mission to help whoever she could, not even questioning what it would take or how much it would cost.

Her generosity was turning me on.

Ridiculous, I know.

The woman was beautiful inside and out.

And to top it off, she was being spontaneous!

Liz pointed her index finger at me. "Don't you dare say it."

I held my palms up. "What?"

"You know what."

I chuckled. "I'm not sure I do."

She crossed her arms. "Then what were you thinking, and why are you looking at me that way?"

"I thought Chitundu was right—you have a beautiful and kind heart."

"This is so true!" Orlando added, cranking his body around and smiling at Liz. "You're the best. The world needs more people like you."

"Thank you—to both of you," Liz said. "Time is precious, and I just want people to be happy. I just want to help."

I felt something stronger than attraction tug in my heart. It was warmth, admiration, and a deep appreciation for Liz. Every little thing she did pulled me closer to her.

I had told Orlando I would marry Liz, and now I was more certain than ever.

CHAPTER EIGHTEEN

LIZ

I was on the other side of the world trying to go through my bucket list, but my mind was only on how I could help other people. Well that, plus maybe a few hundred thoughts about kissing the stuffing out of Adam. I swear I'm going to melt from how the man looks at me. I need to use every ounce of strength I've got to resist him. Maybe focusing on helping others will take my mind off Adam for a few seconds.

Maybe I was dreaming.

Chitundu drove past one small village and made a right turn onto a dirt road.

I looked out the window. "We're not stopping at this village?"

He shook his head. "This village is more for the tourists. It's commercialized. The Maasai you see here come from other villages to work. They wait for tourists coming through on tours and perform for them to sell the souvenirs. This village is a business. There's nothing wrong with that, but I am taking you to where the true Maasai live. To where those women are walking with the water."

Chitundu drove another couple of minutes and parked the Land Rover near a giant acacia tree.

I pointed to the tree. "Is this the tree you were born under?"

He chuckled. "No, but isn't it magnificent?"

"It's beautiful." A few Maasai tribe members walked by and waved to us. I smiled and waved back. "How do you say hello in Swahili?"

Chitundu unfastened his seat belt and turned to me. "One way is to just say *Jambo*."

"*Jambo*. Easy peasy. I like the word." I leaned forward in the seat and tapped Orlando on the shoulder. "Jambo."

Orlando laughed and twisted around to see me. "Jambo."

The four of us got out of the Land Rover.

"Okay." I rubbed my hands together. "Who can I talk to about the water problem here?"

Chitundu held up an index finger. "I know just the person."

"Great—take me to him."

"Her." Chitundu smiled. "This person is a woman."

"Even better." I smiled right back at him. "Lead the way."

I had naturally assumed it would be a man from my research on Africa. It was a well-documented fact that the men were heads of tribes and villages, the ones who made all the decisions. Most of the women took care of the houses and the children. Women rarely had positions of power or decision-making roles in the local and state government. Finding out this person was a woman motivated me more than ever to help the village, and hopefully that would encourage other women to step up and break new ground.

Chitundu led the three of us between a few small houses made of mud and grass to an open area where a woman was tying two goats to a post. He told us most of the people there in the village spoke Maa and Swahili, and only a few spoke English. Luckily, he could translate for us.

Chitundu waved to the woman. "Jambo!"

The woman walked in our direction, her head up, confident. She was wearing a traditional red and black shuka wrapped around her slender frame. I tried not to stare at the colorful beaded necklace around her neck, but it was gorgeous.

"This is Masaka, the most determined woman in the village," Chitundu said.

How could I not like someone with a title like that?

"Jambo." I smiled and gave her a quick bow like they did in China. What was I thinking? I had no idea why I did that, but I felt much less like an idiot when she bowed back.

"Jambo," Masaka said.

Chitundu talked with her while she led us to the side of a hill. She stopped and pointed down toward the ground, gesturing to the water a few times as she spoke with Chitundu.

"She said the spring water flows from the hill year-round," Chitundu said. "But their problem has to do with keeping it clean from the constant contamination from humans, animals, and rain runoff."

I nodded. "What exactly needs to be done to use this water, so they don't have to walk far to get it? Does it need to be filtered?"

Chitundu spoke to Masaka and turned back. "They need to protect the source before it becomes contaminated. That means building a protective reservoir, which would be connected to a collection area protected from the elements. They can build the reservoir and collection area with bricks. She said they have people here who would be proud to do the work. They just need the proper tools and supplies."

I smiled. "That's where I come in. I'm guessing Amazon doesn't deliver here."

Chitundu chuckled. "I'm afraid not."

"That's what I figured." I pulled my cell phone from my pouch and checked the signal strength. "I have two bars on my phone. That's enough to make things happen. Most likely, I'll need a few hours to buy equipment and supplies and arrange for the deliveries. Where would deliveries come from?"

"Nairobi." Chitundu looked at his watch. "This is going to get us to the Four Seasons late. We would need to call them to let them know."

"Okay . . ." I turned to Adam and Orlando. "Are you two okay with this delay?"

"I'm okay with it."

"Me, too. In fact, just a second." Adam pulled out his phone and tapped on the screen. "My signal strength isn't bad. Maybe I can do some research with you."

I refrained from squeezing Adam's arm. "That would be wonderful."

Luckily, it only took two hours to come up with the perfect solution.

Chitundu had heard of a village who had received a solar-powered brick-making machine through some non-profit organization. Adam researched it and found the exact machine for me to buy. It was a modern machine that could press the bricks together without fire, which meant not having to cut down trees. Best of all, after they built the reservoir, they could use the machine to put up new buildings and houses in the village.

I told Chitundu to make sure the leaders knew that Masaka was in charge of the machine and the water project. He was told there shouldn't be an issue because Masaka had made a reputation for herself as an outgoing woman who wouldn't put up with any nonsense from the village men. It helped that she was the daughter of one of the elder tribal leaders.

Satisfied, we turned to walk back toward the Land Rover to snack on some sandwiches that Chitundu had packed for us, before we got back on the road to the Four Seasons.

Chitundu stopped suddenly. "Oh, just a warning about your cellular phone coverage. Although the service is spotty here, it is the best you'll have for a while. Especially, once we cross the border into Tanzania. Unless you don't mind waiting to get to the lodge to make phone calls, it would be best to make any important calls now."

"I'm okay." I could call Josh from the comfort of my room at the lodge tomorrow. Besides, I wanted to do a video call with him, and my signal strength was not strong enough.

"I'm good too," Orlando said.

"Actually . . ." Adam held up an index finger. "I need a minute for a quick call." He pulled his phone out and wandered about twenty yards away. I was curious who he wanted to call.

A few minutes later, Adam returned, his forehead creased. He gave me a smile, but it didn't have its usual sparkle. Something was definitely on his mind. Maybe he'd gotten some bad news.

"Everything okay?" I asked.

"Huh?" Adam looked a little lost in his thoughts. "Oh . . . yeah. Fine." He nodded. "I'm ready if you are."

I had only taken a few steps toward the Land Rover when an older Maasai man grabbed my hand, patting the top. He gestured to my body with his free hand, saying a few things I couldn't understand.

"What is he saying?" I glanced at the man's stretched-out earlobes and piercings. Although I couldn't be certain, I would guess he was around seventy years old. Definitely the oldest Maasai I had seen today.

"This is Zeki, the village doctor," Chitundu said. "He said you're sick and he wants to heal you."

I pulled my hand away from his, shocked he could know I was sick.

I felt perfectly fine today, fantastic actually, and my bruises were hidden under my shorts. This made little sense. How would he know? It was obviously a lucky guess, or he told everyone they were sick and promised to heal them for a fee.

"I'm not sick," I lied. "Tell Dr. Zeki he's mistaken. I'm perfectly fine and don't need healing."

Adam stepped forward, his eyebrows scrunched together in curiosity. "He looks serious. Why not hear what he has to say?"

Because I don't want you to know I'm dying!

"Zeki said you are the one who is mistaken," Chitundu said.

"He wants to heal me for a fee, right?" I asked. "Is Zeki a witch doctor?"

As a history teacher who studied Africa and its history of the Maasai, I knew there were hundreds of witch doctors making a good living telling patients they could help rid them of their evil spirits and illnesses. They were also known to help people find lost items and reunite them with lost loves or family members, but many of the witch doctors were fakes.

Dr. Singh's words came back to my mind, clear and strong.

I'm all for exploring alternative medicine options, but just be careful because there are a lot of scams out there.

Chitundu gestured to Zeki. "Yes, he is a witch doctor, and—"

"We should get going. Tell him thanks, but no thanks."

Part of me wanted to believe that Zeki was sincere and that he could help me. I didn't want to be rude. I also didn't want him to reveal anything just in case he was the real deal. Maybe if Adam and Orlando weren't there, I would've taken him up on his offer.

Chitundu nodded. "You should know he wants no money from you. Yes, people travel from far places to see him and pay him well, but he wants to help you because of your kindness, because of what you have done for the village with the water situation. It's his way of saying thank you. He will not charge you a single penny and he is a man of his word."

This was a surprise. He didn't want to charge me money? Now that got me thinking. Why would he lie if he wanted nothing in return? Maybe this Maasai man was the real deal. Maybe he could really heal me. But if I go, that would be admitting to everyone that I was sick. The last thing I wanted was pity from anyone.

"Let's hear what he has to say," Adam said. "What's the worst thing that can happen?"

"Yeah," Orlando said. "How many times in your life can

you say you had a consultation with a real witch doctor? I heard some of these guys have true powers."

Was it possible for this Maasai doctor to heal me?

I hesitated, not sure what to do, other than sneak into his hut. How exactly would I do that? And even if I did, we wouldn't be able to communicate.

"Let's do it." Adam grabbed my hand and squeezed it.

I glanced down at my hand in his, trying to figure out if I was more shocked that Adam just volunteered me to be a patient or more shocked that we were holding hands.

It didn't matter because I enjoyed it. And I was at a loss for words.

Forget about the witch doctor and his healing powers.

Adam was the one who had a spell over me.

Luckily, I came to my senses, pulling my hand out of Adam's. "Nope. We need to get going. Let's go, people!" I walked toward the Land Rover, hoping I wouldn't regret not visiting Zeki.

I looked over my shoulder to make sure Adam, Orlando, and Chitundu were following me.

They were.

Zeki had gone into one of the mud huts.

The closer we got to the SUV, the more I wanted to change my mind and go back to see him. The only thing I could do was come up with a lie, which seemed to be becoming a habit.

I stopped and turned around after we arrived back at the Land Rover. "You know what? I forgot to go to the bathroom. Do you know where it is?"

"It's just back where we were, behind Zeki's hut. Would you like me to show you?"

"No, no. I'm a big girl. I'll be right back."

I walked back toward Zeki's mud hut. Now, all I had to do was get inside the hut without being seen. How would I do that? Time was running out. Maybe I was worrying about nothing. It would be easy peasy as long as Chitundu, Adam, and Orlando weren't watching.

When I got to the hut, I pulled out my phone and pretended to be looking at it. Keeping my head down, I slowly turned around and peeked toward the Land Rover to make sure the guys weren't watching.

Smooth. I'm a regular undercover operative.

Luckily, they were all getting into the SUV.

That was my opportunity to quickly enter the hut.

Zeki turned around and nodded when he saw me, like he was expecting me. He gestured for me to take a seat on the rug that was sprawled out on the ground in front of him.

I squatted and waited.

Zeki took a few steps toward me, said a few words, and waved his hands in the air over my head before banging on a drum. He chanted for a few minutes and I couldn't help thinking this was taking longer than expected. If he didn't hurry, Adam, Orlando, or Chitundu would come looking for me.

Zeki finished his chant and twisted behind him to mix something into a cup.

Squatting in front of me, he said something that rhymed, and waved his hand over the cup like he was blessing it. Then he held the drink in my direction.

I took the cup from him, staring inside.

It looked like cherry marmalade.

I smelled it, jerked my head back, and grimaced.

It smelled bad, whatever it was.

Zeki gestured for me to drink it.

Thoughts of the volcano water in Cusco and the hours spent on the toilet flashed in my mind. I was also well-aware that some doctors gave goat blood to their patients to help cure them of illnesses and rid them of evil.

I looked inside the cup again.

No way. I can't do it.

As much as I wanted to, I just couldn't drink what was inside the cup. It was an awkward situation because I didn't want to offend the doctor.

Forcing a smile in his direction, I tried to figure out what to do.

The only thing I could think of was to dump the drink outside somewhere and return the empty cup to Zeki, so he would think I drank it.

Easy peasy.

I gestured to the concoction. "I'm just going to take this to go." I pointed toward the door. "I'll bring the cup back."

Before Zeki could say something—not that I would understand it, anyway—I stood, ran from the hut, and immediately ran into something hard.

Adam's chest.

Everything from the cup was now splattered on his shirt and dripping down to his shorts.

At least I wouldn't have to worry anymore about being killed by my disease.

I was going to die of embarrassment first.

CHAPTER NINETEEN

ADAM

I stared down at my shirt and shorts, wondering what the heck Liz had just spilled all over me. Whatever it was, it smelled horrible. At least she didn't get any on my shoes.

Whoops—I spoke too soon.

I didn't like these shoes, anyway.

Liz stood there, staring at me, her mouth open.

"Is everything okay?" I knew everything was not okay.

Liz wasn't in a hurry to answer my question.

Probably because she wasn't okay.

The phone call I had made earlier was to Liz's brother. Josh had informed me she was going to die if she didn't find a bone marrow donor soon. Now I knew why Liz had put together a bucket list on such short notice. I knew something had been going on with her, the way she had been acting on this trip, the way she had been getting sick and passing out.

I had promised Josh I wouldn't let Liz know he had told

me about her condition. I also promised him I would watch over his sister like a hawk and find her a doctor or take her to a hospital if she needed help.

I glanced back at Zeki's hut. "I thought you weren't going to see the doctor."

She shrugged, finally able to speak. "He gave me something to drink, that's all."

I gestured to my stained clothes. "Looks like you have a drinking problem. You do realize that drinks typically go in your mouth?"

Liz nodded and grimaced. "Sorry."

I pointed to the empty cup dangling from her fingers. "Do you want to get a refill?"

She shook her head. "No, no. I'm good." She set the cup on the ground in front of the hut.

That was unfortunate. Zeki didn't work in the hospital and wasn't even a licensed physician, but I honestly thought it couldn't hurt when he offered to heal her. I normally didn't believe in hocus pocus, but Josh had told me to be on the lookout for any alternative medicine.

Josh had also told me the odds of Liz finding a cure with a bone marrow donor, which was ridiculous. Obviously, Dr. Zeki was not going to be the answer, but I wouldn't give up.

"You should see a real doctor," I said.

She glared at me. "Are you going to start this again?"

Josh had also told me that his sister was the most stubborn person in the world. I had witnessed it for myself, but honestly, it was one of the things I liked about her. Headstrong women don't take crap from headstrong men. That meant there was less chance of them getting into a position they didn't want to be in. That didn't mean I wouldn't say anything when she was stubborn, because that was half the fun.

"Yes—I'm starting that again. How many times have you gotten sick?"

Liz sighed. "I told you. Getting sick in Cusco was from something I drank. Passing out twice was because I had no food or water in my system, plus I was dehydrated from the elevation, which happens to just about everyone who isn't careful when they visit Peru. I'm fine. Quit looking at me that way."

Liz played it off well, acting like she was fine. As if whatever she was going through was related to jet lag or the elevation, or something she had drunk. Maybe part of that was true, but I knew what was really going on and I wanted to help so badly. Finding out that there was a possibility of Liz dying did something to me. It made me want to be closer to her. It made me want to care for her.

I glanced down at my stained clothes again. "Maybe it was a good thing you didn't drink it. It smells nasty."

"Call me crazy, but I prefer the greasy hamburger I had in Cusco."

I chuckled. "Glad to see you can still have a sense of humor about this."

"Laughter is the best medicine."

"I could have just told a couple of silly jokes to avoid all this?"

"Yup. You blew it, mister."

"I'm sorry for pushing you to see Zeki."

Liz shook her head. "Hey—I'm kidding. This isn't your fault."

I wasn't so sure.

Who knew if she had gone to see Zeki on her own or because I had pushed her?

What's done is done.

The only thing to do now was make sure she was okay, because I cared about her. I would take care of her and let her know she's not alone. But how was that going to happen without letting her know I knew about her condition?

Liz gazed into my eyes and my heart skipped a beat. "What are you thinking about?"

I decided to just say it. "You."

"Poor me."

"*Beautiful* you."

She snorted. "Right." She glanced down at my shirt, my shorts, and my shoes. "Look what I did to you. I'm so sorry. I'll buy you some new clothes."

"I have expensive taste, as you can tell." I glanced around the village. "Is there a Calvin Klein Store in Kenya?"

"Not funny."

I put my arm around her shoulder and squeezed. "Seriously. Don't worry about it. I have plenty of other clothes in the Land Rover. Come on. Let's get back. I need to change because this smells rancid. These clothes are going straight into the trash." We walked back toward the Land Rover, my arm still around her.

Liz stopped a few seconds later, glancing at her shoulder. "What's going on with your arm here?"

"I'm just helping you back to the car—that's all."

She thought about it. "And who said your help was needed?"

"I'm just making sure. You tripped when you came out of the hut, plus you have this habit of passing out in the weirdest of places. Oh, I get it. Do you want me to carry you?" I pretended to pick her up.

She playfully pushed away my hand. "Behave."

I laughed. "I'll do my best to be a gentleman. I can't make any promises because we're in the wild and there is a temptation to be wild in the wild."

That almost got a smile out of her. She was fighting it again. At least her shoulders seemed to relax, which was a good thing.

We arrived back at the Land Rover, and both Chitundu and Orlando got out.

"Whoa." Orlando pointed to my clothes. "What happened to you?"

I didn't want Liz to feel bad, so I said, "I fell. It's no big deal. I need to change and then burn these clothes."

"It looks like someone sacrificed a goat on you." Orlando waved his hand in front of his face. "Wow, that stinks."

Chitundu arched an eyebrow. "Did you go see Dr. Zeki?"

The question surprised me. "Me? Why do you ask?"

"Because that looks like the drink he gives his patients."

"I didn't see the doctor," I said, which wasn't a lie. "I told you—I fell."

Okay, that part was a lie.

I walked around to the back of the Land Rover to open it and get to my suitcase.

Liz took a few steps toward me and whispered, "You didn't have to do that."

I whispered back, "You've been through enough. And what can I say? I care about you."

There. I said it.

She squeezed my arm. "Well, thank you."

"You're welcome."

Chitundu ran over and grabbed the handle of my suitcase. "Please. Let me get that for you." He pulled out the suitcase and set it on the ground.

"Thank you." I opened the suitcase and pulled out a fresh shirt, setting it inside the tailgate of the Land Rover. "This will be quick, and we can be on our way." I pulled off my soiled shirt and dropped it on the ground.

Liz was watching.

She glanced at my chest and my midsection, before turning around.

Was she blushing?

I chuckled. "We're all adults here."

"Yes—we are." She kept her back facing me, and I couldn't help smiling.

"I can change over here." I walked around to the other side of the Land Rover and quickly changed clothes.

When I came back to the other side Chitundu said, "I can dispose of that for you."

"Thank you."

He returned a minute later. "We're running behind, as you can imagine. We can snack in the car on the road to make up for lost time."

We all agreed it was a good idea.

Before we could get back in the Land Rover, a beautiful African boy approached and smiled at Liz. "*Asante.*"

Chitundu placed a hand on the boy's shoulder and smiled. "*Asante* means thank you."

The boy grabbed Liz's hand, said something else in Swahili, and tried to pull her back toward the village.

Liz laughed and pulled him to a stop. "Where does he want to take me?"

"His name is Ayo. He has just invited us all to join them for a meal." He chuckled. "I guess we will be arriving late to the lodge, because a meal with the Maasai is not something you can pass up. You're in for a treat."

We followed Ayo to an open area and sat on the ground on colorful blankets that surrounded a pile of green grass about as wide as a hula-hoop.

One of the Maasai went from person to person, pouring water over our hands from a jug, while another tribe member approached with a giant sizzling platter of meat that was cooked on an open fire.

He placed the platter on the pile of grass in the center between us and gestured for everyone to eat. It looked and smelled amazing.

Soon, we were pulling the delicious meat from the platter and eating with our fingers.

Liz didn't ask what type of meat it was.

She didn't seem to care.

It was a simple meal with an extraordinary culture.

No plates. No silverware. No pretension.

After we ate, the Maasai told lively stories in Swahili. We couldn't understand a word, but we enjoyed it just the same. I could feel their enthusiasm. I could admire their beautiful smiles. I could hear the fullness of their heartfelt laughter.

Liz glanced over at me and gave me a knowing smile, stealing another piece of my heart in the process.

How could someone who knew she was possibly going to die be so strong and courageous? And then still have the heart and compassion to help complete strangers.

She amazed me.

A few minutes later, a couple of the male members of the Maasai grabbed Orlando and me from our places on the blankets and invited us to join them in a circle for the jumping dance.

Chitundu had explained to us that it was sort of a mating dance, a way for a young Maasai man to demonstrate his strength and agility to the other members of the tribe, quite possibly attracting a bride as well.

I was over twice the age of most of them. I knew it would be impossible to out-jump them, but that didn't mean I couldn't have some fun.

The women gathered around and cheered us on, singing and clapping. One by one, a member of the tribe stepped into the circle and jumped as high as he could.

When it came my turn, I stepped into the center, jumping higher and higher with each try.

Liz was the bride I was trying to attract.

She smiled and danced along with the female members of the tribe, her eyes never leaving mine.

I was out of breath and decided to stop before I pulled a muscle.

Liz squeezed my shoulder as I returned to stand next to her. "Impressive."

"Thank you."

I didn't end up telling Liz I was falling for her. At least she now knew that I cared for her. That was important because it was the truth. I take care of the people I care about. I didn't want anything to happen to Liz. I was falling in love with her. Crazy, but true.

And now more than ever I wanted her to be mine.

CHAPTER TWENTY

ADAM

The next morning, Orlando and I were in our terrace suite at the Four Seasons Safari Lodge, preparing to leave for the safari. It was early since the alarm had gone off at six, just before the sun came up. At least we'd already had a wonderful buffet breakfast with Liz and Chitundu in Kula's, a restaurant on the property in the main lodge. We'd returned to the room to brush our teeth and grab our backpacks, before heading out for the adventure of a lifetime.

Orlando rinsed his mouth and spit it out in the sink. "How are we ever going to stay in a normal hotel again after this?" He wiped his mouth, set the toothbrush on the bathroom counter, and walked toward our private sundeck and infinity pool. "This place is ridiculous."

I knew he meant *ridiculous* in a good way because we were staying in a five-star resort again. Thanks to Liz.

Orlando spun around in the room, admiring it, just as he

had done when we stayed at Giraffe Manor and at the hotel in Cusco. "I could get used to this. Can you hurry and marry that woman? Then you can spoil me for the rest of my life."

I chuckled. "Is that how it works? I get married and *you* reap the rewards?"

"I'm your best friend and I need to be compensated for putting up with your—"

I held up a finger. "Watch it or I'll cut you out of my will."

He threw his hands up in defense. "Whoa. Don't be so drastic. Sorry." Orlando pointed outside. "Look. A family of elephants in our backyard."

"Backyard?" I laughed, considering our "backyard" was the Serengeti, which was in reality twelve thousand square miles.

I walked over and stood by him, looking outside into the not-too-far distance. Seeing the elephants crossing the savannah and stopping at the watering hole was a surreal moment. It put things into perspective at just how lucky we were to be there, and how amazing this place was. We were in a luxury resort in the middle of the Serengeti.

How could it get any better than that?

"Beautiful." I took a moment to appreciate the elephants, even though we needed to get going. I knew we would see more of them on the safari. "Okay, we'd better get going. Don't want to upset the boss."

Orlando laughed. "I doubt that'll happen. You're back in her good graces. Just be a good boy, would ya? Did you see the way she was looking at you at the breakfast table? The woman is smitten with you."

Believe me, I had noticed.

Something had changed between me and Liz yesterday

after visiting the Maasai village. She seemed more relaxed. It was almost as if she didn't see me as just a pilot for-hire.

We felt closer, more intimate than that.

There was even a moment at breakfast where we brushed hands when we were both reaching for the salt. She blushed.

"That woman is a rock—I'll tell you that much," Orlando said. "Especially considering all that she's going through with her disease."

I had told Orlando everything Josh had told me on the phone about Liz, her illness, and being on the waiting list for a bone marrow donor. I had to. He was my best friend, and he knew something had been on my mind.

I had him promise me he wouldn't say anything to Liz about us knowing about her condition. The only thing I could do was hope he would keep the promise. Especially after he told her about the nosocomephobia, which I now knew I did have.

"Remember." I grabbed my backpack and headed to the door. "She doesn't know we know about her condition and I want to keep it that way. Liz needs to enjoy this trip. Got it?"

"Got it!" Orlando pretended to insert a key into his mouth and lock it.

We made our way to the front of the lodge to meet Liz and the new driver, Jabali. He was an employee of the Four Seasons and our guide for the safari today since Chitundu was already making his way back to Nairobi.

An hour later, we were deep in the heart of one of the world's most celebrated wildlife reserves, where the beautiful animals ran free and the tourists came by the thousands each day to be awed by them.

We popped our heads out of the open-top Jeep and

watched as a cheetah and her three cubs casually strolled over the savannah toward a large tree. A minute later, a group of buffalo appeared, stopping to graze in the bush. Liz took picture after picture after picture, occasionally showing one to me.

"Look!" Liz raised her hand and smacked me in the eye with a finger. "Oh! I'm so sorry! Are you okay?"

"I'm fine, I'm fine." I held my hand over my eye, rubbing it and trying to make the sting go away. She had gotten me good and my eye watered.

"Let me see." Liz moved closer.

I shook my head. "I said it's fine. Don't worry about it."

"Look this way."

"No!" I pointed in front of the Jeep. "Hey look, it's a weird bird!"

"I'm not falling for that again. Quit being stubborn." She practically crawled up my chest, trying to pry my hand from my eye.

I lost the urge to push her away when I got another whiff of her hair. "Mmm. Strawberries."

She stopped tugging on my arm and glared at me. "Are you smelling my hair again?"

"It's hard not to when you're practically jamming it in my face, like your finger."

"I'm worried about you. Let me see your eye or I'll poke the other one by accident, and then I'll feel terrible."

I gave up and pulled my hand away, squinting with one eye. "See? Just like new."

She leaned forward, inspecting my eye. "Yeah . . . it's very red." She gently made a circle around my eye with her two fingers and caressed my cheek with her hand. "I'm sorry." Her gaze dropped to my lips.

I swallowed hard. "I told you, don't worry about it." I couldn't help dropping my gaze to her lips. Her sexy lips.

We were both silent for a moment.

I wished I could read her mind. I wanted to kiss her so badly it hurt.

It was almost as if she was asking me to kiss her, but I couldn't take a chance, in case my instincts were wrong. I couldn't forget even for a moment that she was my client.

Orlando snickered, causing me to crank my neck in his direction.

Unbelievable.

"Have you been recording a video of us?" I stared at his phone pointed at us.

"Yes, siree!" He smiled and wiggled his fingers. "Just documenting the safari for you, so you have memories. Say hi!"

"Say goodbye." I stuck my palm in front of the camera lens on his phone.

"Party pooper." Orlando frowned and lowered his phone.

I turned back to Liz and cleared my throat. "Anyway, what were you trying to show me before you almost decapitated me?"

She laughed and shook her head. "A hot-air balloon. Turn to your right carefully and look up. I'll keep my hands to my sides, to avoid injury."

I turned and looked up. "Oh, yeah. That's cool." I glanced toward our driver. "Hey, Jabali, have you ever gone up in one of those?"

"Yes—I have, sir. They're a real treat to get a wonderful view of the plains and the wildlife."

"You should be able to fly one of those," Liz said. "With all your experience."

I shook my head. "Not at all. That takes a specific skill and you are at the mercy of the wind. I'll stick to flying jets, thank you very much."

"I never asked you why you wanted to be a pilot."

I smiled. "My dad was a pilot. I thought what he did was cool, and I wanted to be like him."

"That's sweet."

"There's nothing else I'd rather do. Plus, how many people can say they have an office at forty-one-thousand feet in the sky?"

Liz smiled. "Not too many."

"Okay, we need to get moving again," Jabali said. "Hold on."

There were bars around the top of the Jeep for us to hold on to, so we could stand up and look out as he drove.

"I got radioed that there's a dazzle of zebras only a few miles from here," Jabali added. "Maybe a hundred. You're in for a treat."

Liz clapped her hands together. "Yay!"

The Jeep hit a bump and Liz was thrust into my chest.

I kept one hand gripped to the bar and used the other to hold Liz against me, so she wouldn't fall. Taking care of her was becoming a regular occurrence, and I had no problem with that.

"Oooh," Orlando said. "I need a video of this."

"Take it and you're a dead man."

Liz laughed, and it was the sweetest sound my ears would want to hear.

She steadied herself and grabbed the bar again.

Later when we got back to the lodge, Orlando and I agreed to meet Liz for a sunset dinner, but that would give us a couple of hours to relax in the room.

At least that's what I thought.

When we arrived, Liz told us she was exhausted and going to her room to take a nap before dinner. She also told us the front desk had something for us.

The man at the front desk said we had twenty minutes before our appointment at the spa.

"There must be some kind of mistake," I said, hoping to clear it up, so it didn't end up on Liz's bill.

He typed something on his computer. "You're traveling with Miss Liz Parker, correct?"

"Yes."

"Well then, there's no mistake at all. You're in for a special treat. She has arranged for the both of you to enjoy ninety-minute massages and facials."

Orlando practically jumped in the air after hearing the news. "Liz is the best!"

She was.

Just when I thought she couldn't surprise me anymore, she did this. Still, I didn't like that she was spending so much money on us, and I wasn't doing anything for her. I know I was working for her, but that didn't matter. I was doing my job and getting paid for it.

"You will *love* this," Orlando said. "I have been trying to get you to have a facial forever, and it will finally happen, thanks to Liz. Your face will feel baby soft."

I grimaced. "I don't want my face to feel baby soft."

"Yes—you do! Come on, we only have twenty minutes to clean up." Orlando grabbed me by the shoulders, twisted me around, and pushed me toward the hallway leading to our room.

Honestly, I could use a good massage and was looking forward to it, however I wasn't sharing Orlando's enthusiasm about the facial. I wasn't so sure I'd enjoy someone getting all handsy with my face and rubbing all kinds of products on it. I didn't mind it when Liz caressed my cheek out on the safari today, but that was different.

That was Liz.

How could a simple touch from a woman do so much to a guy?

And how could Liz be so selfless when her own future and life hung in the balance?

I was sure I'd never met a woman like her in my entire life.

Enough was enough.

I would let her know my feelings this evening at dinner.

I would ask her out on a date.

This was going to be a special night. I was sure of it.

CHAPTER TWENTY-ONE

ADAM

I had come to the realization that this was the most anti-climactic dinner in the history of the universe. I'd had high hopes. I'd imagined a wonderful evening with a special lady. I was wrong, wrong, wrong.

I stared at the empty chair across from me where Liz should have been sitting.

She wasn't coming.

After waiting twenty minutes in the restaurant, I sent her a text to see if she was on her way. When Liz hadn't replied to my text, I ran by her room to check on her, but there was a "Do Not Disturb" sign hanging from the door. I was tempted to knock on the door to make sure she was okay, but I didn't want to seem paranoid and wake her up if she decided to rest instead of eat dinner. I had even texted her brother Josh to let him know I was worried about her but hadn't gotten a reply from him.

Not only was I worried about her, but I also had wanted to profess my feelings to Liz this evening. I had rehearsed what I would say to her more than a few times. I even had the perfect answer for each reason she would most likely give for not wanting to go out with me, just in case the conversation headed in that direction.

The way I saw it, Liz would most likely use one of four reasons to turn down my invitation for a date. I was ready for them all.

Reason #1: This is strictly business.

My answer: I quit.

Reason #2: I'm just not in a good place right now for relationships.

My answer: Tell me where that good place is. I'll fly you there.

Reason #3: I'm not looking to date anyone at the moment.

My answer: I'm not just anyone.

Reason #4: I just got out of a bad relationship.

My answer: Then it's time to get into a good one.

I thought those were darn good. And I had a few other comebacks in case she was in one of her extreme stubborn moods.

Orlando and I were on the dessert portion of our evening, even though I hadn't touched mine. I had barely gotten through my main course since I had lost my appetite at the thought of Liz not feeling well.

I took another sip of my wine and stared off into the distance. The sun had set over an hour ago and they told us we would most likely see the glowing eyes of nocturnal animals staring back at us as we ate. Even if I'd seen an animal, it wouldn't have been the same without Liz.

"You need to turn that frown upside down, my man." Orlando took the last bite of his cheesecake and nodded his approval. "It's not the end of the world. You can ask her out tomorrow or the next day or when you get back home. You'll have plenty of opportunities."

I stared at my chocolate brownie covered in chocolate syrup, wondering if I would touch it. "It's not just that. I'm worried about her. Liz is not only a planner, but she's also efficient, dependable, and organized. It's not like her to miss dinner or lunch or any appointment without saying something. I hope she's okay."

Orlando pushed his empty dessert plate toward the center of the table. "You know her well. You also need to know that even the most rigid people have to alter their plans when unexpected things come up. Look, we already knew she was tired before we went to the spa, right? She probably fell asleep in her room and there's nothing wrong with that. She needed to rest. Fatigue is a symptom of her disease, remember?"

"Of course, I remember."

"Well, there you go! This is completely expected. She's off in snoozeville, dreaming of you. It's not like I didn't want to see her, too! I need to thank her for the best massage and facial of my life."

The massage was amazing.

Considering I wasn't even looking forward to the facial, I kind of liked it too, although I was tired of Orlando asking if he could touch my face to see if it was baby-soft.

My phone vibrated in my pocket and I quickly pulled it out. "Bingo. It's a text from Josh."

Orlando sat up in his chair. "What did he say?"

"Let's see."

. . .

Josh: Hi, Adam. I got your message. Thanks for checking in. I talked with Liz and she's fine.

Me: Good to know. Do you know why she skipped dinner? She needs to eat.

Josh: She was exhausted after the safari and stayed in her suite to order room service. Don't be too alarmed if you see her with low energy. It may get worse as the disease continues its course. By the way, she said she sent you a text to let you know she was skipping dinner in the restaurant, but never heard back from you.

Me: I never got her text. At least, I don't think I did. Hang on. Let me check again.

Josh: No problem.

"Unbelievable." I closed my text conversation with Josh to check my other text messages.

"What?" Orlando asked.

"Josh said Liz sent me a text telling me she wasn't going to make dinner. I'm checking to see if it came through and I missed it somehow."

Sure enough, there it was, a text from Liz.

Liz: Hey, Adam. I know you and Orlando are at the spa. I wanted to let you know I'm going to skip dinner at the restaurant this evening and order in. I hope you don't mind. I'm exhausted. Please forgive me. Hope you guys enjoy your massages and facials. I had the most amazing time with you today. One of the best days of my life. Thank you. I'm looking forward to Paris next. See you in the morning!

"Josh was right." I shook my head in disbelief. "I had a text from Liz letting me know she wouldn't make it."

Orlando poked me in the shoulder with his finger. "See? All that worrying for nothing."

"Yeah." I read her message again. "She said she had one of the best days in her life and said thank you. Why would she thank me? I had nothing to do with the safari. It's not like I planned it or arranged for the animals to show up."

"Tsk, tsk, tsk. That's where you are wrong. You had everything to do with it. That's why she was thanking you! She was telling you that your company made it special today. Come on, don't be so surprised. You two have a thing for each other. It's adorable."

I couldn't help smiling.

Orlando pointed to my face. "There you go. Your frown is officially upside down. Good job. Now, eat your dessert or I'll do it for you."

"You will lose a finger if you touch my brownie." I grabbed my fork to take a bite and quickly set it back down. "Oops. I need to finish my conversation with Josh."

Me: You're right. I checked and there was a message from Liz. I don't know how I missed it. Sorry to worry you.

Josh: No worries at all. Better safe than sorry, right? And thanks for caring about my sister and watching over her. She told me about her fainting episodes in Peru and the bloody drink at the Maasai village. You're a good man.

Me: It helps that she's an amazing woman. She's got a heart of gold.

Josh: Can't argue there. She has always been like that.

Orlando tapped me on the arm with the back of his hand. "Tell him I said hi."

I stared at my best friend, who had obviously lost his mind. "Are you serious?"

"What's the big deal? Just tell him."

"No. If you want to say hi, text him, and tell him yourself."

Orlando crossed his arms. "Remember when we were flying here, and you kept asking about Liz every time I entered the cockpit, if she said anything about you, and blah blah blah blah blah?"

"That was different."

"No—it wasn't." He pointed to my phone. "All I'm asking is for a simple gesture."

I hesitated and blew out a frustrated breath. "I can't believe I'm going to do this."

Orlando smiled, but wisely stayed quiet.

Me: Orlando says hi.

Josh: Tell him I said hi! Is he enjoying the trip?

I shook my head and turned back to Orlando. "He said hi and

wants to know if you're enjoying yourself."

"Tell him yes, and that the safari was fabulous! And make sure you put *fabulous* in capital letters. Or split up the word like fab-u-lous. Oh, and add a few exclamation points at the end. You can never have too many exclamation points."

"I will write it how normal people write it and you can forget about the exclamation points."

"*You* are a party pooper."

"That's what you keep telling me." I lifted the phone again to text Josh.

Me: Orlando said the safari was fabulous.

Josh: I can't wait to see the pictures. Ask him to send me some, if you don't mind.

I sighed.

"What?" Orlando asked.

"Why do I feel like I'm running a gay dating service now?"

"Because you are. What did he say?"

"He said he can't wait to see the pictures and asked if you would send him some."

"Fab-u-lous! Your job is done. I'll take over from here. See? That wasn't so hard, was it?"

"Yes, it was."

"Quit being a big baby. Oh, and don't forget to reply to Liz's text."

"Good call. That's the smartest thing you've said all day." I went to Liz's text message on my phone and replied.

. . .

Me: Sorry, Liz. I'm not sure how I missed your text from earlier. I understand if you needed to rest up in your room. Yes, Orlando and I both enjoyed the massages and facials. Thank you. You didn't have to do that, but I won't complain. Hope you had a great dinner and I'll see you in the morning. We missed you. Good night.

"There. Done." I stuck the phone back in my pocket. "I was tempted to ask her if she wanted me to tuck her in, but I knew that would be pushing it."

"Smart man. You'll have your chance. Have patience. Speaking of which, I have zero patience for your pathetic display of culinary improprieties."

"I'm not even sure what that's supposed to mean."

"Well, let me spell it out for you then: You have run out of time to eat your dessert."

Orlando reached for my brownie and—

"Don't you dare." I pushed his hand away and grabbed my fork, taking a big bite.

My appetite suddenly returned after finding out Liz was okay.

It helped that she told me she had one of the best days of her life.

With me.

Now, I just needed to make it through the Paris portion without having a meltdown.

CHAPTER TWENTY-TWO

Two Days Later . . .

ADAM

Orlando paced back and forth in our fifteen-hundred-square-foot suite at the Five-Star Shangri-La Hotel near the water's edge of the Seine in Paris, France. "This is ridiculous, and I can't take it anymore. If you don't marry Liz, I will. Are you listening?"

I chuckled. "I don't see that happening, I mean, with you being gay and all."

"That's just a tiny technicality, because this woman has spoiled me for good. We've stayed in some nice hotels before, but this one is amazing. I mean look at this place!" He spun around in the room, just like he had done at every hotel room on this trip.

I glanced around our huge suite, which was almost as big

as my home back in San Diego. Our accommodations included two queen beds, a living room, a dining room, a marble-clad bathroom with a heated floor, and our own private one-thousand-square-foot glass terrace that had a sweeping panoramic view of Paris. It was unbelievable.

The Shangri-La was originally a private mansion that belonged to Prince Roland Bonaparte, the great-nephew of Napoleon. It's not a surprise we were staying there since Liz had a thing for world history. All the rooms had been redone to recall the grand French lifestyle of the late 1800s. Impressive was an understatement.

What was Liz thinking? I was a simple man who didn't need much, and the woman was treating us like royalty. It was like she tried to outdo herself with every hotel we stayed in.

Orlando stepped out onto the terrace, leaned against the glass rail, and reached his hand out as far as he could. "I can almost touch the Eiffel Tower! Can you believe this? And we're in the city of love, the city of lights. Hello, Paris! I love you!"

I laughed again. "Keep it down—I don't want to be arrested. And come back in here and get ready. We need to head downstairs to meet Liz."

After flying almost nine hours from Nairobi to Paris, you'd think we'd both be a little tired. That double espresso we'd had at the airport while waiting for customs to clear us did the trick. It also helped that the city was electric, and we were obviously absorbing the Parisian energy into our systems.

Since we arrived in Paris later in the day, the plan was to take a night-time cruise on the river Seine and watch the Bastille Day Fireworks celebration from the Champ de Mars gardens in front of the Eiffel Tower. Tomorrow we would get an early start for a full day of sightseeing.

Surprisingly, I had thought little about Mary since we'd touched down at the airport, which was such a relief. I'm sure that had something to do with Liz, since she was occupying all of my thoughts at the moment. I needed to keep my mind in the present and not dwell in the past.

"I can't believe we were in Peru not long ago, then Africa, and now in France. This has got to be the most insane itinerary ever. Who spends only a few days in Africa?"

"Liz does, although now we know the reason. She wants to see as many things as possible on her bucket list in the shortest amount of time possible, before she heads back to spend time with her brother before, well, you know."

Orlando nodded. "Yeah. Well, I have a feeling everything will turn out just fine for Liz."

"I do, too."

"I'm curious how she got so much money, though. She seems calm and normal. There's not even one hint of snooty in that booty. She's as down to earth as they come. I need to Google her."

"I told you before, *do not* Google her."

"Why not? Aren't you curious?"

"No," I lied.

Orlando crossed his arms. "Puh-lease. I *know* you're curious. Let's Google her."

I gestured to the door. "Let's leave."

"Ooops!" Orlando's eyes were ping-ponging back and forth as he read something on his phone. "I accidentally Googled her. And wow. Wow, wow, wow."

"I don't want to know."

"You don't want to know she won the lottery and is worth over five hundred million dollars? Well, it looks like she took the cash option instead of payments over thirty years, so after taxes she got a paltry two hundred million."

"What?" I snatched the phone from his hand and checked.

Sure enough, Liz had won one of the biggest lottery jackpots in the country. I stared at the news, deep in thought. I couldn't imagine having that much money. It changed nothing.

I handed the phone back to Orlando. "I don't care how much money she has. Health is more important, and money can't buy that. I wish she were healthy."

"Me, too! But if she hadn't won the lottery, you would have never met her, and she would still be sick."

"Good point. Now forget you saw that, and don't you dare mention to Liz that we know about this. Regardless of our feelings for her, we need to remember that she's a client and we need to respect her privacy."

"I won't forget." Orlando slid his phone back in his pocket. "And you worry too much. Her winning the lottery is public knowledge. It's not like we broke into her home and stole secret information from her computer. Anyway, relax. I won't say a thing."

I wasn't convinced. "Just like you wouldn't say a thing about my fear of hospitals?"

He pointed at me. "Ha! You finally admit it!"

"You're annoying me." I pointed to the door. "Can we go, please?"

We went downstairs and made our way through the lobby to the entrance. An older, regal man in a coat and a top hat swung the front door open for us.

"Did you see that?" Orlando pointed behind him as we

stepped out onto the sidewalk. "That's what I'm talking about. Pure class."

I glanced down the sidewalk to the left and to the right. "I don't see Liz."

"That's because I'm right behind you," she said.

Orlando and I both swung around.

She smiled. "Ready?"

"Ready," I said.

"Wait," Orlando said. "I need to say something. It's about the room."

"I know, I know," Liz said. "I tried to get you guys a better room. That was all they had. You don't like it?" She grinned.

Orlando choked. "I can't tell if you're being serious or not. Of course, I like it! I want to live there for the rest of my life! You can bury me there too. That's not my point. It's not necessary. You don't have to get us the most expensive room in the hotel."

She held up her hand like she was being sworn in during a court proceeding. "Full disclosure, it's not like I had a choice. This is one of the biggest weekends of the year in Paris. There are millions of people here just for the Bastille Day celebration and every hotel in the city is sold out. I got our rooms because they were the only two rooms available in the hotel, yes, most likely because they were the most expensive. I had to do it. Frankly, I was surprised they were even available. And the rooms came with the boat tour tickets, which was perfect, because those were sold out, too. By the way, you're worth every penny, and I would do it all over again in a heartbeat. Just enjoy it! Can we go now?"

"Yes." Orlando reached over and squeezed Liz's hand. "You're the best. Thank you."

"Yes," I said. "Thank you for everything."

Liz gave me a smile that nearly knocked me over. "Thank *you.*"

"Me? What did *I* do?"

She placed her hands on her hips. "Well, you're the one who brought me here, silly."

"Oh . . . right."

That was the power Liz had over me. She could make me forget my name and occupation. Honestly, this hadn't felt like work, even the long-haul flights. Except for maybe when she was passing out or not feeling well, it felt like I was on vacation with the most beautiful girl in the world.

Orlando winked at me as we walked toward the corner to cross the street into Trocadéro Gardens. I mouthed *stop* to him. I guess I wasn't intimidating enough because he was still smiling.

A little boy yelled frantically in French and pulled hard toward the street as his mother tried to restrain him.

"What is he saying?" Orlando asked.

"I have no idea," I said. I was fluent in four languages, but French wasn't one.

"Oh no!" Liz pointed to a fluffy white Pomeranian with a pink collar who was running through the traffic. "That must be his dog over there that's loose. It's going to get hit by a car."

"Not if I can help it." I stepped off the curb and—

A black Mercedes Benz honked and came within inches of hitting me. Luckily, I jumped back just in time.

"Whoa." I watched the car disappear around the corner, not even slowing down for me. "That was a close one."

"Be careful, please." Liz squeezed my arm.

"Maybe I'll look both ways this time." I glanced to the left and the right. This time I saw the opening and took it. I ran between a truck and a scooter, then between a taxi and a BMW. I had to hurry because a motorcycle was approaching, weaving in and out of the cars.

"Gotcha!" I snagged the dog with both hands, pulling her against my chest and jumping onto the curb on the other side of the street.

The motorcycle zoomed by a second later.

I walked toward the corner and waited for the light to change.

I scratched the dog between the ears. "Hey there, girl. You need to watch where you're going." The dog licked me on the face, making me laugh. "No need to thank me. Please stay off the street."

When the light turned green, I crossed the street, and handed the dog back to the boy.

The boy hugged the dog and kissed her on the head. "Merci! Merci!"

At least I knew what that meant. "You're welcome."

I made a mental note to study up on some basic French words since I had no idea how to say *you're welcome* in French.

Liz smiled. "That was wonderful what you did."

"You're a hero." Orlando slapped me on the back. "Good job, Superman."

Liz scratched her chin and eyed my shoulders and chest. "I think you'd look good in a cape."

Orlando pointed at my legs. "And spandex."

I shook my finger at him. "Uh—no. No spandex."

Liz laughed. "It's green—we should cross."

We crossed the street and entered Trocadéro Gardens, walking past the ice cream stand and the carousel. We stopped near the Fountain of Warsaw to take selfies in front of the cannons that shot water in the air.

Liz glanced up at the Eiffel Tower and her eyes lit up. "We're going to the top tomorrow."

"I can't wait," I said.

We continued on our way toward the Bateaux-Mouches pier where we boarded an open-air excursion boat that would cruise the river Seine. Liz and I sat together on the upper deck toward the front while Orlando opted for a seat all the way in the back in the last row.

A few minutes later, the boat took off.

"Here we go," I said.

Paris illuminated at night was truly a sight to see, but it didn't compare to the way the floodlights from the bridges we passed under lit up Liz's face.

She was glowing like an angel.

Liz glanced at me and cocked her head to the side. "What?"

"Nothing. I'm just admiring all the beautiful things I see in Paris. Isn't that what we're supposed to be doing?"

She shook her head. "What am I going to do with you?"

I grinned. "I know you're a planner. Would you like a list of all the things in alphabetical order?"

She laughed. "You're impossible."

"Wrong. I'm easy peasy. Hey, maybe I should get a T-shirt with that saying printed on the front. Nah, nobody would dare wear such a thing."

She crossed her arms. "You have a comeback for everything."

"Not true. Sometimes you render me speechless."

"Yeah? When is that?"

"When you smile."

She stared at me for a beat and blushed before turning away.

So beautiful.

A minute later, Liz sat up straight and pointed. "There's the Louvre. It's the world's largest art museum *and* also the world's most visited museum."

"We are now passing the Louvre museum," said the tour guide on the microphone. "It's the world's largest art museum *and* also the world's most visited museum."

I pointed to the tour guide. "You could easily take that guy's job."

"You're making fun of me now."

"Not at all. I admire you for how you embrace the past and are so passionate about history."

"Well, thank you. And I admire you for how you embrace the present."

"Thanks, although I wasn't always this way."

She studied me for a moment. "What changed?"

"I'll probably need to be drunk for you to get that out of me." I laughed, even though I wasn't kidding.

She nodded. "Okay—I'll remember that. Look on the other side, Musée d'Orsay. The museum building used to be a railway station."

"Now, we are passing Musée d'Orsay," the guide said on the microphone. "The museum building used to be a railway station."

Liz cranked her head in my direction and pointed a finger at me. "Don't say it."

"Watch it with that thing." I laughed and grabbed her finger. "This is a lethal weapon."

She shook her head. "Superman can't handle it?"

"Not when he's dealing with Wonder Woman."

"Good to know I can put you in your place if I need to."

We were quiet for a few moments, admiring the city as the boat continued to cruise the Seine.

"Uh, Adam?"

"Yeah?"

"Can I have my finger back?"

"Oh . . ." I glanced down at my hand wrapped around her finger. "Right. I guess you'll be needing that." I let go and forced a smile in her direction.

The tour guide talked about Notre Dame and the fire that happened there, as we passed it.

Liz frowned. "So much history . . . It would have been great to see it before the fire."

I nodded. "Yeah . . ."

"Life is unpredictable."

I had the feeling that she wasn't talking about Notre Dame anymore.

After the tour on the water, we walked to the gardens in front of the Eiffel Tower and squeezed our way among the throngs of people to get closer to the stage and the live classical music. We lost Orlando, but he was a big boy and could find his way back to the hotel.

Then came the magical display of fireworks above us, the dazzling bursts of light shooting across the Parisian night sky. I would glance over and get a peek of Liz's face as she marveled at the show. And every now and then she would catch me watching her and would just smile back. I pretended to not see the tears rolling down her cheeks, probably from the emotion of being there. I only hoped this wouldn't be the last time she would visit Paris.

Back at the hotel, we were quiet as we entered the elevator.

We got out on the top floor and both paused, staring at each other.

Liz hesitated and gestured with her thumb behind her. "I'm *this* way."

I gestured with my thumb in the opposite direction. "I'm *this* way."

"It was another perfect day," Liz said. "Just perfect." She fidgeted with one of her fingernails and smiled. "Well, good night."

"Good night." I turned and walked toward my room at the end of the hallway. When I got there, I pulled out the card key, pausing, and looking back since I hadn't heard her door open or close.

Liz was standing in front of her door, card key in hand, looking back in my direction.

I'm not sure if it was my imagination, but it sure seemed like she was trying to tell me she wanted me to rush over there and kiss her goodnight. Or maybe she didn't want to sleep alone.

The feelings are mutual.

She gave me a little wave and inserted the card key, entering her room. The door automatically closed behind her.

I continued to stare back toward her door, sure of one thing.

I wouldn't be sleeping much tonight.

CHAPTER TWENTY-THREE

LIZ

After an early breakfast with Adam and Orlando in the hotel restaurant, we headed out to tackle our first full day in Paris. We had a lot to see in a short amount of time. I had it all planned out perfectly. After visiting Luxembourg Gardens, we'd head back to the Eiffel Tower to go to the top before lunch. Everything was right on schedule and according to plan.

Just a block away from the Eiffel Tower, I saw a poster of a castle in the window of a small travel agency. "Look at this beautiful castle. Is that in Germany?"

Orlando and Adam moved closer to look.

"I have no idea," Adam said.

Orlando leaned closer. "Neither do I. Do you want to ask?"

I put my hands against the window to look inside. There were two women at their desks on their computers, but nobody else.

I shrugged. "Why not? They don't seem to be too busy at the moment. You don't mind?"

"Not at all." Adam stepped toward the door and pushed it open for me. "After you."

"Thank you." I stepped inside and smiled at the first woman who lifted her head from her computer.

"Americans?" She smiled, stood, and moved toward us.

Adam chuckled. "That obvious, huh?"

She nodded. "After a while you notice things about people, mannerisms, the clothes they wear. If that's not enough I could hear you talking outside through the open window." She laughed. "How can I help you?"

I gestured to the poster. "Where is that castle? Is that Germany?"

She shook her head. "That's right here in France. We have many beautiful castles in a region just south of the city. In English it's called the Loire Valley."

"Oh, I've heard of it," I said.

"It's a well-known region of our country and not far from here. Let me show you." She opened a file cabinet and flipped through a few things before pulling a thick binder out. "Here we go." She gestured toward the round table with the four chairs. "Please have a seat and I'll show you."

"Thank you." I sat next to her, while Adam and Orlando sat across from us.

She opened a binder and pointed to a few laminated images. "All these castles are in that region. Le Château de Chambord is one of my favorites." She pointed to the next picture. "Also, this one, Le Château de Chenonceau."

I leaned in to get a better look and pointed to a picture. "That's the one on the poster, right?"

"Yes."

I turned the binder around on the table for the guys to see. "Look at this. Isn't it amazing?"

"Incredible," Adam said.

"I love it," Orlando said. "It looks familiar. Have they ever filmed a movie there?"

"They have shot many movies in that region and specifically in that castle," the woman said. "Would you like to plan a day-trip there? I can definitely help you."

I shook my head. "I'm more interested in staying the night in a castle. Actually, a few nights would be even better. We have something already booked in Germany, but staying in a castle here would give us more time in France. Is it possible to spend the night in one of these castles?"

She studied me for a moment, her gaze dropping to my clothes and purse, most likely checking for quality. Is that how she would determine if I had enough money to make it happen? By the brand names I was wearing?

Or maybe my ego was getting the best of me. When I had won the lottery that was one of my biggest fears. That people would judge me and stick me in a certain category because I had money. Well, I wasn't like other people. My jean shorts from Target only set me back twenty-five dollars, but I felt like a million bucks in them. I've always been more concerned about comfort than about the name on the label.

"Are you a head of state or foreign dignitary?" she finally asked.

I snorted. "No. I'm just a simple history teacher from San

Diego, California. Well, I *was* a history teacher. I quit recently."

Oops. Didn't mean to say that.

Adam and Orlando were both staring at me, expecting me to elaborate on quitting my job, I'm guessing, but that wasn't going to happen.

"You're saying it's not possible to stay a night in these castles?" I asked, trying to get back on the topic.

The woman shook her head. "I'm afraid not. Not those castles. I have a wonderful option for you in another castle. Let me find it." She pulled the binder closer and turned it around. She flipped the pages toward the back, stopping on another castle that was gorgeous and reminded me a little of the English estate in the show *Downton Abbey.* "You can stay here, if you would like, assuming they have availability."

I moved closer to inspect the picture of the castle. "It's lovely. Do you know much about the place?"

She nodded. "It is a castle steeped in romance, the Neo-Gothic Jewel of Anjou." She glanced at some information she had in the binder. "It says here that the staff will serve you a feast at the royal table in your royal attire. It's the fairytale coming to life."

That got my attention. "You're serious? I can dress up?"

"Just like the Queen." She gestured to Adam and Orlando. "They will dress like royalty as well."

"I've always wanted to be a prince," Orlando said. "Adam —you're the king."

"I thought I was Superman," Adam said. "Make up your mind."

"You can be both," I said to Adam, although I'm not sure why.

He glanced at me and winked. "As you wish, your majesty."

I giggled like a giddy schoolgirl.

Something about this place was telling me, *Yes. Do it.*

This sounded like a fairytale and what woman didn't want that?

"Here's a little more information," the woman said. "If it sounds good to you, I can check availability and get a price for you as well."

I read the description underneath. "Listen to this; it says they designed the chateau to commemorate the passing of time. Its four towers represent the seasons, twelve turrets represent the lunar months, twenty-six spiral staircases represent the fortnights per year, fifty-two fireplaces represent the weeks of the year, and three hundred and sixty-five windows represent each passing day." I looked up and smiled at Adam and Orlando. "I want to stay here."

"What about the castle in Germany that you already have planned, Miss Planner?" Adam asked. "I mean, your highness."

I waved off his question because it wasn't an issue. "We'll just cancel it. It was nice, but it was actually a castle converted into a hotel." I tapped on the picture in the binder with my finger. " *This* is a true castle. Who's with me?"

Orlando's hand shot up. "I am!"

Adam chuckled. "I'm game."

"Great!" I turned to the woman. "We need to book this. How far is it from here and how can we get there? Can you check the availability? What do I need to do?" I needed to breathe, or I would pass out again. I also needed to find my manners. "I'm sorry, I'm being rude. What's your name?"

She laughed. "Estelle."

"Nice to meet you. I'm Liz, and this is Adam and Orlando." I was going to burst with enthusiasm.

"A pleasure to meet you all," Estelle said. "To answer your question—this castle is two hours from Paris by train. I'll check the availability now."

"Thanks so much."

I crossed my fingers and glanced across the table to Adam and Orlando.

They both crossed their fingers, waiting with me in anticipation of the answer.

I was like a kid waiting to find out if she was going to Disneyland.

Estelle slid back into the chair behind her desk, immediately going to work on her computer. She nodded and talked to herself in French as she typed.

I shrugged, wishing I could understand French.

Estelle sighed. "This doesn't look good. The castle is sold out for the summer." She kept her eyes on the computer screen.

"Oh." I felt a little dejected. "Well, that's too bad. I guess I shouldn't have gotten my hopes up until I knew there was something available."

"Unless . . ."

I scooted to the edge on my seat. "Unless what?"

She held up her index finger. "One moment, the system just updated, and it looks like . . ." She leaned in closer to her monitor. "This is interesting."

"What? What is it?" This couldn't be good for my heart.

"Well, it looks like something just became available. It's short notice, but they have availability for tomorrow. It says in the notes that the customers who have it booked for the week will be delayed one day. It looks like it is available for just one night only."

I jumped to my feet. "We'll take it! Book it!"

Estelle seemed a little shocked by my enthusiasm. "Okay —I can tell you the price for the evening."

"It doesn't matter! Book it before it disappears. Please." I opened my purse, pulled out my credit card, and dropped it on her desk. "Here you go. What else do you need? My passport?" I pulled out my passport and dropped it on her desk next to my credit card. "Here you go. Anything else? Another form of ID? A blood sample?"

Estella laughed. "Your passport and credit card are sufficient."

Orlando clapped his hands. "Yay! This is destiny, Liz. You and Adam will be king and queen."

I smiled. "And you will be a prince!"

Twenty minutes later, the castle was booked for the next day, along with the tickets for the train to get there. We would leave in the morning, bright and early.

We thanked Estelle, headed back outside, and walked toward the Eiffel Tower.

Even though I wouldn't bring attention to it, my spontaneity amazed me. I had done it on my own. What a feeling! I was a different person. I'm not sure exactly how to describe it. I felt relaxed and free. I knew the reason for my change, and he was now standing next to me in line at the bottom of the Eiffel Tower.

King Adam.

I couldn't wait to call him that when we were inside the castle.

"What's on your mind there, Miss Smiley Face?" Adam asked.

"Nothing at all, Mr. Inquisitive. I'll tell you tomorrow." There would be plenty of time to tell him how grateful I was for his friendship. Right now, I was ready to double down on the spontaneity since they told us we would have to be in line for two to three hours. I was hungry. "Would you mind grabbing something for us to eat since we'll be in line a while?"

"Don't mind at all," Adam said. "What are you in the mood for?"

I shrugged. "Surprise me."

Adam gave me a knowing smile and winked. "You got it."

"Oh . . ." I grabbed him by the arm before he took off. "No frog legs or escargot."

He chuckled. "Not a problem."

Twenty minutes later, Adam found me and Orlando farther up in the line and handed us both something warm in a white wrapper. "Here you go."

"Thank you." I took it from him. "What is it?"

"Open it."

I unfolded the wrapper. "A crepe?"

He nodded. "Ham and cheese crepes."

"Yum!" Orlando ripped open his wrapper and took a huge bite.

"Where did you find them?" I took a bite. "Mmmmm."

Adam gestured behind us. "Over by the carousel. And I've got chocolate for dessert."

A man after my heart.

We ate the most delicious, warm crepes ever and nibbled

on the chocolate as we inched closer and closer to the elevator that would take us to heaven.

Finally, we made it to the summit of the Eiffel Tower and stood there admiring one of the most popular cities in the world. We could see every major landmark and every place we would visit over the next few days. I swore I could almost see the roundness of the earth in the horizon, although I was sure it was my imagination.

Orlando browsed through the handout of facts about the Eiffel Tower and read a part to us. "Witness to thousands of promises of undying love, the Eiffel Tower stirs emotions."

Right on cue, a man dropped to his knees in front of us to propose.

"I hope he knows her," Orlando whispered.

The woman nodded emphatically. "Yes!"

The man put the ring on her finger and jumped back up to kiss her passionately.

Everyone clapped and cheered, while some tourists took photos and videos.

Orlando pointed. "Look. Another proposal over there."

This time it was a couple that had to be closer to our ages.

The woman said, "Of course, I'll marry you! Now get up from there, that's not good for your knees."

"My knees are fine," the man replied.

"That's not what the doctor says."

"Forget about him and kiss me!"

Adam smirked. "They already sound like they're married."

I laughed. "Love is in the air."

"It is," Orlando agreed. "We are in the city of love, you know." He winked.

"That we are."

I shouldn't have been surprised at how many couples were kissing at the top.

Even the couple to our right started to kiss.

I did my best not to look because they were literally inches from my face, and I couldn't move away since it was packed with people.

The couple to our left began to kiss, too.

Adam's eyes were darting back and forth between the dueling kissers. I couldn't help laughing.

"What?" Adam whispered.

"Nothing." There was no way I would tell him that my bucket list included being kissed at the top of the Eiffel Tower.

Maybe he was reading my mind because he glanced down at my lips.

Kiss me, Adam. Kiss me.

Someone bumped into my back, pushing me right into Adam's chest.

"Sorry." I nervously brushed his chest, as if I had gotten his shirt dirty from bumping into him.

Adam smiled. "Not a problem. It's getting a little crowded up here."

I glanced at his lips and looked away after he caught me.

Another person bumped into my back, pushing me into Adam again.

This time he grabbed me by the waist to steady me, and we locked gazes.

Our bodies were completely touching from my knees to my breasts.

"She said yes, she said yes!" a man yelled.

Another proposal.

Adam and I didn't look this time.

We were in our own little world.

I could feel his heartbeat banging against me.

He swallowed. "Liz . . ."

"Yes . . ."

He glanced down at my lips again.

Please don't ask me if you can kiss me.

That had to be the least romantic thing in the world a man could do, and we were in the most romantic city in the world. If he was going to kiss me, he just needed to do it.

Kiss me now. I'm begging you, put me out of my misery.

To my surprise and delight, Adam inched closer and closer to my lips.

This was going to happen.

Then he kissed me.

First slowly, then with more passion once our lips parted and our tongues touched for the first time. Pleasure ricocheted through my body in every direction, and I pulled him tighter against me. I couldn't get him close enough.

My feelings for Adam were strong and I'd been denying them all along. I couldn't take it anymore. I was bursting at the seams for him, but it was almost too much.

I had to breathe.

I pulled away slightly, dazed and confused, blinking a few times.

We were both out of breath, our foreheads touching.

I was still staring up at his lips. "What just happened there?"

"I'm not sure." Adam caressed the side of my face. "I guess we got caught up in the moment."

"You were okay with it?"

"I wouldn't change a thing. It was perfect."

Orlando had his back to us, but turned around, his gaze darting back and forth between us. "What's going on here?"

"Nothing," Adam and I said at the same time.

We both laughed.

Orlando arched an eyebrow. "*Something* happened here. I turn my back for one minute . . . Wait a minute, did you finally kiss?"

Finally? He was expecting this to happen?

Oddly enough, both Adam and I stayed quiet.

Like we had a secret, and we wouldn't tell anyone, not even Orlando.

"Hallelujah!" he said, obviously not needing an answer from either of us to confirm his suspicions. "It's about time."

We both remained quiet.

"Fine, be that way, but I wasn't born yesterday, you know. Anyway, I'm going to head over to the Marais District, if you don't mind."

"Never heard of it." Adam's hands were still gripping my waist, and it seemed he had no intentions of letting go, which was fine by me.

"It's the Jewish Quarter but there's also a gay community over there. Hot dogs and falafels, cafes and bookstores, you get the idea."

"I thought you were going to go with us to Montmartre and the Sacré-Coeur," I said.

"I'll catch up with you there later. I want to check out the Marais District for a couple of hours and see what it's all about. I'll text you to see where you are later."

"Sounds good."

And just like that, Orlando was gone.

Adam and I walked around the top of the Eiffel Tower a

little more before heading back down the elevator, neither of us saying much. It was like we were in this awkward space, neither of us knowing what to say or do. Not a surprise. We were caught up in the passion and love of the city, and it almost consumed us and swallowed us whole.

Back down at street level, we walked side by side toward the Sacré-Coeur. It was a gorgeous day, and we weren't in a hurry like the woman who just ran past us, looking frantic.

"Mary!" a man yelled, running toward us, most likely chasing after the woman. He weaved in and out of a few people, but ran straight into Adam's shoulder, knocking him off balance. The man continued past us, not even saying sorry to Adam. "Mary! Wait! Mary! I'm sorry!"

Adam turned around, startled, watching the man run after the woman. He continued to stare even after the man had disappeared around the corner.

I rubbed Adam on the shoulder. "Are you okay? He hit you pretty hard."

Adam turned toward me. "Huh?"

"How's your shoulder?"

He rotated his shoulder in a circular motion. "Yeah, yeah, I'm fine." He hesitated. "Shall we continue?" He gestured ahead of us toward the Sacré-Coeur.

"Sounds good," I said.

He was acting a little odd, but maybe the man injured Adam and he was too stubborn or embarrassed to say anything.

A few seconds later, Adam stopped and stared across the street at a restaurant, shaking his head.

"What?"

He didn't answer.

I stepped closer. "Adam? Are you okay?"

His eyes were dull. His energy was gone. It was like Adam was hit by a truck, instead of a man.

"Adam? Talk to me."

He pointed to the restaurant.

I was more confused than ever. "What? The restaurant? What about it? Are you hungry?"

"The name," he said, his voice cracking as he stared at his feet.

I read the sign. "Le Mary Celeste." I still didn't get it.

He picked at one of his fingernails. "That was my wife's name. Mary Celeste."

Now, it made sense.

And the man who ran by us was yelling Adam's wife's name, too.

Got it.

Adam was getting emotional and memories of his wife were getting the best of him.

Did he still love Mary? Of course he did. You don't stop loving people just because they die.

Death.

I had forgotten about that for a while.

Adam lifted his head but avoided eye contact. "You know what? I'm going to head back to the hotel, if you don't mind."

"Okay—I'll go back with you."

"No."

His reply was so direct it shocked me.

And it made me sad. He didn't want my company.

How could he dismiss me this way after that kiss?

He cleared his throat. "Go see the Sacré-Coeur and all the

things you wanted to see over there. You've been looking forward to it and I don't want to ruin your plans."

"Adam—"

"Seriously," he added. "I'll be fine. This is your bucket list and you need to go. I won't take no for an answer." He shooed me away with his hand. "Go. Please."

Then he turned and walked back toward the hotel.

CHAPTER TWENTY-FOUR

LIZ

I walked up the street toward Montmartre, deep in thought, glancing at a few monuments on the way. I couldn't summon the enthusiasm to stop or take a picture.

This vacation day had taken a turn for the worse.

It was like someone had taken the wind out of my sails and grabbed a pair of scissors to cut the sails into a thousand pieces. I needed to get what happened with Adam off my mind, so I could enjoy the sights. How could I do that when I cared about him so much? And now that I really thought about it, it went far beyond just caring for the man.

I was falling for him. I was sure of it.

This was not good.

I didn't want to fall in love with a man. Worse than that, I didn't want to fall in love with a man who couldn't return the feelings because he was still in love with his late wife.

It would be wrong.

Maybe my brother Josh could give me some advice, because right now I didn't know what to do or what to think, and I had to talk to someone. I sent him a text.

Liz: I need your help. Call me when you get a chance. No, I'm not dying.

I waited for a minute to hear from him. He didn't call me back. Maybe he was in the middle of something at work. I put my phone away, figuring that I couldn't do much else at the moment. Hopefully, I would hear from him soon.

I arrived at Montmartre and walked up the cobblestone street, past the ivy-covered building facades, and an old water tower. There were flowers everywhere, but I wasn't motivated to sniff them like I usually did.

I looked around at the many cafes and shops and sighed. The neighborhood on the hill was mostly known for the Roman Catholic church, the Sacré-Coeur. It was also a former artists' village once inhabited by Picasso and Dalí. I should have been excited to be there. My energy was low, feeling empty without Adam.

A minute later, I wandered into a pastry shop and glanced at the delectables behind the glass display. I ate when I was worried or sad, and right now I was both.

I pointed to the chocolate croissant and paid for it, taking my first bite before stepping back out onto the sidewalk. Maybe another view of the city would help me clear my head. I finished eating the croissant and entered the Sacré-Coeur.

Once inside, I immediately climbed the three hundred

stairs inside the Roman Catholic church to the dome to try to burn off some of the calories.

Lots of sugar today, but that won't kill me.

Sadness, worry, and guilt didn't make the best combination.

I tried to appreciate the view at the top of the dome, the streets, and the landmarks. All I could focus on was the Eiffel Tower I saw in the distance.

What a kiss.

Okay, it was worse than I thought.

Maybe breathing exercises would clear my mind.

I took a deep breath in and let it out. "Out with the bad, in with the good." I repeated the process again. "Out with the bad, in with the good." I thought about how I felt now. "Nope. Didn't help at all."

They told me to allow an hour or two to see the church and take pictures, but I was out of there in twenty minutes. I wandered down the street and stopped near a crowd gathering around a wall. People were waiting in line to take pictures in front of the wall.

"It's the *I Love You* wall," someone said. "Let's kiss in front of it and get someone to take a picture of us!"

I moved closer to read the sign. The wall had six hundred and twelve lava tiles and featured the words "I Love You" in three hundred and eleven languages. The wall was created by two artists as a rendezvous location for lovers and a lasting monument to eternal adoration.

I adore Adam.

A woman said something to me in French and held her camera in my direction.

She wanted a picture in front of the wall with her man.

"Merci," she said.

She grabbed him by the hand and pulled him toward the wall. They turned around to face me, looking so happy and in love.

He kissed her and I took the picture.

Then he dipped her and kissed her again.

I took another picture.

She laughed, trying to dip him, almost falling over.

They kissed again.

I snapped a few more pictures.

Then he dipped her again and kissed her.

I snapped a few more.

This last kiss seemed to go on forever, taunting me, torturing me, telling me I just wasn't lucky enough to have a man kissing me like that in front of the wall.

They finally ended their kissing marathon, and I handed the camera back to the woman.

"Merci," she said.

Okay, it was time for another escape before I started picturing Adam kissing me in the front of the wall.

I ended up in Place du Tertre, where I was surrounded by a thousand different colors and street artists everywhere. Most of them were caricaturists and watercolor painters. One particular artist had a handful of people standing behind him, watching as he painted.

I moved closer to see what was piquing everyone's interest and looked over his shoulder.

My head flinched back slightly after his painting caught me off guard. I thought for sure the artist would be painting a caricature, like most of the other artists. Or maybe the view of

Paris or the cafes or shops in Montmartre with the tourists frequenting them.

Not even close.

It was one of the most interesting, thought-provoking paintings I had ever seen.

Biting my lip, I continued to study it. I couldn't come up with anything except that it must have something to do with time.

I slid between two people and came up beside the artist. "Excuse me for interrupting. Do you speak English?"

The artist set his paintbrush down and turned, smiling. "I hope so since I was born in Chicago."

"Oh, wow!" I laughed. "Are you on vacation?"

He shook his head. "Nope. I live here."

"How did you end up in Montmartre of all places?"

He shrugged. "Not that difficult, actually. I was busting my butt in the IT industry, unfulfilled and overworked. It wasn't what I wanted to be doing. I wanted to paint. Some of the most famous painters in the world have painted here in Montmartre, so I took a vacation to visit. I ended up staying and going to art school here. It was a moment of spontaneity that changed my life."

"Spontaneity." I shook my head in amazement.

He nodded. "The heart of pleasure is spontaneity."

Just wonderful.

The artist was channeling Adam.

"I had a question about what you're painting, if you don't mind."

"I don't mind at all." He stood up and stretched. "I was ready for a break. What would you like to know?"

I pointed to the piece. "What are you trying to say here?"

He laughed. "That is the million-dollar question. Many times, the interpretation is in the beholder's eye. Sometimes you need to tap into your own feelings to come up with the answer. Don't get caught in the trap of trying to figure out what *I* meant. Try to focus instead on what it says to you. What do you see?"

I narrowed my eyes and studied the painting, trying to figure out what the painting was saying to me. There was a man and woman dancing in an elegant ballroom. She was wearing a beautiful red dress, and he was wearing a tuxedo. They looked happy. In love. There was a giant chandelier above their heads with thousands of crystal hearts dangling from it. Hundreds of people were standing, forming a circle around them as they danced on the dance floor.

Here was the curious part . . . the people watching the couple dance had clocks as heads.

All of them.

"Okay." I analyzed it a little more. "Well, it has something to do with time, there's no doubt about that."

"Time is watching you," a woman said. "Or it's *time* to dance. You're running out of time!"

"You can't escape time," a man said. "Time is on your side. Time to give it up because my guesses are ridiculous."

Everyone laughed.

I scratched the side of my face. "The clocks are watching the couple dance. It's the same time on all the clocks."

The artist smiled. "Very good."

"I think this is more about the couple, though."

"What are they feeling?"

I closed my eyes and pictured myself dancing with Adam.

A few seconds later, I opened them and looked at the painting again.

The artist pointed to my face. "You look like you've got it."

I smiled. "Time stands still when I'm with you."

"Bingo!" the artist said, high-fiving me.

The people standing around us clapped and cheered for me.

I didn't care about that.

I cared about Adam.

I had barely thought about having my disease, barely thought about the urgent need for a bone marrow donor, barely thought about the possibility of dying.

It was because of Adam.

Time truly stood still when I was with him.

He made me feel alive.

Oh no. I've made a horrible mistake.

I had been having a Paris pity party walking around Montmartre, like it was all about me, when Adam was the one who was truly hurting and needed someone.

How many times had he taken care of me on this trip so far?

How many times did he make me feel better without judging me?

How many times had he been there for me?

Too many times to count.

He never hesitated. Ever.

And what had I done when he needed me most?

I abandoned him.

The one time he needed someone I wasn't there for him. Yes, I offered to go back to the hotel with him, and he said no.

I should have insisted, like he would have if it had been me in his shoes.

I felt like crap and had to redeem myself. There was only one thing I could do now. I needed to get back to the hotel. Well, there were two things. First, I needed to buy that painting for Adam. I saw the two of us when I looked at it. Even if I would never see him again, I would love for him to have it.

"I'm assuming you're going to sell this piece?" I asked.

"Well, it will be for sale, yes. It's not done yet, obviously."

"I'll wait until you're done."

He stared at me like I was crazy.

"I don't mean I'll wait right here next to you right now while you finish painting it. I want to buy it. Will you ship it to the US?"

"Of course."

"Great." I gave him my contact and credit card info along with Adam's address, so he could ship it to his office as a surprise. Then I left as fast as I could to head back to the hotel.

I needed to see Adam.

I'd made a big mistake leaving him and coming here by myself. Sure, maybe it was meant to be. Maybe I had to meet that artist, so he could open my eyes and sell me the painting.

Time to get back.

I walked to the hotel and made my way through the lobby toward the elevator, glancing inside the bar as I passed it.

I stopped and took a few steps back to look inside the bar again.

Adam was there.

He was sitting in a booth with his elbows on the table and a drink in his hand. I wondered if he had been there drinking the entire time since I had abandoned him on the street.

I took a deep breath and walked toward his table, ready to apologize.

Adam's head was hanging down, like he was looking for something on the floor.

Or maybe he was drunk and just didn't have the energy to keep his head upright.

I stopped in front of his table and waited for him to look up.

Adam's eyes fluttered when he saw my feet, but he didn't lift his head.

He continued to stare at my feet, finally letting his eyes wander up slowly to my shins, to my knees, and finally to my thighs where he stopped and held his gaze there.

"How are your bruises?" he asked.

I held back a smile, flattered he recognized my legs.

"You have the sexiest legs, you know that?" he added, finally looking up at me.

There he went saying sweet, romantic things again, even while he was heartbroken by his wife's death.

I smiled and shook my head.

"There's that smile I love." He took another sip of his drink, finished it, and set the glass down. "You never told me if the bruises were gone."

"They're gone." I slid into the booth across from him. "How are you?"

Adam gestured to my legs under the table. "I don't think we're finished talking about your legs. They're masterpieces—I'm telling you. They belong in the Louvre next to Mona Lisa. Did you know she doesn't have eyebrows?"

"Adam . . ."

"Awww, don't get mad because I'm talking about your legs. I'm just doing that, so I don't have to talk about what happened earlier."

I glanced at his glass. "How many drinks have you had?"

"Not enough." He raised his hand, calling the waiter over. "Can I have another, please?"

"Of course." The waiter turned to me. "Can I get you anything?"

"A strawberry daiquiri?"

The waiter nodded. "Of course."

"Thank you." I turned back to Adam. "We need to talk."

"I know, I know. I'm sorry for ruining your vacation."

"You didn't ruin my vacation."

"Yes, I did."

"The only thing you've done was make it special. And I'm sorry I left you when you needed me. I shouldn't have gone to Montmartre without you." I reached across the table and placed my hand on top of his. "How are you doing? Do you want to talk about Mary?"

Adam pulled his hand away from mine and sat up, glancing over at the bartender shaking some concoction in his shaker.

"It might help to talk, you know. Do you still love her?"

I was sure he still loved her. Otherwise, Adam wouldn't have had that reaction when he'd heard that man calling out for Mary. Or when he saw her name on the front of the restaurant.

He shook his head. "I will always love her. I'm not *in love* with her anymore. Hell, we were married for twenty-three years, you know? She'll always have a special place in my heart. That's not it."

"Then what is it?"

"Guilt."

"Guilt?"

"One hundred percent guilt."

"Why would you feel guilty?" It suddenly dawned on me. "Oh, I get it. You feel guilty because you kissed me? That's it."

He squeezed his eyes shut. "No, no, no. That kiss was sublime and almost as sexy as your legs. Why would I have a problem with that? Geez, I wanted to kiss you until the cows came home, even if there aren't any cows in Paris. Are there cows in Paris?"

"I don't know."

"Anyway, take it as a compliment, cows or no cows."

This man was adorable. I figured he must be drunk.

"So, what were you feeling guilty about?"

He hesitated. "Okay, look, here it is. I'm just going to tell it like it is. Today is the two-year anniversary of Mary's death. There. I said it. I was doing my best to keep my mind off it. I'll tell you that is not an easy thing to do."

"I understand completely. She was a big part of your life. That's not something you can easily erase."

The waiter brought our drinks. "Here you go."

"Thank you," I said.

Adam took a sip of his drink and stared into the glass. "I had promised to bring Mary here to Paris and kept putting it off and putting it off. She died before that ever happened." He looked down again and raised his eyes to me. "You told me you admired me for embracing the present. I wasn't always this way. I didn't learn how precious time was until after I had lost

Mary. I should've brought her to Paris. And now, I'm here without her on the anniversary of her death kissing the woman I can't get out of my mind. You."

I felt flattered for a moment, but this wasn't about me right now. I could understand how he would feel, even though I hadn't been there myself. I would have felt the same way if I were in his shoes.

"She would want you to be happy, you know. That's how most women are. Life goes on, as they say."

He nodded, thinking about it, but didn't say anything.

I took a sip of my strawberry daiquiri. "Anyway, why didn't you tell me about this when we were planning the trip?"

"We didn't know each other well, plus you said you had to be here today. And I had no right to give my opinion because you were a client. My job is to take you wherever you want."

I arched an eyebrow as I took another sip of my drink. "*Were* a client? I'm not your client anymore?"

"Technically, yes. It doesn't feel like you're a client anymore."

I knew I should avoid talking about feelings. I couldn't help it. "What does it feel like?"

"It feels good, I'll tell you that. It's like I've known you for months instead of days."

I felt the same way.

"Let me ask *you* a question." He set his drink down and leaned closer across the table. "Are you attracted to me?"

The temperature seemed to shoot up in the bar. Or maybe I was feeling the effects of that smoldering look he was giving me. I grabbed my daiquiri and sucked hard through the straw, draining half my drink in a heartbeat. Maybe if I kept quiet, I wouldn't have to answer the question or maybe I'd get lucky, and he would change the subject.

"It's a simple question," he continued. "I'm just curious, because I'm *definitely* attracted to you."

Maybe I should just tell him how I feel. He didn't seem to have a problem telling me his thoughts. He wasn't going to remember any of this conversation, anyway.

I swallowed hard and hoped that was the case. "I'm attracted to you. Yes."

He grinned. "Good. You think about me then?"

"I've been thinking about you a lot lately. Anyway, I think I should head up to my room."

"I only think of you on two occasions. Day and night."

Goodness gracious, he shouldn't say things like that.

My hands were getting sweaty, longing for another one of those kisses. He needed to turn down his charm dial before I became unhinged in a public place. By the look on his face, he wasn't even close to being done.

He grinned. "I've got a crush on the teacher."

I let out a nervous laugh. "Oh, do you now? I'm not your teacher."

"You'd be surprised. You've taught me a thing or two." He reached across the table and grabbed both of my hands. "You're an amazing woman, Liz. You're beautiful, intelligent, compassionate, generous, and I love your sense of humor. You're stubborn as hell, which I love too, did you know that? Because you keep me on my toes. While we're on the topic, toes are connected to legs, and I've already made it perfectly clear how I feel about your legs. And your kiss."

Why couldn't I look away from him?

Adam made me feel like a woman should feel.

I was close to jumping over the table and kissing him hard, right there in the bar.

"And you know what else I love about you?" Adam asked.

I couldn't take it anymore. "Shut up, Adam."

He needed to kiss me, or I was going to explode.

"Pardon me?" He lifted an eyebrow.

"I need a little less talk and a lot more action." I leaned across the table and grabbed him by the collar. "So, shut up and kiss me. Now."

After another amazing kiss that rivaled the one on top of the Eiffel Tower, I guided Adam upstairs to make sure he got back to his room okay.

I walked to my suite, and plopped myself down on the sofa, sighing.

It had been tempting to stay there with Adam in his room.

So tempting.

Not this time.

CHAPTER TWENTY-FIVE

LIZ

It had been a dream of mine to spend the night in a castle ever since I was a little girl visiting Disneyland for the first time. Call me silly, but I had always wanted to dress up like a member of the royal family and walk around a castle like I owned the place.

Now, at the age of fifty, I was finally getting my chance.

A white Rolls Royce Phantom picked us up from the train station in the Loire Valley, an area in central France known for its vineyards and castles. Orlando was in the front passenger seat talking to the driver, while Adam and I were seated in the back behind the privacy glass.

I turned to Adam. "I was hoping to talk with you on the train. I didn't want to interrupt you and Orlando while you were working."

Adam nodded. "Sorry about that. We were trying to work out a conflict in our schedules for a trip we have with a corporate client when we get back. Anyway, all is good. We figured out a solution, and Orlando can fly with me."

"You two seem close."

Adam glanced through the privacy glass at Orlando in the front seat and smiled. "He's my best friend. We've been through a lot together. He has always been there for me, especially when Mary passed away."

It surprised me that Adam brought up the topic of Mary on his own, since I had wanted to talk with him today to see if he was feeling better.

Now, I didn't have to worry about bringing it up.

"I don't know how much you remember from the bar yesterday—"

Adam glanced at me. "I remember everything."

I arched an eyebrow, hoping he was joking. "Really?"

"Of course! Did you think I was drunk or something?'"

"Well . . . yeah!"

Adam chuckled. "I'm not really a drinker, and know how to control my alcohol, even when I'm sulking, which isn't often. Plus, the two drinks were pretty watered-down. Anyway, I wanted to talk to you about yesterday as well. I want to thank you."

Another surprise. "For what?"

He shrugged. "For caring, and for what you said. It meant a lot to me. I agree that Mary would want me to be happy. She was that kind of woman. I thought I'd feel guilty about being in Paris without her on the anniversary of her death. I didn't. Not at all. So, basically, I was feeling guilty about not feeling guilty." He chuckled. "It sounds kind of pathetic when I say it out loud, but I'm at peace with it now. The guilt has disappeared, so thank you."

"You're welcome."

Adam leaned back in the seat and clasped his hands behind his head. "And now that we've gotten that out of the way, let's talk about how you're attracted to me and how you think about me all the time."

I crossed my arms. "You weren't supposed to remember that. Strike it from the record."

He smirked. "I'm sorry, I just can't do that. It's tattooed on my brain for life."

"And I didn't say *all* the time. I said I think about you *a lot*. That could mean three times a day."

"Or three hundred."

I laughed.

Orlando knocked on the privacy glass, and I lowered it so he could talk to us.

"Check it out." He pointed directly in front of the Rolls Royce. "We're here."

The driver pulled up to the enormous gate, and a few seconds later it slid open, little by little, revealing the most amazing French Renaissance castle and its immense towers at each corner.

It was stunning.

I lowered my window and breathed in the floral scents of the huge garden in front of the castle. There must have been thousands of plants, shrubs, and rose bushes.

Orlando stuck his head out the window. "Somebody slap me back to reality because I must be dreaming." He shook his head in disbelief. "This place makes *Downton Abbey* look like a backyard tool shed. How long did it take to build?"

"Twenty years," the driver answered, as he drove the Rolls Royce up the driveway that split the garden right down the middle. "With eight hundred full-time workers and over one hundred thousand tons of stone."

"How many rooms are there?" Adam asked.

"Two hundred and forty, sir." The driver pulled up to the front of the castle where a man and woman were standing by, smiling. "One hundred and sixty rooms are accessible to you on the first and third floors. The royal suites for your overnight accommodations are on the second floor."

Orlando popped out of the car before the driver could open his door. "The prince has arrived! Where's the red carpet?"

I laughed and turned to Adam. "I guess he's a little excited."

He shook his head. "He hasn't even stepped inside yet."

The driver opened my door, and I slid out of the Rolls Royce. Adam must have been excited too, because he slid out behind me instead of waiting for the driver to open his door.

"Bienvenue! Welcome!" The man bowed. "My name is Jean-Luc, and this is my beautiful wife, Monique. We are the property managers in charge of making sure you have the most delightful time."

"Thank you." Orlando stepped forward and grinned. "I'm Prince Orlando of San Diego. These are my parents, Queen Elizabeth and King Adam."

"Your parents?" Jean-Luc's gaze popped back and forth between the three of us.

Orlando pointed his index finger at Jean-Luc and shot it like a gun. "Gotcha!"

Jean-Luc nodded his appreciation of Orlando's joke and chuckled. "Very good. You got me."

I laughed. "Orlando is just *a tad* excited to be here."

"As he should be. You're all in for a royally good time." He gestured to our suitcases that the driver took out of the Rolls Royce. "We will have someone take your luggage to your suites, and your first guided tour will start momentarily. There are many fascinating, historical parts of the castle we will share with you, including the Gallery of Portraits, the Royal Library, and the Hall of Mirrors. Your schedule for the evening has been meticulously planned and we even have special attire for you to wear at the royal dinner. Please let us know if you have any questions at all."

Jean-Luc handed the three of us a schedule for the evening, which included dinner and three separate guided tours.

I glanced down at the document and lost a little bit of my enthusiasm.

It was structured, right down to the minute. That's not how I envisioned my night in the castle, and it was a little bit of a letdown.

Adam leaned forward and looked in my eyes. "Is everything okay?"

I thought about it, deciding to say something. "I was hoping for something a little different than this, that's all."

"Like what?" Orlando asked.

I sighed and held up the itinerary. "I mean—this is not bad, don't get me wrong. Normally, I like to geek-out on history, and these tours would serve that purpose perfectly. I don't know, I'd just love to explore the property on our own and see what we find. I think that would be fun." I avoided eye contact with Adam, knowing he would give me crap about spontaneity.

"Wait a minute . . ." Adam studied me.

Right on cue.

"You mean, you want to be—"

"Spontaneous!" I practically yelled. "Yes—I admit it. I want to be spontaneous, just like you. Happy?"

He grinned. "Very."

"Let's not make a big deal about it. I want to try something different. I would like to explore the castle on our own, like you." I turned to him. "For instance, what first comes to your mind when you think about entering the castle? What would you do first?"

Adam looked up at the enormous castle, thinking about it. "I would want to go to the top of the tower and look out."

"Well then, *that's* what we should do!" I turned to Jean-Luc. "I hope you won't be offended. I know you have the guided tours planned."

"This is not a problem at all," Jean-Luc said. "We typically have this program for tourists who are intimidated by the size of the castle and don't know where to begin. I will gladly take those back from you." He grabbed the schedules from us, stuck them inside his folder, and pulled out maps. "Take these instead. You can explore without getting lost. The castle is yours for the evening. You are free to do exactly as you choose. Just keep in mind the dinner will be served promptly at seven in the main dining room on the first floor. You will hear a loud gong throughout the castle ten minutes before the first course is served." He checked his watch. "That gives you exactly three hours to explore the property before dinner. And since you are in an adventurous mood, there are a few secret passageways you might enjoy. Try to not get trapped in the dungeon because there is no way out and there are alligators down there, I'm afraid."

"What?" Orlando looked horrified. "You have alligators on the property?"

Jean-Luc shot an index finger back at Orlando. "Gotcha!"

Orlando pretended to wipe sweat from his brow and chuckled. "Yeah—you got me good."

Jean-Luc laughed. "It looks like we are in for a wonderful evening, indeed. Monique and I are at your disposal throughout your stay, no matter the hour. Let us know if you need anything or have any questions."

"I'm going to head to my suite first to unpack a few things and freshen up," Orlando said.

"I would be happy to show you the way," Monique said.

"Thank you." He turned to me and Adam. "I'll find you both later."

"Sounds great. Let's go!" I grabbed Adam by the arm and pulled him into the castle, excited to explore. We paused in the massive marble entryway, looking around. "Which way? You choose."

Adam checked the map and pointed to the spiral stone staircase. "We need to go up."

"Then let's do it." I pulled Adam by the hand, practically dragging him up the stairs, on a mission to get to the tower.

He laughed hysterically. "I'm loving your enthusiasm right now, but I would like to get there without breaking a leg."

I laughed and slowed down, out of breath. "Sorry. I guess I'm a little excited."

"A little?" He laughed again.

We made it to the top of the steps and walked hand-in-hand down the long corridor lined with paintings.

Adam pulled me to a stop in front of a portrait of Louis

XIV in a gold frame. "Hey, I know that guy. I recognize him from the hair."

I nodded. "Louis the fourteenth."

Adam shook his head. "No, no, no. You're definitely mistaken. This guy played lead guitar for Bon Jovi."

I laughed, pulling him down the hallway again. "Come on. The king is being silly, but we need to get to the tower."

We arrived at the tower door, and I tried to pull it open, but it wouldn't budge. "Wow. This thing is heavy. I wonder if it's the original."

"Let me try." Adam yanked it. The hinges squeaked in protest, but he was able to open the door. "After you."

"Thank you. You go first, since you wanted to see it."

"As you wish, my queen." Adam climbed the spiral stairs of the tower ahead of me.

I couldn't help admiring his assets.

The man was definitely in good shape.

That had to be the firmest fifty-year-old butt I'd ever seen in my life.

Okay, maybe it was wrong to stare like that.

Don't look at his butt. Don't look at his butt.

Adam laughed. "You can look."

I stopped before the last step.

Please, no. Did I say that out loud? Somebody kill me.

Adam continued to laugh and held out his hand. "It's okay. Come on."

I took his hand again and made it to the top, shaking my head. "I have arrived at the age where I don't know if I'm thinking something or saying it out loud. That's a little bit scary, to be honest."

He stared at me. "Were you going to say something?"

I crossed my arms and laughed. "*Not* funny." I turned to look at the view from the tower and froze. "Oh, wow." It didn't seem like we went that high, but the view was amazing.

We had a 360-degree view of the Loire Valley, including a few other castles in the region, the churches, the many vineyards and orchards, and the Loire River, which wasn't far away.

"This is spectacular." Adam took a deep breath and appreciated the view.

"Look!" I pointed across the valley. "That's the castle from the poster at the travel agency in Paris."

We ended up staying up in the tower for almost an hour, pointing out things we discovered, chatting, laughing, and enjoying each other's company. It was the perfect start to our night in the castle, and I wouldn't have changed it for the world.

After we climbed back down from the tower, we explored many other rooms on that floor, including the Hall of Mirrors, several grand ballrooms, a lapidary room, the hunting room, and the Tapestries Room—no surprise that it was full of tapestries.

We walked down a long hallway when I heard the sound of a piano. "Wait. Listen."

Adam stopped next to me. "Someone plays well."

"Let's see where it's coming from."

I turned the corner and followed the sound down another long corridor to the Royal Library, of all places.

Adam pushed the door open and we stepped inside.

To our surprise, Jean-Luc was playing the piano in the middle of the library, surrounded by thousands of books from floor to ceiling.

He stopped and swiveled around on the piano bench. "Welcome to the Royal Library. Are you enjoying yourselves so far?"

I nodded. "Very much so. You play beautifully."

"Merci, merci. It is something I do truly enjoy."

"I'm surprised there's a piano in the library, though."

He chuckled. "It would have to be one of the many peculiarities of this castle, I would say. Something else you might find odd is that just about all of the leather-bound books you see on the shelves around you have never been read." He pointed to one of the shelves. "See for yourself. Grab one."

Adam took a few steps toward one of the shelves, pulled a book from it, and inspected it. "It's like new."

"Exactly." Jean-Luc stood and gestured to the rest of the books in the library. "You will find some great French literature in this room, *Les Misérables*, *Madame Bovary*, *The Hunchback of Notre Dame*, *The Count of Monte Cristo*, and *The Phantom of the Opera*, to name a few. And almost all of them have never been opened. Never been touched or read. By the way, sorry about the dust. We hire a person every other month to dust the shelves and books. It takes hours."

I glanced around the library. "Strange . . . Why have books if you're not going to read them?"

"That's a good question. The owner of the castle intended this to be a normal reading library, but his wife lost her eyesight. He didn't think it was fair that anyone else should be able to read, so he forbade reading in the castle, and turned the library into a showcase for entertaining. That's why the piano is here, because his wife played the piano well, even after she became blind. In fact, there are fourteen pianos in the castle. He wanted to make sure she always had one close by."

"That's so romantic and tragic at the same time." I pointed to the book Adam had taken off the shelf. "Don't you dare read that."

Adam chuckled. "It would be difficult for me, since it's in French."

Jean-Luc laughed and checked his watch. "Just a warning —you have forty-five minutes until dinner."

"Oh." I needed to get a move on. "I should get ready."

"Monique is in the next room and can show you to your suite."

"Thank you." I gave Adam a smile. "See you at dinner."

Adam bowed. "I look forward to it."

I found Monique in the next room, and she took me to my suite.

She opened my suite door and smiled. "I will be close by, in case you need anything at all."

"Thank you so much." I stepped inside the suite, closed the door behind me, and blinked. "Wow."

The suite was big enough to sleep ten people.

I glanced up at the vaulted ceiling and over to the upholstered walls that perfectly framed the windows overlooking the marble courtyard. Then I checked the firmness of the mattress on the king-size canopy bed with the red silk curtains.

I nodded my approval and sat down on the bed, marveling at the suite. "It's perfect. Just perfect."

Directly across from me, hanging from the armoire, was a red silk gown. Just below it on the table was a gold crown with rubies, sapphires, and pearls.

They were gorgeous and I was going to wear them to dinner.

I took a quick shower and was happy I didn't have to wash my hair since I had done it that morning.

I took the gown off the hanger and slipped into it. I placed the crown on my head and stared at myself in the mirror.

"I'm a queen." I adjusted the crown on my head and turned to the side to admire my gown.

Thirty minutes later, and with Monique's help for the long zipper on the back, I was ready to head down for dinner with Adam and Orlando.

There was a knock at my door, and my mind went to Adam, hoping he was there to escort me to the main dining room.

I swung the door open and—

"Pardon me." Jean-Luc bowed and handed me a bouquet of flowers with a card. "These are for you."

"Wow." I smelled the flowers and smiled. "Lilies. My favorite."

He nodded. "Fleur-de-lis. They are a special symbol of our country and the royal crown."

"They're beautiful. Thank you so much. That was kind of you."

"Please do not thank me. I'm the delivery person."

"Who are they from?"

"I am not at liberty to say." Jean-Luc pointed to the card. "You will find the answer in the card." He winked as a loud gong reverberated throughout the castle. "And it looks like we will see you at dinner shortly."

"Thank you. I'll be right down." I closed the door, set the

flowers on the table by the window, and opened the card to read it.

Dear Liz,

I want to express my gratitude for this wonderful time together with you, some of the best days of my life. I admire you, Liz. Your compassion, generosity, sense of humor, and your beautiful self. You never stop amazing me. Please, don't change. And thank you for choosing us to be part of this adventure with you. I'd like this journey to last forever. Accept these special flowers for a very special woman. Looking forward to our royal dinner together.

Love,

Adam.

I sighed, and closed the card, placing it on the table next to the flowers.

I'd like this journey to last forever.

"You're not the only one," I said to myself as I headed downstairs for dinner.

CHAPTER TWENTY-SIX

LIZ

I entered the main dining room and struck what I thought was a decent pose, doing my best to make a grand entrance. I cleared my throat and waited for Orlando and Adam to turn around. I assumed by the two jaws dropping open that being dressed up as a queen suited me well.

"You look amazing, your highness." Orlando bowed in his all-white ensemble—high-waisted short pants, a long jacket, and a waistcoat with gold trim.

"Thank you, Prince Orlando. I must say you're looking quite dashing this evening." I eyed his white knee-high socks. "Oh, and nice legs."

He bowed again, this time with a proud smile. "Thank you. I was hoping you'd notice."

Adam took a few steps toward me, looking dapper in his tuxedo. "You look ravishing, your majesty." He grabbed my hand and kissed the top, his eyes never leaving mine.

Can't take my eyes off of you.

I tried to get the Frankie Valli song out of my head.

Did I sing that out loud?

Adam didn't say anything, so I was pretty sure I had escaped embarrassment this time.

"Thank you, King Adam. You're looking as handsome as ever."

He bowed. "You are too kind, your highness."

Jean-Luc entered the dining room and smiled. "Welcome. Meal service will begin in just a moment, and Chef Pierre will make an appearance!" He pointed to the far end of the large rectangular wood table with twelve chairs. "Queen Elizabeth, you will be sitting at *that* end." He pointed to the opposite end of the table. "King Adam, that will be your place for dinner."

Orlando pointed to the chair with the only other setting in the middle of the table. "I guess this is me."

"Correct, Prince Orlando! We shall return with your first course." Jean-Luc left the dining room.

The three of us sat and stared at each other for a long beat across the table that seemed to go on forever.

"This just doesn't feel right." Orlando stood and slid his table setting next to me. "Much better." He took a seat and grabbed the napkin, placing it on his lap. "This is where the party is at, right next to the queen. I was in another time zone over there."

Orlando and I glanced down to the far end of the table where Adam was sitting, watching us.

He blew out a deep breath. "I feel alone down here, and I'm not going to let Orlando hog the queen all to himself." He stood to move his place setting down to my end of the table, sitting across from Orlando to my right. He turned to me and smiled. "Much better."

I leaned closer to Adam and whispered, "Thank you for the beautiful flowers and card."

"My pleasure. I meant what I said."

"I know you did. That was sweet of you."

"This proves you *do* like surprises."

I smirked. "You got lucky this time—let's not make a habit of it."

"Sorry. I just can't make that promise." He grinned.

I crossed my arms. "What are you up to, King Adam?"

"Nothing, nothing at all."

Four staff members came out from where I could only assume was the kitchen, three of them carrying plates, and the fourth carrying a bottle of wine. They set one plate in front of each of us and poured the wine.

The door flew open again, and a man dressed in white pants, white shirt, and a puffy chef's hat threw his hands up in the air and flamboyantly glided toward us like he was floating on air. "Welcome, welcome, welcome, my friends! My name is Pierre, and it is a *wonderful* pleasure to have you here this evening. I have prepared with *great* love many of my favorite dishes for you. Your first course is baked chicken cordon bleu with maple Dijon and a side of ratatouille. Bon appétit!"

We thanked him, and he glided back into the kitchen.

Orlando pointed toward the kitchen. "I *love* that man. Did you see the way he moved?"

Adam chuckled and grabbed his wine glass, raising it in the air. "To Queen Elizabeth. Thank you for an adventure to remember."

"To Queen Elizabeth," Orlando said.

We all clinked glasses and sipped our wine.

"This *has* been unforgettable," Orlando added. "I can't believe we're going to see the northern lights. Thanks again."

"It's nothing," I said, not wanting to make a big deal out of it.

"Are you kidding me? This has been amazing with a capital A and a *zing*! Thank you, thank you. I know you're a client, but I'm hoping we can continue being friends after this trip."

"That would be lovely."

"Good, because I have a date with your brother when we get back."

I almost spit out my wine. "What? When did that happen?"

"He gave me his business card at the airport the day we met. I sent him an email with some pictures from the safari, and one thing led to another."

"Well, I'm sure you two will hit it off. I'm grateful to have such an amazing brother."

We finished our chicken cordon bleu, and they cleared our plates.

Chef Pierre glided in again. I glanced to the floor to see if he was wearing roller-skates. He had on normal shoes. How did he do that?

"How was it, my friends?" Pierre said. "Please tell me you loved it."

"We did," I said. "It was the best chicken I've ever had."

"This is music to my ears! Well, you're in for a treat because your next course is called potatoes dauphinoise." He clapped his hands twice, and the servants entered with three more plates, placing them in front of us.

Adam leaned down and sniffed it. "This smells wonderful."

Pierre smiled proudly. "Merci. It is simple but *bursting* with flavor. Potatoes, cream, cheese, and a hint of garlic and thyme. That's it! Your next course will be even better! I'll give you a hint, it may have lobster! I'd better get back to the kitchen."

"Out of curiosity, how many courses are there?" Adam asked. "Just so I can try to pace myself."

Pierre walked around the table and placed a hand on Adam's shoulder. "We did not want to overwhelm you with too much. There will only be seven courses."

Adam choked. "Seven? You're serious?"

"But of course, I'm serious. In our country we believe eating is *a pleasure* rather than a necessity. I shall return!"

Sure enough, we had seven of the most amazing courses I have ever eaten in my life, finishing the meal off with a cup of French roast coffee and chocolate soufflé. The dinner lasted almost three hours, but the courses were nicely spaced out so that we had a chance to enjoy each and every dish. I had the best time chatting with Adam, Orlando, and Pierre.

"This is the life." Orlando pushed his chair out a little and glanced around the dining room. "Imagine living in a place like this."

I looked around and shrugged. "Don't get me wrong, this place is amazing, and it's a dream come true to stay here tonight. I love my cozy life in San Diego. I don't need a big house. Maybe I'll get something closer to the ocean at some point. Size doesn't matter."

Adam and Orlando stared at me, both on the verge of laughter.

"You know what I mean!" I shook my head, laughing. "Men."

Adam chuckled and gave me a knowing smile. "I know exactly what you mean. I prefer cozy, too. And a bigger house means more to clean. Who wants that?"

"Not me," Orlando and I said at the same time. We laughed together.

We spent the next hour exploring the castle, without the map, trying to burn off the calories from the seven courses, even though we knew we wouldn't even come close. We never got to see all the rooms. I'm guessing we saw maybe fifty or so, including two secret passageways leading to a wine cellar and a cigar room.

After Orlando said goodnight and went back to his suite, Adam and I continued exploring. We strolled through the hallways, admiring paintings on the walls, and chatting about life. We talked about my life as a teacher and his as a pilot.

"What's in here?" Adam stopped and opened a door, frowning. "It's just a closet."

I peeked inside. "Any skeletons in there?"

He laughed and closed the door. "You don't want to know."

"Listen." I stopped after a few more steps in the hallway. "Do you hear that?"

Adam stopped and listened, nodding. "The piano again." He listened a little more. "It's in a different room this time. Let's go find it."

We headed down one of the spiral staircases back to the first floor and turned right.

Adam stopped in front of the first closed door, putting his ear against it. "It's coming from in here. Let's check it out." He grabbed the handle to open the door.

I pulled his arm back to stop him. "Wait. I don't think this is one of the rooms we have access to."

"Of course, it is. It's fine."

"I'm not so sure, and I don't want to barge in on anyone."

"Okay, I'll tell you what. Let's do this . . ." Adam knocked on the door.

"Adam!" I said in my loudest whisper. "It's getting late."

"They're obviously awake!" He chuckled. "You worry too much."

The door flew open, startling me.

"We meet again!" Jean-Luc waved us inside the room. "Please. Don't be shy. Come in."

I stepped inside and glanced around at the enormous room with the four crystal chandeliers hanging from the ceiling. It was completely empty except for a piano near the center of the room.

"Wow. Is this a ballroom?"

"It is!" Jean-Luc smiled proudly. "This is *the grand* ballroom. Many royal events were hosted here, some with upwards of three hundred people. Presidents, heads of state, foreign dignitaries, you name it, they've all been here. Even some Hollywood celebrities. We also rent it out for wedding receptions."

It certainly was a magnificent ballroom.

Jean-Luc held up an index finger, indicating for us to wait. He walked toward the piano, sat down, and began to play, "La Vie en Rose."

"I *love* this song. It's one of my favorites."

Adam grinned. "Well, in that case . . ." He held out his hand. "Shall we dance?"

"I would love to." I placed my hand in Adam's, and he led me to the middle of the room.

He spun me around and slowly slid his hand around my hip to my lower back, pulling me closer.

Oooh, I like this.

We swayed back and forth as Jean-Luc continued to play the song on the piano.

"This is from one of my favorite movies, *French Kiss*, with Meg Ryan and Kevin Kline. A French song from *French Kiss* while we're in France. I love this."

Adam grinned. "It's also from the movie, *The Bucket List.*"

I thought about it for a moment. "You're right!" I laughed. "I can't believe we're dancing to a song from the movie *The Bucket List* while I'm experiencing my own personal bucket list."

"What a coinkydink." Adam chuckled.

"Okay, something's going on because you hate that word." I pulled away from him slightly, studying him. "Wait a minute. Did you plan this?"

Adam didn't answer, but his bottom lip quivered.

"Oh, my goodness, you planned this whole thing!"

"Maybe I did, maybe I didn't."

Jean-Luc winked at me.

"How?" I asked.

Adam shrugged, keeping his body close to mine. "I just did a little research. You know how that goes." He smiled. "You were right all along; research does come in handy every now and then."

"This is crazy. I'm becoming you and you're becoming me."

"We bring out the best in each other, don't we?"

"Yeah. I think we do."

I put my head against his shoulder, enjoying every second of the dance, thinking about how I was in heaven at the moment. How it felt so perfect in his arms.

How it felt like home.

Time stands still when I'm with you.

I thought of the painting I had bought for Adam.

We were a live version of those two people dancing in front of the clocks.

I couldn't wait for him to have the painting.

We thanked Jean-Luc after the song ended, ready to head to our suites for the night.

We walked down the long corridor of the north wing in silence.

Adam pointed to his door. "This is me."

I nodded, looking forward to one of his kisses. "Okay then."

"But I'll walk you to your room."

Much better.

I smiled. "Such a gentleman, King Adam."

"Only for you, Queen Elizabeth."

We arrived at my door and I swung around to face Adam, putting my hands behind my back, and leaning against the door.

I wanted a kiss, but on the other hand, I didn't want to say goodnight.

Not yet.

"What an evening." Adam took a step closer.

"It was perfect," I said.

Adam glanced down at my mouth. "I think there's only

one way we can make it better." He pulled my body against his, leaned down, and pressed his lips to mine.

It was another one of *those* kisses.

The kind of kiss that made my knees weak.

The kind of kiss that made me almost lose my mind.

The kind of kiss that made me want to do something I didn't think I would do in the castle tonight, or at any time during this entire trip, or in the near future.

I forced myself to pull away from his lips. "There *is* another way to make this night better."

"Do tell."

I shook my head. "Talking is overrated." I opened the door, stepped inside my suite, and walked toward my bed, not looking back.

A few seconds later, I heard the door close behind me.

"You're right," Adam said. "This is *much* better."

CHAPTER TWENTY-SEVEN

ADAM

I was feeling on top of the world, walking back to Liz's suite, whistling "La Vie en Rose," and carrying a tray of chocolate croissants with French press coffee. Liz was still asleep when I snuck out this morning, and I was looking forward to surprising her with breakfast in bed.

She had told me she didn't like surprises, and I had been skeptical. Now, I knew that wasn't the case at all, judging by her reaction after receiving the flowers and the card, and by how much she enjoyed that private dance in the grand ballroom.

What a dance.

What a night.

Liz was just as passionate as I knew she would be.

I didn't know how much time I had with her, or what the future held.

There was one thing I knew for sure: I loved her.

And I wanted to spend every minute possible with her.

I balanced the tray on the palm of one hand and used my other hand to carefully open the door to the suite. I stepped inside and closed the door behind me, surprised when I saw the bed empty.

Liz was sitting by the window in her *Easy Peasy* T-shirt, looking out to the garden, the phone in her hand.

I hoped she still appreciated the gesture and had an appetite.

"Good morning, my queen." I placed the tray on the table next to her. "Breakfast is served."

I leaned down to kiss her and—

Uh-oh.

She turned away from me.

That wasn't a good sign.

"Is everything okay?" I asked.

She didn't answer.

Maybe she'd gotten some bad news from the doctor. Whatever it was, I just needed to be there for her, and let her know that everything would be fine. I knew there was a possibility of something happening with her condition, but I wasn't going anywhere.

"Did you get some bad news?" I asked, pointing to her phone in her hand.

"You could say that." She turned to me, holding up the phone. "It was a text from Josh. He wanted to know if the symptoms from my disease were getting any worse."

I jerked my head back, surprised she was telling me about her disease. She had kept it a secret from day one, and it didn't make sense why she would share that information with me now, and this way.

Unless things had taken a turn for the worse, which I hoped wasn't the case.

"And?" I sat down at the table across from her. "What did you tell Josh? How are you feeling?"

She shook her head. "I didn't tell him *anything*. You don't understand." She held up the phone again. "The text from Josh was *to you*. This is *your* phone."

I blinked twice and glanced back at the bedside table where I had left my phone. "What do you mean *my* phone?"

"You know we have the exact same phone. I thought yours was mine! When it vibrated, I naturally picked it up and saw part of the text message on the screen. That doesn't matter. You knew about my condition and never said a word."

"I'm sorry about that. I promised Josh I wouldn't say anything."

"How long have you known?" she demanded.

I hesitated, feeling that if I answered I would only make it worse.

Liz clenched her fist. "How long, Adam?"

I sighed. "Since the Maasai village, right before you spilled the cup of blood on me. I called Josh and told him I was worried about you. He told me everything about the disease. About you needing a bone marrow donor. Everything."

"Unbelievable . . ." She stood and paced the room, turning back to me. "What about Orlando? Does he know?"

I nodded.

Liz squeezed her eyes shut and shook her head. "I can't believe this."

"Look—it's not a big deal."

"*It is* a big deal." She crossed her arms and glared at me. "What else do you know about me?"

I looked away, which most likely made me appear guilty, which I was.

"Adam? Spill it. You know something else and I want to know what it is."

I ran my fingers through my hair, realizing that I had to tell her everything now. Relationships couldn't be based on lies. "Okay, okay. I know you won the lottery. And I know how much money you won. That's it. Nothing else, although that part didn't come from Josh. It came from Google."

Her nostrils flared and I could see the whites around her eyes. "You *Googled* me? Are you serious?" She dropped her arms to her side, pacing again. "I can't believe this."

I couldn't throw Orlando under the bus for that, because it wasn't going to make a difference how I found out she had won the lottery. In Liz's eyes, all that mattered was I had known and hadn't said anything. She felt betrayed.

I sighed, hoping she would calm down. "None of this matters."

"It matters! You were hiding things from me. How do I not know you weren't just humoring me this entire trip?"

"What? You can't be serious."

"I'm serious! How do I know you weren't pretending you cared? Complimenting my legs? Giving me flowers and the card? And that dance? How am I supposed to believe you didn't do it *all* out of pity? Huh?"

I stood there, shocked she would even consider such a thing.

"That's what I thought." She turned her back on me, looking out the window again.

"I would *never* do that!"

"How do I know?"

"Because!"

"That's not a reason."

I moved closer and just blurted it out. "Because I love you! That's the reason."

She swung back around, her shoulders tightening. "What?"

"You heard me. I love you."

"That's *not* possible." Liz blinked rapidly.

I let out a nervous laugh. "Well, I didn't think it was possible either, yet here I am, standing before you, in love. Go figure."

Her eyes teared up.

I wanted to grab her and hold her tight and never let her go. I knew it wasn't what she wanted. She was fighting this too hard.

She was scared.

"What if I die?" Liz barely got the words out.

"What if you don't?"

"What if I do?"

"You're not going to die!"

"How do you know that?"

"Because you're much too stubborn to die!"

I didn't mean to yell—she was driving me crazy.

I sat down on the edge of the bed and closed my eyes, shocked this was happening after one of the best nights of my life. "Liz . . ."

She didn't answer.

Josh was right. His sister was the most stubborn woman in the world. I was the one who was going to pay the price because my love life was imploding at this very minute.

"Liz," I tried again.

She finally turned back to me. "None of this is real, you know."

"Last night wasn't real to you?"

"No. It wasn't." She couldn't hold my gaze long, so I knew she was lying.

"Right . . . Don't tell me that didn't feel real to you. *Everything* about last night was real. The food, the conversation, the laughter, the intimate moments with you. Everything. It doesn't get any more real than what we experienced. Some people go their entire lives without something that real. And here you are, wanting to deny it all." I shook my head.

She crossed her arms. "Last night was a fantasy that spiraled out of control. Now I need to get back to the real world." She set my phone down on the table, walked to the closet, and pulled out her suitcase.

"What are you doing?"

She didn't look at me. "I'm going home."

"What? You can't be serious?"

"Believe me, I'm serious."

We had now reached worst case scenario.

Liz wheeled the suitcase around me, and tipped it over to the floor, unzipping it. She walked over to the dresser and started pulling out her clothes.

"Liz, listen to me. You can't deny there's something between us."

No answer.

I sat on the bed and watched her stuff clothes into her suitcase in the most unorganized way possible. She was on a mission to get out of there ASAP.

My heart ached and my eyes watered. I was going to hold

it together, because I wasn't going to give up on her. I just didn't know what else to say.

I sighed. "You're making a big mistake."

She didn't answer.

"And what about the rest of your trip? You were so excited to see the other parts of Paris. And the northern lights? We were saving the best for last."

She shook her head. "I'm going home—I told you. Don't let that stop you and Orlando from continuing with the trip. It's all paid for. Knock yourself out. I'll catch a commercial flight home from Paris."

"Look—you can cancel the rest of the trip, if you want to, even though I think you're making a huge mistake. You hired me to do a job, and that's exactly what I will do. I'm flying you home."

"You're relieved of your duties. You're fired."

"Liz . . ." This was going to be my last shot. "Forget about me working for you, or not working for you, since you apparently just gave me the ax. That's all minor stuff compared to the big picture. The big picture involves you and me. Nothing else. No flights, no clients, no castles, no vacations, no diseases. Just you and me. I want you to do something for me and then I promise I won't ask for anything else. I want you to look me in the eyes and tell me you don't love me."

She avoided eye contact with me again.

I had only known her for a few short weeks. I could read her like a book.

She loved me.

"Liz?" I patiently waited for her to say something. "Talk to me. Do you love me? Yes or no. It's a simple question. Tell me you don't love me, and I'll leave. I'll be out that door. I promise."

She turned, staring at me, hesitating.

Say it. Say you love me. I know you do.

Everything would be all right, if she would just admit it.

Liz felt trapped. She was scared. I could see that.

Love would set her free.

Say you love me. Please. That's all I want to hear.

Liz finally opened her mouth to speak.

I held my breath.

"I don't love you," she said.

She held my gaze just long enough to try to make me believe she was serious, which I didn't buy for a minute. Then she turned her attention back to stuffing her suitcase.

My pulse slowed down.

My eyes were on her, but it was like I was looking right through her now.

I had given it everything I had. My energy was completely drained.

She wasn't going to change her mind, and I promised to leave her alone.

I had to let her take the commercial flight back to San Diego.

She was dreaming if she thought this was over.

I would be leaving her room, not her life.

We were far from over.

"You can't fight love." I grabbed my phone from the table. "Love *always* wins."

I walked out the door.

CHAPTER TWENTY-EIGHT

Three Weeks Later . . .

LIZ

Today was the day that would change the rest of my life. The doctors had found a bone marrow donor match for me, and Josh was going to drive me to the hospital for the transplant.

Barring any unusual complications, I would live a normal and happy life.

Too bad I didn't feel happy.

In fact, I had been depressed ever since I had gotten back from the trip.

I hadn't slept much.

I hadn't eaten much.

I hadn't really been doing anything at all.

Josh had told me there were dark circles under my eyes. I would've never known if he hadn't said something since I was too embarrassed to look at myself in the mirror after the way I had treated Adam.

When they had called me to tell me they had found a one-in-a-million bone marrow donor match for me, I had cried for an entire hour. It had been like winning the lottery all over again, only a million times better. But any positive thoughts about being able to continue living had been immediately replaced by grief and sorrow and a heaviness in my heart so strong it almost suffocated me.

It was my own fault for pushing Adam out of my life.

I missed him terribly and had thought about calling him many times, but then my pride had squashed the idea because I was just too embarrassed about my behavior.

The only thing I had done since I had gotten back was watch the National Geographic Channel. All day and all night. But when they had shown the program about Machu Picchu, I bawled uncontrollably. Then there had been the program about the Maasai tribe in Africa. More crying. And just when I had thought I had run out of tears, I surprised myself with more.

Josh had yelled at me more than a few times when he had found out I had lost weight from not eating. He had told me I needed to be strong for the transplant.

He was right, but I had lost hope.

Hope for finding a bone marrow donor.

Hope that I would ever hear from Adam again.

He's gone. He moved on.

Who could blame him?

The honking horn in front of the house snapped me out of my torturous thoughts.

I went out the front door, locked it behind me, and then

walked down the driveway toward Josh's brand-new BMW that I had purchased for him last week. He had brought me home to pick up a few things before heading to the hospital but had stayed in the car to finish a phone call with his boss.

I reached for the passenger door handle.

"Wait!" Snoop Dolly Dog frantically ran across the street toward me like her bunny slippers were on fire. "Liz!"

So close to escaping.

"Hi, Dolly. I'd love to chat, but I can't be late for my appointment."

"I know exactly where you're going *and* what your appointment is for," Dolly said.

Of course, she knew.

Dolly held her arms out. "I just wanted to say good luck and give you a hug before you go. Come here. Everything will be fine, sweetheart."

Dolly being affectionate was new to me. She hadn't been her normal self lately. She wasn't bitter anymore and had become the kindest I had seen her in years. And not one time had she gossiped in the last three weeks. She said she was a changed woman after meeting and falling for a man while I was gone. That was proof that love could change a person.

Or it could make them run and hide, like I had done.

Dolly pulled me into a bear hug so tight that I was sure some of my internal organs had shifted to a different part of my body.

"You're good people, Liz Parker. Do you hear me?"

Actually, it wasn't easy to hear since my face was buried deep in her bosom.

"We need to get going," Josh said out the window.

Dolly loosened her full-body-death-grip, but kept a hand

on each of my shoulders, looking me straight in the eyes. "Everything is going to be fine. Do you hear me?"

"Thanks, Dolly. I appreciate it."

I got in Josh's car and closed the door, putting on my seat belt.

Josh gave me a comforting smile. "Ready to do this?"

I nodded. "Ready as I'll ever be."

Josh drove to the hospital.

I was quiet, listening to the music on the radio, thinking of Adam.

I wondered if the guilt would ever go away.

Josh shot a glance over at me and got his eyes back on the road. "You're going to run out of fingernails."

I pulled my finger out of my mouth. "Yeah . . ."

"Everything is going to be fine."

"It's natural for a person to get a little anxious before going to the hospital." I thought of Adam and his phobia, which was more extreme. "What if something goes wrong? What if I wake up in the middle of the procedure and can feel pain because the anesthesia wasn't working well enough?"

"Yeah, that happens *all* the time, and they usually hit the patient on the head with a coconut to put them back to sleep." He chuckled. "Don't worry. They told you this was a simple procedure and the success rate is high. You've got nothing to worry about."

"Honestly, I wasn't even thinking about that."

"Don't tell me . . . Adam?"

"Bingo. I finally broke down yesterday and sent him a text saying I was sorry, and to share the news about finding a bone marrow donor. I also told him I had been thinking about him. Anyway, he never replied."

"He's probably just busy. Didn't you say he had a bunch of back-to-back trips to the East Coast?"

I nodded. "That's what he told me when we were in France."

"Well, there you go. He must be in the air as we speak."

Still, sending a text reply only took a few seconds. He couldn't have been *that* busy. Not that I expected him to visit me in the hospital, but he could have wished me good luck and told me he'd call me after. Just knowing he still cared about me is all I wanted at this point.

I couldn't blame him one bit for not wanting anything to do with me.

We arrived at the hospital and checked in, and a nurse took me straight to my private room.

Dr. Singh came in and smiled, giving me a big hug. "Good to see you again."

"You, too." I sat down on the edge of the bed.

He explained the bone marrow transplant procedure to me, even though I had already been briefed by Dr. Anna Nguyen from the Hematology and Oncology Department. She was the one who would be performing the transplant. It wasn't actually a surgery, so everything would happen right there in my hospital room while the transplant team watched me closely.

Amazingly, the procedure would only take two to three hours.

Dr. Nguyen entered the room with a file and a smile. "Nice to see you again, Liz."

"You too, Dr. Nguyen."

"I'd like to start preparing you for the transplant. Let me

just check a couple of things." She looked over the file and made a few notes.

"I'm going to let her do her job," Dr. Singh said. "I'll be close by if you need anything at all. Oh, and my wife and I would love to have you over for chicken tikka masala after you have made a full recovery."

I smiled. "Yum. That's the kind of motivation I need to recover faster."

"I'm just curious . . ." Josh said. "Does that invitation extend to family members?"

Dr. Singh laughed. "Of course. It would be a pleasure to have you over as well, Josh. I'll see you both again soon." He had a few words with Dr. Nguyen and left.

Josh sat on the bed next to me. "Okay, sis, I'll let you go. I'll be in the lobby, waiting to hear the good news that everything went according to plan. I love you."

I hugged Josh. "Love you."

After he left, I sat back on the bed and waited for instructions from Dr. Nguyen.

I glanced over at the magazine rack on the wall. There was a travel magazine with the Eiffel Tower on the cover.

My heart clenched.

I wanted to ask Dr. Nguyen if she could fix the hole in my heart first.

Tears leaked from my eyes, remembering the first kiss I shared with Adam.

I shook my head, wondering if I was going to think of him and that amazing kiss every time I saw anything related to France or the Eiffel Tower.

Of course, I would.

Because I loved him.

I love Adam.

And in a moment of spontaneity I can only attribute to the man I loved, I made an important decision. I needed to tell Adam the truth.

Dr. Nguyen turned to me and smiled. "I think we're just about ready to begin."

I grimaced and held up an index finger. "Do you mind if I send one more text? It's important. This will be quick."

"No problem."

I pulled my phone from my purse and typed a message to Adam.

Liz: I lied to you when I said I didn't love you. I do love you, with all my heart and soul. Will you forgive me?

I slipped my phone back in my purse, satisfied.

I should've said that a long time ago.

Now, I would just have to wait and see if he responded this time.

If not, it just wasn't meant to be. I would need to move on. I would be grateful to have met a man who taught me the meaning of spontaneity and fun, while making me feel like the sexiest woman on the planet.

I glanced at Dr. Nguyen and blew out a deep breath. "Okay. Let's do this."

CHAPTER TWENTY-NINE

Eight Days Later . . .

LIZ

Dr. Nguyen entered my hospital room early in the morning, smiling. "Good morning."

I sat up in the bed. "Good morning. I'm surprised to see you here so early today."

"Well, that's because I have some good news. *Amazing* news, actually."

"What is it?"

"You have engraftment. Your new cells are growing and making new cells."

I stared at her. "How is that possible? I thought you said it usually takes two to four weeks?"

Dr. Nguyen shrugged. "We're just as baffled as you. We've never seen engraftment happen so quickly, but you did have a rare form of the disease we had never seen before. Honestly, we weren't sure what to expect. The bottom line is, you've already reached an important milestone because you have passed the stage with the highest risk of infection. You're way ahead of the game right now. I shouldn't have been surprised since your daily walks around the hospital were getting longer each day. You've got a strong immune system, that's for sure. Congratulations."

"Th-thank . . . you." I could barely get words out as tears traveled down my face.

"My pleasure. It was a team effort." She erased some numbers on the whiteboard related to my blood counts and wrote in updated numbers.

I wanted to text Adam the good news, but he'd never responded to my last text before the transplant, telling him I loved him.

Forget about him.

"We've already contacted your brother to give him the update," Dr. Nguyen said. "I'm going to run a few more follow-up tests later this afternoon. The next step is getting you discharged, so you can continue the recovery at home."

"Great. Thank you."

The door swung open and Josh came in. "Hi, sis." He walked over and kissed me on the cheek. "Didn't I tell you not to worry?"

I smiled and wiped my eyes. "You did. Many times."

"I'll see you a little later." Dr. Nguyen smiled and left.

Josh sat on the bed next to me. "How do you feel?"

"I'm a little bit in shock, actually."

"That's to be expected. It must be an emotional rollercoaster for you."

"It is. It's crazy to think that they took something from somebody else's body and stuck it inside my body, so I could live." I slapped Josh on the leg. "Hey, I want to do something special for the donor, maybe send her on a vacation. Or buy her a car. Or a house. Whatever she wants. You can't put a price tag on life, and I'm beyond grateful." I slapped him on the leg again. "You need to find out who she is."

"That's not going to happen."

"You're training to be a detective. You could *easily* find out."

Josh shook his head. "You know the rules. No gifts over fifty dollars. And no contacting the donor for a year. It's the law and I'm a police officer."

"I don't care if you're a cop. My brother loves me too much to say no."

He looked away, biting his lower lip, and avoiding eye contact with me.

I cocked my head to the side. "What's going on, Josh?"

He didn't answer.

"Josh?"

"Okay, okay. I can't do this anymore." Josh blew out a deep breath and sat back down on the bed. "It's Adam."

"What do you mean it's Adam? We were talking about the donor."

"*Adam* was your donor."

I flinched. "Adam?"

He nodded. "Yes. Adam."

It took all my strength to swallow, as I considered the magnitude of what Josh had just revealed to me.

The man I loved had donated the bone marrow that saved my life.

A part of Adam was now a part of me.

It was kind.

It was romantic.

Not to mention the odds of him being a donor match for me.

It was almost too much, too overwhelming for my mind.

Adam had said *I* was stubborn? Ha! He was the stubborn one. He hadn't given up on me, even after the way I had treated him.

That just made me love him even more.

And something else just occurred to me that was even more unbelievable . . .

Adam didn't go into hospitals.

I shook my head in disbelief. "I don't understand. He has nosocomephobia."

"Not anymore, thanks to you." Josh sighed. "But there's something else I need to tell you."

"What?"

Josh stood and took a few steps away from me. He turned around to face me, running his hand through his hair. "He's . . . in a coma."

I felt my chest breaking in two.

My hand flew up to my throat, and I sucked in a quick breath. "What? No! How did that happen?"

"I didn't get the whole story. Something about a kid climbing the vending machine here in the hospital. The machine was going to fall. Adam saved the boy from getting injured but hit his head and was knocked out. That was the same day he donated his bone marrow."

"Eight days!" I gasped, suddenly finding it difficult to breathe.

This was a nightmare, and somebody needed to wake me.

"Take it easy, sis. Breathe."

I hugged my legs with my arms, rocking back and forth. "No, no, no, no, no. This can't be happening." Tears streamed down my face. "This is not right, and it's all my fault!"

"Calm down. This is not good for your health."

"I'm your sister and I had the right to know," I yelled. "You know I love him!"

"Of course, I do."

My blood pressure must have been going through the roof. "You should've told me."

"I didn't tell you because of *this*!" He gestured to me. "Look at you. I wanted to say something, believe me. Dr. Nguyen told me *any* stress or *any* anxiety could be detrimental to your recovery. There was no way in hell I was going to jeopardize that."

I sniffled and wiped my nose. "How serious is it? How is he?"

"The doctor said that recovery from a coma is completely unpredictable. He can breathe on his own and his vital signs are stable. That's a good thing, from what I was told." He took a step toward me. "I'm sorry. Orlando has been here in the hospital every day visiting Adam. He wanted to come see you. We didn't want you to find out about Adam and get stressed out. It was eating me up inside not telling you. I had to do what was best for you."

I wiped my eyes. "Do you want to know what's best for me right now? I need to see Adam."

I couldn't believe we were both in the hospital at the same time.

Swinging my legs out of the bed, I stepped into my

slippers. "Take me to him. If you say no, I'll go find him myself."

He stared at me. "Fine. Don't cry in front of him. You need to be strong. You can talk to him, tell him stories, jokes, read to him. Heck, you can sing, if you want to. You can even touch him. Just keep it positive and encouraging."

I nodded. "How do you know all this?"

"Orlando told me. Coma patients need familiar things. Familiar voices."

"If I have to talk with him all day and all night, that's what I'm going to do until he comes out of that coma."

"Hey, don't forget you're still recovering yourself."

"I know," I said, to make Josh feel better, even though that was the least of my concerns. I grabbed my robe, put it on, and tied it around my waist. "Let's go."

I let the nurse know I was going for my morning walk.

Josh took me up to the next floor, gesturing to Adam's door. "This is it."

Don't cry. Don't cry. Don't cry.

Josh pushed open the door, and gestured for me to go in. "I'll be in the waiting area at the end of the hall. Stay positive, and don't blame yourself. This is not your fault."

I stepped inside the room, closing the door behind me.

Glancing over at the bed, I swallowed hard.

Adam lay there, his eyes closed, the blanket pulled up neatly across his chest. His arms were outside of the blanket, and one of them was hooked up to a drip system.

I walked around to the far side of the bed and placed my hand on his arm.

My eyes started to burn.

Don't cry. Be strong. Do it for Adam.

I kissed him on the forehead and on the lips then grabbed the chair by the window, sliding it over next to the bed.

I sat down and smiled. "Hi, Adam. It's me."

I didn't expect him to respond just like that.

It wasn't like I had magical powers and could snap him out of his coma with a few words, like in the movies.

I placed my hand on his arm again. "Thank you for saving my life. Sounds like you saved a kid's life, too. Looks like I need to start calling you Superman again. I know, no spandex." I smiled. "You'll be happy to know I've been spontaneous here in the hospital. When the nurse took my order for dinner last night, she asked me what I wanted for dessert. I told her to surprise me. Can you believe that? *You* did that to me. You've done a lot of things that have made me a better person. A happier person."

I slid my hand down his arm and grabbed his hand. "Anyway, I think you should know there's a good chance we're both going to be arrested today. You need to prepare for that because it appears we're breaking the law at the moment. I'm not supposed to know who my donor is. I'm not supposed to know anything about you, actually. I'm not supposed to know that you're fifty years young and devastatingly attractive. I'm not supposed to know that you're an amazing pilot. I'm not supposed to know you're the kindest man I have ever met in my life. And I'm definitely not supposed to know you're the best kisser the world has ever known." I paused for a moment, trying to keep it together. "There *is* something you should know that I haven't told you in person. I love you. I love you *so* much." I squeezed his hand.

My eyes started to burn again, and they filled.

Uh-oh. Not good.

I held up an index finger for Adam. "Just one moment. I'll be right back."

I quickly walked outside the room, closed the door, and leaned against the wall.

I placed a hand over my mouth and sobbed uncontrollably.

I couldn't let him hear me cry in the room.

It was so much harder than I thought it would be.

Suck it up. He needs you. Do it for him.

I wiped my nose and my eyes, nodding, ready to give it another try.

Josh walked over from the waiting area. "Hey, sis. You need to get back to your room. This is upsetting you too much. Plus, you haven't eaten your breakfast."

I sniffled. "I'm not hungry. Adam needs me and I can't leave him."

"I'll carry you back to the room if I have to."

"You told me he needed familiar things. Here I am."

"He does, but—"

"Wait a minute." I put my hand on Josh's shoulder. "I just thought of something. I need you to do me a huge favor and then I'll eat breakfast. I promise."

"What do you need?"

"Can you bring me my phone and charger from the room?"

"Now?"

I nodded. "Please."

"Okay, then you're going to eat breakfast. You promised."

"I will."

I waited for Josh to return with my phone and entered the room again. I walked around to the far side of the bed again, rubbing Adam's arm. "I'm back. Did you miss me? Well, not as much as I missed you! Hang on, because I have a surprise for you. Do you like surprises?" I smiled. "Well, *I* have grown to appreciate them, you'll be happy to know."

I plugged my phone into the electrical outlet and searched my music folder for "La Vie en Rose" by Louis Armstrong. I had purchased the song after I had returned home from the trip and had played it a few hundred times since then.

I tapped the button on my phone, so it would automatically repeat the song over and over again, then set the phone down on the table next to Adam's head.

The song began to play, and I grabbed his hand again, dancing next to his bed. I closed my eyes, transporting myself back to the grand ballroom with Adam at the castle in France.

I swayed back and forth, not letting go of his hand.

I opened my eyes. "Do you remember this song, Adam?" I kissed his hand softly, continuing to dance with him.

"I have lived more during the short time we spent together traveling, than I have lived my entire life. I plan on growing old with you, did you know that? You just need to wake up, so we can continue our journey together. If you don't, I'll spend the rest of my life sitting by your bed, reminding you how much I love you. Wake up, my love."

The song ended and began to repeat again.

"I promised Josh I'd go eat breakfast. I'll be back." I kissed Adam on the cheek and turned to leave.

I reached for the door handle and stopped, almost positive I heard a noise.

I turned around slowly, not sure if it was my imagination.

My heart slammed into my ribs and I pressed my palms to my cheeks.

Adam's eyes were open.

He was blinking.

I flew to the bed.

Tears streamed down my face.

I pushed the nurse call button even though I could barely see through the tears.

I grabbed Adam's hand, kissed it, and smiled. "Welcome back, my love."

He blinked. "La . . . Vie . . ."

He couldn't finish his sentence.

It didn't matter.

"Yes." I squeezed his hand. "That's 'La Vie en Rose.' Our song."

He gave me the slightest nod and the hint of a grin. "Our . . . song."

EPILOGUE

Eight Months Later . . .

LIZ

I still remember the conversation I'd had with Adam the day I'd met him for the first time in his office. We had been talking about the Taj Mahal, and how the emperor of India hadn't met his soulmate until his third marriage. I had no idea that day I would have something in common with the emperor.

Life had surprised me with a third husband.

My soulmate.

Maybe even more surprising would be the fact that Adam and I were on a double honeymoon with Josh and Orlando. Life couldn't have been any better, and I was guaranteed to never be bored with these three guys around.

"My buns are frozen," Orlando said. "Seriously, I can't feel a thing at all."

Josh grimaced. "Mine, too."

"I'm President of the Frozen Buns Club," Adam said. "I think it should be illegal to be outside when the temperature is lower than your age. Do you think we can get a law passed like that, officer?"

"That's out of my jurisdiction, since I am now officially a detective." Josh grinned.

"Okay, detective, solve the mystery of the coldness."

I crossed my arms. "Would you guys quit being such wimps? Call me crazy, but I think it's okay to be a little cold in the capital of the Arctic. I offered to buy you all wool jackets. You could be warm and toasty like me, but did you take me up on the offer? No."

"You've been spoiling us too much," Orlando said.

"Fine. Do you want me to cancel the hotel reservations? I'd be happy to look for a camping area where we can all sleep on the ground in the snow."

"No!" the three guys bellowed together.

"That's what I thought. Oh—the show is starting."

The four of us gazed up into the sky above Tromsø, Norway, admiring the glow of the aurora borealis, the legendary northern nights. There was nothing more magical in the world than watching the green, pink, and violet light dance across the night sky.

"I've never seen anything like this before in my life," Adam said.

"Mother nature is putting on quite a show," Josh said.

"It's so incredible that I even forgot my buns were frozen," Orlando said.

I laughed. "I wonder what it would be like to see this from an airplane." I squeezed Adam's arm. "What do you think?"

"I'm sure it's even more spectacular at forty thousand feet. I prefer being down here with you in my arms." He pulled me closer.

"Awwww." I twisted around and reached up to kiss my husband on the lips.

A lot had happened in our lives since we had met last year.

Adam and I had made full recoveries.

We were happy, healthy, and madly in love.

I had sold my house and moved in with him.

The painting I had bought for Adam in Montmartre was now hanging in our living room over the fireplace.

We even started a non-profit organization called On the Wings of Love, offering free flights to hospitals across America for patients with limited financial means. Adam was the president and had already lined up fifty volunteer pilots. Of course, I had to buy him a brand-new jet.

Meeting Adam was like winning the lottery again. He had taught me to enjoy the present, because we didn't know what tomorrow would bring. For so many years I had been skipping vacations, preferring to save money for the future. I had been filling my bank account when I should've been filling my heart with unforgettable experiences.

I smiled and kissed Adam again, grateful to have him in my life.

Josh sighed. "Okay, I've had enough of my sister smooching for this lifetime. I declare a kissing moratorium in the country of Norway."

I laughed. "I guess that means I need to plan our next trip."

"You still have Greece and India on your bucket list."

"Wait—I have a great idea."

Adam chuckled. "This wouldn't be the first time."

"Why not a little spontaneity? I'll spin one of my old classroom globes around when we get home, close my eyes, and stop it with my finger. Whatever country my finger lands on, *that* will be the destination of our next trip."

Adam's mouth was hanging open. "I've created a monster."

"I'm serious!"

"And what if your finger lands on North Korea or Iraq?"

"Well then . . . I'll spin again. Easy peasy."

Adam smirked. "You know what's easy peasy?"

"What?"

"Loving you."

"Awwww." I reached up to kiss him again.

"Moratorium!" Josh yelled.

I ignored my brother, and kissed Adam hard.

He sure was right about one thing . . .

Love always wins.

THE END

FREE romantic comedy!
All of my newsletter subscribers
get a free copy of my fun story,
Happy to be Stuck with You, plus
updates on new releases and sales.
http://www.richamooi.com/newsletter.

**You can also browse my entire list of
romantic comedies on Amazon here:**
Author.to/AmazonRichAmooi

ACKNOWLEDGMENTS

Dear Reader,

I hope you enjoyed *Dying to Meet You*. This story almost killed me. LOL. Okay, maybe not, but I think I have a lot less hair. Some books are harder to write than others, even though I don't think I can give you a reason why. Maybe because this one was deeper since it was about life and death. Whatever the reason, I'm so proud of this book and grateful you took the time to read it.

I would just like to take a moment to thank you for your support. Without you, I would not be able to write romantic comedies for a living. I love your emails and communication on Facebook and Twitter. You motivate me to write faster! Don't be shy. Send an email to me at rich@richamooi.com to say hello. I personally respond to all emails and would love to hear from you.

Please LIKE my Facebook page and follow me here:

https://www.facebook.com/author.richamooi/

Also, please consider leaving a review of the book on Amazon and Goodreads! I'd appreciate it very much and it would help new readers find my stories.

It takes more than a few people to publish a book so I want to send out a big THANK YOU to everyone who helped make *Dying to Meet You* possible.

First, thank you to my amazing wife, the love of my life, Silvi Martin. I LOVE MY WIFE! She's the first person to read my stories and always gives me the best feedback. I couldn't publish a book without her. Thank you, my angel! I love, love, love, love you!

Thanks to Meg Stinson for editing.

A big thank you to Paula Bothwell, Sherry Stevenson, and Graham Toseland for proofreading. You rock!

Thanks to Tammi Labrecque for helping me with the amazing cover!

Special thanks to Teresa Carpenter and Hannah Jayne for helping me brainstorm before I started writing the story.

Thanks to Teresa O'Kane for answering my questions about the Maasai tribe and Africa while she was on vacation in

Australia. Find her amazing book, *Safari Jema: A Journey of Love and Adventure from Casablanca to Cape Town* on Amazon HERE.

A huge thank you to my beta readers Marsha, Allan, Robert, Cheryl, Maché, and Deb for helping make this story even better with their feedback.

Thanks to Author's Corner and Deb Julienne for your support.

Becoming a bone marrow donor is easier than you think and is painless. You could save a life! For more information, please visit https://bethematch.org/

With gratitude,

Rich

ABOUT THE AUTHOR

Rich Amooi is a former Silicon Valley radio personality and wedding DJ who now writes romantic comedies full-time in San Diego, California. He is happily married to a kiss monster imported from Spain. Rich believes in public displays of affection, silliness, infinite possibilities, donuts, gratitude, laughter, and happily ever after.

Connect with Rich!
www.richamooi.com
rich@richamooi.com
https://www.facebook.com/author.richamooi
https://twitter.com/richamooi

Printed in Great Britain
by Amazon